3|13

WITHDRAWN

WITHDRAWN

Deep
Betrayal

ALSO BY ANNE GREENWOOD BROWN

Lies Beneath

Deep
Betrayal

ANNE GREENWOOD BROWN

delacorte press

Text copyright © 2013 by Anne Greenwood Brown
Jacket photograph copyright © 2013 by Elena Kalis

Visit us on the Web! randomhouse.com/teens

Educators and librarians, for a variety of teaching tools, visit us at RHTeachersLibrarians.com

Library of Congress Cataloging-in-Publication Data
Brown, Anne Greenwood.
Deep betrayal / Anne Greenwood Brown.
p.   cm.
Sequel to: Lies beneath.
Summary: "As dead bodies start washing ashore, Lily and Calder realize someone's on a killing spree—and they fear it's either Calder's mermaid sisters or Lily's father." — Provided by publisher.
ISBN 978-0-385-74203-0 (hc) – ISBN 978-0-375-98909-4 (ebook) –
ISBN 978-0-375-99037-3 (glb)
[1. Mermen–Fiction.   2. Mermaids–Fiction.   3. Brothers and sisters–Fiction.
4. Love–Fiction.   5. Revenge–Fiction.   6. Superior, Lake–Fiction.]   I. Title.
PZ7.B812742Dee 2013
[Fic]–dc23
2012030598

The text of this book is set in 11.5-point Caslon Book.
Book design by Angela Carlino

Printed in the United States of America
10 9 8 7 6 5 4 3 2 1
First Edition

For Laura and Stephanie

I hold it true, whate'er befall;
I feel it, when I sorrow most;
'Tis better to have loved and lost
Than never to have loved at all.

—Alfred, Lord Tennyson, "In Memoriam A.H.H."

1

NO COWARD SOUL

Death finds us all. Yet I was impatient and had gone looking for it; now there was no going back. My toes curled over the edge of the rock. I welcomed the feeling. Hard and cold. Wet and rough. The wind whipped my dress around my legs, sucking it close to my body, then ripping it away like a flag unfurled–a white flag–because this was my surrender.

Somewhere out there in the black water, she was watching. If she doubted me now, she wouldn't for long. This was nothing. One small step. Nothing. The fall would be over before I could be afraid. I didn't look down. I'd made this fall before. I couldn't let the rocks deter me. And if I saw her . . .

No, I couldn't think about that. I could do this if I didn't see my fate lashing at the water, cursing in my ear. If I could take this small step, I could save my dad, and with him, my whole family. If I could only be brave enough. Just enough.

My stomach turned, and I rocked back on my heels. I hoped Calder wouldn't see. The mermaid said he was far away. She said he wouldn't save me, even if he could. I hoped she was right.

A wave crashed against the rocks, sending a fine mist into the air. It settled on my cheeks and lips. The air had never smelled cleaner. The sky had never been so clear. I had never felt so huge. I was enormous. A giant. My mind buzzed over the roar of waves, the scream of gulls, the whisper of the trees.

No coward soul have I. No coward soul have I. No coward soul . . .

One small step. My toes dug into the rocky precipice, feeling its pockmarked surface. The shiny lacquer of my toenails reflected a bird overhead. We made eye contact–the bird and I–he with a questioning expression, raising a feathered eyebrow.

One small step. Tensing, I leaned forward.

One small step. I closed my eyes and inhaled the perfumed air.

One small step.
And I was falling.
A rush
of adrenaline
surged from
my stomach
to my heart.

2

EXILED

The memory of the mermaid dissolved as I woke up and my eyes adjusted to the light, making out the white wicker bed and the floral wallpaper. A matching duvet lay in a twisted jumble on the floor. A silver-filigreed clock read 8:32 p.m. None of this stuff was mine.

Well, that wasn't entirely true. The paper chain I'd made hung from the corner of the bedpost. Somehow, in my fitful sleep, I'd managed to get tangled in its length. I unwrapped the chain from around my neck and dropped its loose end to the floor. As of this morning, it had thirty links: one marking every day since my exile from Lake Superior and my parentally enforced separation from Calder White.

Thirty links, thirty days since I'd heard from him. No calls. No texts. *Where the heck is he?*

Counting had become something of an obsession with me lately. As in, fifty-two days since Dad had dragged me away from Minneapolis, from my school, from all my friends, to go live in a falling-down house on the shores of Lake Superior. Fifty days since I'd been rescued by what I naively believed to be a freshwater dolphin. Thirty-three days since my pathetic attempt at martyrdom had resulted in Tallulah's death and revealed a family secret that I still could not fathom (and that sent me into a cold sweat every time I tried). And now thirty days, two hours, and seventeen minutes of exile.

I flopped back on the bed and threw a pillow over my face, muttering into it. *Damn you, Calder White.*

I'd make him eat this paper chain next time I saw him. When he'd swum away, he'd promised to come back for me. Wherever I was. So what was taking so long? How hard could it be to pick up a phone? Had he found a new girlfriend? Was he dead? In my darkest moments I thought, *He better be dead.* That would be the only acceptable explanation for his silence. But I didn't really mean it, and I quickly traced the sign of the cross over my chest.

The bedroom door knob rattled, and my best friend, Jules Badzin, swished in with a twirl, wearing a royal-blue graduation cap over her flat-ironed black hair. She carried another cap in her teeth and two gowns on hangers.

I really should have been excited. The only good thing about being forced away from Lake Superior was getting to graduate with my class. Jules's parents had been generous enough to let me crash at their house, but I had to fake every ounce of enthusiasm. And faking it was exhausting.

"Oh!" Jules said. "Were you going to bed already? It's not even nine yet."

"No, I'm good. I'm up." I picked off the strands of hair that were stuck to my sweaty face.

Jules hung my cap and gown from the top of the closet door. We'd been friends since kindergarten. I could tell her anything. Well, almost anything.

She flipped her hair to one side and wriggled out of her jeans. "I've got to start buying pants a size bigger. I swear these are giving me a rash."

"Thanks for sharing," I said. My phone vibrated on the bedside table. It was a text from an unknown number. It was the seventh time that day. The first time it happened, I thought, *This is it!* Calder probably got a new phone, right? That would make sense. Now that he had his freedom, he wouldn't want his sister Maris to know how to reach him. But when I clicked on it, there was no message—only a link to a website, just some hacker sending me a virus. Now it was just plain annoying.

"Figure-flattering," Jules said, trying on her graduation gown. "We're going to look like saggy blueberries. Remember that *Willy Wonka* girl after she goes through the juicer? I wonder what they'd look like belted?"

"Stupid," I said, sliding my phone open and closed, open and closed.

"Geez, Lily, what's got your undies in a bunch?" She laughed. Everyone was always laughing these days. Or maybe they always had been. Had I ever laughed so easily? Nothing seemed funny anymore. I gathered my strength and forced a smile.

Jules rolled her eyes and muttered, "Nice try," while she scrounged through my closet.

"Sorry. Just tired," I said. "Are you looking for something in particular?"

Jules bypassed a paisley blouse, a chenille poncho, and a 1970s denim jumpsuit (my latest thrift-store purchase). She tossed a belt and a tuxedo cummerbund onto the bed and wrapped a skinny necktie around her waist.

"You've been grumpy for weeks, Lil, and you always say it's nothing. It's something, all right. It's that guy again, isn't it?" She checked herself out in the full-length mirror. "Want me to get the frozen yogurt?"

That guy. Dark curly hair, hypnotic green eyes, voice like liquid, each word pouring into the next like water tumbling over rocks when he got excited. Calder White. The most amazingly beautiful boy who'd ever tried to kill my father.

It wasn't funny. Not at all. But I couldn't help smiling when I thought of how far we'd come. I'd told Jules plenty about him: how we'd worked together at the Blue Moon Café and how he'd taught me to use the cappuccino maker and steam milk to a perfect foam; how he'd rescued me from a near drowning and later given me a personal tour of the shipwrecks and natural wonders of the Apostle Islands. Of course, I'd never mentioned the most amazing part: that the tours had been underwater, with his perfect lips pressed to mine.

Jules walked gingerly across the floor to the bed. A semester's worth of white loose-leaf paper littered the guest-room floor. Now that my last final was behind me, I planned to toss it all, but I was enjoying the look of the room, kinda snow-covered.

A stack of books leaned like the Tower of Pisa in the corner of the room. Trig, physics, humanities, French, three dog-eared novels, and a copy of *Hamlet*. A tattered anthology of Victorian poetry teetered at the top, flopped open to Tennyson's "Mariana." That poem was what I'd fallen asleep to the night before: a poor girl asking when her true love would return. It probably should have made me feel worse, but it was the one thing that made me feel closer to Calder, remembering the sound of his voice as we recited Tennyson on Manitou Island, the cool air evaporating the water off my skin. . . .

Jules plunked herself down on the bed and put her hand on my shoulder. "He still hasn't called?"

I shrugged.

"Do you think maybe you should move on? It's not like this was a long-term romance or anything, right?"

"Right," I said.

"I mean, it's not like you're *in love* with the guy, right?"

Love. I wasn't sure what I felt for Calder White. When I first met him, he made me nervous, partly because of his unnaturally good looks, but mostly because he was always just *there*, too close and too fast.

Later, I was proud of myself when I figured out what he was, and, after that, repulsed when he told me what he did. I had to work hard to keep my face composed. It wasn't easy repressing my disgust for his hunting past, just so he'd keep talking and feeding me the information I so desperately wanted—information that would explain my family's history and put my father's shame to rest.

So, okay, I used him at first. But after learning how hard Calder worked against his nature, after really coming to *understand* him, and now, after all we'd been through . . . What did I feel for him now? Respect, maybe? Longing? Fascination?

Whatever it was, it wasn't as mundane as what Jules was suggesting.

"Well, if *he's* not going to call *you*," Jules said, "have you thought about—"

"I can't call him. He's got a new number. The one I have doesn't work anymore."

Jules crinkled her nose at me. "That's a bad sign. Is it possible that maybe he just wasn't that into you?"

I nodded. I had already considered that. Making the reality of his silence sync with the fantasy of my memories was like trying to fit square pegs into round holes. I'd given up after only a few painful attempts.

"Don't be sad," Jules said. "It's not like he's the only fish in the sea. I'm sure if you put yourself out there again, the guys will be lining up."

"Heh." *Hilarious.* "Yeah. I could do that."

"Sure you could. We both could. We've got a whole summer ahead of us before everyone splits up for college.

The last hurrah, right? Let's get out there and break some hearts."

I didn't answer, so Jules wisely changed the subject and asked, "When are your mom and dad getting in?"

"Supposedly tomorrow, but I'll believe it when I see it."

"Oh, shut up. It's not that far of a drive. There's no way they're missing your graduation."

"I don't mean they don't *want* to come. I just don't know if they can." I'd been calling home every day to talk to Mom and subtly keep tabs on Dad. After what had happened in the lake, I wasn't surprised when Mom said he'd been on edge.

She, of course, had no idea about the mermaids, and Dad still didn't know the truth about himself, but it was only natural that plunging into his birth waters would set something in motion.

"My dad hasn't been feeling well," I said. I wished Jules hadn't brought it up. What if the urge to swim got too strong for my dad? What if he jumped in? I couldn't help obsessing over where and when and how he'd learn the truth for himself.

I'd hoped things would be better now that he was no longer the target of a mermaid assassination plot, but I was afraid my attempt at heroics had only made things worse. A part of me wished I'd told him right away, but how do you tell your father he's a merman? Particularly with our family history for crazy.

Instead, I'd tried to limit my worry to something else: If Dad was a merman, what did that make me? My eyes went automatically to *MY SCRIBBLINGS,* half buried under the flurry of paper. Recently I'd scribbled the cover of my poetry notebook with my answer:

Mutt, MUTANT, Mixed-breed

At least I finally had an explanation for my abnormal ability to endure the freezing lake temperatures. I wasn't normal. Not by a long shot.

"Your parents will be here," Jules said. "Don't worry. Hey, what's with the paper chain?" She swirled her finger through one of the blue links.

"It's nothing."

My phone went off again. Same website link again. Damn spammers.

"Lily, quit saying that. Give me something to work with."

"I guess I'm just nervous about graduation tomorrow."

"You mean with Phillip's thing? No one's going to get in trouble. Every grad class has some stupid prank. It'll be easy. When you go up onstage to shake Principal Landsem's hand, just drop a penny into his palm. It'll be funny. By the time he gets to the N's, he'll have collected about three hundred. His pockets will be bulging."

"Couldn't we just go with a streaker?" I asked. "Or maybe a flasher? It's been a few years since a class did that. I bet Mikey'd be up for it."

"No doubt. Which is why no one asked him. Have you ever seen that guy naked?"

"No. Have you?"

"Kelly Moeller's pool party last year. My eyes are

still burning." Jules picked up my poetry notebook. The word *mutant* stood out the most, in all caps, centered on the cover.

"What's with the self-loathing?"

I ripped the notebook from her hands. "Who says it's about me? I was actually commenting on you."

She grabbed it back and thwacked me over the head with it.

"I'm going to give your dad a big hug when I see him. Seriously, the coolest thing any parent ever did, sending you home where you belong. I doubt my parents would have done it."

Jules's phone went off and she slid it open. Her thumbs worked furiously over the keypad as she sent back her response, then snapped the phone shut.

"Good news," she said. "Robby and Zach are going to make it after all."

Jules's mother had planned a catered dinner party at their house for our friends. She was loath to celebrate what she called a "milestone event" at the Olive Garden.

"Now, can I help you clean this mess up? My mom's going to freak when she sees this floor."

We spent the next hour sweeping my senior year into a trash can and throwing dirty clothes into a hamper. Jules commented on several of my favorite pieces: a navy velvet jacket and a yellow beret. "You're the only one I know who can pull this stuff off. I'd look like a deranged clown."

"I was going more for a modern-day Charlotte Brontë." I hung the jacket in the closet. I hadn't worn it since coming back to the Twin Cities. I could still smell the lake air in its fibers.

"Who?" Jules asked as she turned on the TV. The 1939 film version of *The Hound of the Baskervilles* was playing. Jules flopped down on the bed, resting her head in her hands. I wrapped up in an afghan on the floor and tried to focus on the movie. Something about a curse and some girl who got away.

Neither of us was awake for the end of the movie, and I was dreaming again:

I sank through the floor, through the joists, past the tangle of wires to the downstairs, and on past the basement. I dropped like a weighted line below the foundation into a watery underworld. The cold cut my skin and my lungs burned. A mermaid's arms crushed my chest. Tighter, tighter. I called out, but no one answered. I reached for something that wasn't there, then the sudden explosion of sound, and the mermaid's unexpected release, the copper taste of blood in my mouth, red pooling around my face, and the tug of two arms pulling me onto the rocks, a silver ring appearing around a throat . . . the howling sound of voices calling my name . . .

I woke up with a shout. "Dad!"

Ugh. Groggy and stiff, I looked around to get my bearings. The movie was over, the lead actor's voice replaced by a late-night talk-show host's. I clicked off the TV and stood up. Jules slept peacefully in my bed, her hands curled under her cheek. It wasn't nice, but I gave her a swift shove, and she rolled off the edge, hitting the floor with a satisfying *thud.*

"Hey!"

"You fell," I said, crawling into the warm sheets. "Better go back to your own room. Graduation and all. Get some sleep."

3

BLUE

"Geez, it's so blue," Jules said as we walked into Humphrey Auditorium. She was right. The decorating committee had gone overboard: blue balloons, blue banners, a curtain of blue and white streamers hanging behind the stage. Add in six hundred kids in blue caps and gowns and the effect was a little overwhelming. It was the first time in a long time that I was dressed like everyone else. It made me feel a little off balance.

"I got to get to my seat," Jules said. "Good luck."

I nodded, exhaling slowly. "Yeah, you too."

I found the *H* row and my metal folding chair with only minutes to spare. Rob Hache slapped my hand as I squeezed by him. Besides Jules, Rob was my oldest friend—ever since we tied for third grade spelling-bee champ. Sometimes he tried to cross the friendship line, but lately we'd reached a truce in that debate.

Up front, the superintendent stood at a shiny blue podium, coughing into his sleeve before making some comments about how we were all heading off into a *grand adventure.* It wasn't long before the name butchering began with "Mary Margaret An . . . An . . . drze . . . ze . . . jewski."

The superintendent continued to trudge through the alphabet, while Principal Landsem, who was handing out the diplomas, quickly began to lose his enthusiasm for the ceremony. By the time we got to the *H*'s, my classmates had already deposited two hundred pennies into his palm, and the pockets of his suit coat bulged and begged for the floor.

Brian Halvorson turned and winked at me as his name was called, saying "Penny for your thoughts," then he strode confidently across the stage. I clenched my penny tight in my fist. It might have been a boulder for how heavy it felt.

"Lily Anne Hancock."

Principal Landsem, his mouth pinched at the corners, stood with his hand outstretched. I shifted the penny from my sweaty palm to my fingers and walked forward with an apologetic smile.

When I was halfway across the stage, an air horn blasted me out of my embarrassment. I turned toward the audience and caught, for just the briefest of seconds, a familiar dark head in the standing-room-only section. I stopped in my tracks and stared. No. Why would he be here? Now?

But I lost track of the beautiful figure ghosting through the crowd. And then I lost faith in my eyesight. *Wishful thinking*, I decided. Calder didn't like crowds.

Mom and my ten-year-old sister, Sophie, screamed my name and waved blue pompons in the air. Dad sat stoically beside them, mirroring my wide-eyed expression, his face pale as paste. The sight of my family shook me out of my befuddlement. I refocused on my diploma and finished the trip across the stage.

"Congratulations, Miss Hancock," Principal Landsem said. He handed me a black certificate case as I slipped him the penny. He added, "Although I expected a little more maturity from you." The penny made a plinking sound as he dropped it into his pocket.

And then I was free! Thirteen years of school were over!

Jules high-fived me as I passed the *B* row and made my way back to my seat. I collapsed onto my folding chair and Rob reached across a couple of laps to shake my hand.

"Good going," he whispered. His red-brown hair curled around the edges of his cap. "You didn't wimp out."

I rolled my eyes. *As if.* I'd wrestled with sea creatures. It would take more than a stupid, juvenile gag to undo me. Really, there was only one thing that could make me lose it, and that day was drawing near. Back in the Badzins' guest room, thirty-one paper links hung from my bedpost.

The drone of names continued. I let the sounds blend like the beads of sweat that met and blossomed under my cap band. The back of my neck prickled, and I was sure I was being watched. There was no mistaking the burn. I turned in my chair, expecting to see Calder White standing there, his shockingly beautiful face mocking my exhibition. But still there was nothing.

"Elizabeth Marie Smith,

Sandra Ellen Smith,

Zachary David So-beach . . . Sobee-eck . . . Sobee-ack."

Our beleaguered and weighted-down principal looked two inches shorter than when we started. When the superintendent finally called Yousef and Zinn, Principal Landsem slunk to the back table and emptied both pockets of our goodwill offering while the band struck up the school anthem. No one knew the words.

Caps flew into the air. I got up and walked to the back of the auditorium, toward my parents. At least, that was where I tried to go. My body bounced off my classmates as I battled against the stream of people. The blare of air horns ricocheted off the ceiling and into my ears, along with the girls' woot-woots and the boys' loud guffaws. I couldn't believe I'd grown up among these faces. Everyone was a stranger.

"Lily!"

A hand clasped my arm and snagged me from the crowd. Dad pulled me against his chest and whispered something in my ear. I wrapped my arms around him, and held on tight. Having him here, intact, standing on two legs . . . I wasn't prepared for the rush of relief.

He led me to a corner at the back of the gym where Mom swiveled her wheelchair in an excited dance at the bottom of the ramp. Sophie stood with one hand on a handle.

"Oooooh, Bay! Bee!" Mom cried, her hands waving in the air. "How do you feel? Tell me. How do you *feel*?"

She didn't give me the chance to put together an answer, or to beg to come home, or to even say hello.

"You look so much older," she gushed. "Doesn't she look all grown up, Jason?"

I glanced nervously at my dad, wondering if I could find the answer to a different question in his eyes, like "Yes, you can come home now."

"Oh, honey," Mom continued, "I've missed you, but I'm so glad you got to walk with your class. Now bend down, we've got a present for you."

I knelt in front of her chair and she fixed a fine silver chain around my neck. "It's a family heirloom from your dad's side. The original chain was broken, so this one's new, but the pendant . . . I think it must be very old. Isn't it beautiful?"

"Grandpa gave it to me before he died," Dad said. "He wanted you to have it."

"A real keepsake," Mom said as I studied the beach-glass pendant hanging from its copper fob. Softened by sand and water, the glass was the same green as Calder's eyes, and it lay strangely hot against my chest.

"I'm glad you made it, Mom. You too, Dad."

He said, "We've missed you, too, kiddo. It hasn't been the same since you left."

I didn't correct him by saying that I hadn't left, I'd been *sent.* I didn't want to pick a fight; it felt too good to have them here.

An hour later, we arrived at the Badzins' house. Inside, the air conditioner hummed and aromatic candles laced the air. Mrs. Badzin had brought out her white linens and good silver service. Several parents hovered around the buffet table where a platter of sushi and sashimi had center stage. I dunked a spicy tuna roll into soy sauce and shoved it in my mouth whole, bending over the table so the drips rolling down my chin wouldn't stain my lace minidress.

Rob grabbed me as I came around the corner, and he pulled me into a bear hug. "Congratulations, beautiful," he said, stumbling a little.

I pried myself free and shook my head. My mouth still full, I mumbled, "Knock it off, Wobby."

He laughed, saying, "C'mon. Everyone's in the basement." He pulled me by the arm, down the steps to where our friends were hanging out.

Jules announced my arrival ceremoniously as I tripped in my vinyl platform shoes and fell awkwardly onto the futon with a self-deprecating "Ta-da!"

I lay my head on Jules's shoulder. "I'm so glad it's over."

"Over?" Zach asked as he aimed a dart toward a small plastic target hanging on the wall. "It's just beginning." He let the dart fly, but it glanced sideways off the bottom rim and barely missed Jules's foot.

"Careful! You nearly killed me," Jules said, pulling her feet up and under her. Zach shrugged.

"So what's up for tomorrow?" Phillip asked.

Colleen Gilligan lounged on a lumpy, basement-worthy couch, her head in Scott Whiting's lap. The two had been an item since sophomore year. "Beach?" they both suggested in unison.

I couldn't help but watch as Scott twirled a lock of Colleen's dark brown hair around and around his finger. She looked up at him, her lips pulling into a small smile as he took off his thick glasses and curled his body to kiss her. For a second, I thought I could feel it myself. The soft meeting. The momentary heat. Voyeuristic, I know. But there it was.

"What do *you* want to do, Lil?" Rob asked. "Does the beach sound good?" He dropped onto the futon next to me and swung an arm around my shoulders.

"What? Oh. Yeah. That sounds good." I let him leave his arm where it was. It was graduation after all.

Phillip laughed. "We've got the Hancock seal of approval. Beach it is!"

"Are you going to Square Lake?" Sophie asked, her small feet tripping silently down the carpeted stairs. "Can I come, too?"

"Of course," I said before anyone else could answer. I slipped off the futon onto the floor and pulled my sister into my lap. The baby-powder scent of her made me homesick. "I've missed you," I whispered in her ear.

"Me too," she whispered back. "It's been really bad without you."

The shine in her eyes brought on the guilt. All this time I'd been focused on *me*. How alone *I* felt. How worried *I* was. Why hadn't I ever considered Sophie in all of this?

She might have been completely in the dark about what had gone down with Dad, but she was still left with the fallout of the mess I'd made.

"Let's get something to drink," I said. She crawled out of my lap, and I led her outside through the sliding-glass patio door. I grabbed two bottles of water from a cooler and screwed off the top for Sophie, passing her one.

"Y'know you could have called me. Or got on the phone when I called Mom."

"Mom said you were busy with finals and I shouldn't bother you."

"Well, school's over. Start bothering me."

Sophie peeled at the label around her bottle and pouted her lips. Her once-curled hair flopped in the humidity and clung to her neck. Finally, she said, "Did you see Dad's face?"

"Yeah. He looks old."

Sophie kept peeling and picking.

"Sophie, tell me."

"He's acting weird. I watch him from my window. Every night he's down at the dock. After Mom goes to bed . . . he gets down low, like he's going to get in the water. Then he stands up and comes back to the house. Sometimes he'll turn around again and touch the water, and then he pulls back like it's biting him or something."

My arms stiffened at my sides. "Has he gone in?" I asked, dreading the answer.

"No. It's like he really, really wants to, but he's afraid. Do you think it's because of me falling out of the boat that one time? Is it my fault?"

I inhaled and let it go slowly. "Don't be silly. And I wouldn't be too worried, Soph. You know Dad can't swim. He's probably trying to get over his fear, and he was looking to do that in private. You probably shouldn't tell him you've been watching."

"Oh, I wouldn't. When he's not at the dock, he's in his room." She dropped her voice lower. "I think he's crying. He hides it from Mom, but I can hear him. Last few times after church, me and Mom will go to the car, but he stays on his knees for, like, an extra ten minutes. Sometimes more."

My first reaction was that it served him right for sending me away, but that quickly gave way to pity. Even if he'd allowed me to stay, what help could I have been to him? He needed someone who could actually explain things. He needed Calder.

There it was again. *Where the hell is he?*

A drop of water hit my arm, and I glanced up at the slate-colored sky. "Let's get in," I said. "It's starting to rain."

With the crack of thunder, the elegant graduation party turned into a refugee camp. The wind shook the house, and the lights flickered. All the adults came down to the basement as the sky went prematurely dark. Rain lashed at the windows and when lightning lit up the sky, we'd get a look at the backyard trees, twisting and arching like a landscaped yoga class. No one wanted to venture out onto the roads.

Instead, we all hunkered down around the television,

watching the giddy weatherman gesture at the Minnesota map. A big red patch covered the metro area with the words Tornado Warning. After he warned the viewing public to stay indoors (as if we needed convincing) and away from windows (harder to do), the screen cut away to the news anchors and the scripted stories of the day.

Mr. Badzin leaned forward and reached for the remote. He turned down the volume just as the picture cut to a young blond reporter. Behind her was a familiar dark lake with spotlights focused on the brambles along the shore. I pulled closer to the flat screen so I could listen.

"Thanks, Geoff," said the reporter. "This afternoon, twenty miles north of Ashland, Wisconsin, a young man discovered part of an enormous fish that washed up on the shores of Lake Superior."

The studio cut to video of agents from the Department of Natural Resources carrying something bulky and wrapped in a tarp to a waiting truck. They struggled with its weight. I glanced around the room. No one was watching but me, their heads all turned to watch the storm.

The reporter continued. "DNR officials believe it to be the remains of the largest sturgeon on record. However, one young man has a different theory for us to consider."

The studio cut to a prerecorded interview, the camera lens tightly focused on a face I knew too well. Jack Pettit was staring intently at the camera, his dark eyes looking directly at me.

"It's pretty big for a fish," he said, not blinking. "Even a sturgeon. Makes you wonder."

The reporter pressed on, capitalizing on the story. "Makes you wonder what?"

Jack seemed unaware that she was making fun of him with her question. "Whether the legends are true," he said. "The ones about mermaids in the lake. Anyone who looks at those scales has to wonder. It doesn't look like any fish I've ever seen."

The camera cut back live to the studio, and the male anchor laughed warmly. "That kid's got quite a theory, Lindsay."

"Well, he is right about one thing, Geoff. It is a sensational find, and the DNR is investigating it as an unusual specimen, possibly a new species, but not anything mythical. Although I have to admit, that would be a lot more fun."

More chuckling between the two anchors, as they cut to footage of the DNR picking over the decomposing remains. The remains of Tallulah White.

I grabbed my stomach and ran upstairs to the bathroom, vomiting half-digested tuna roll into the toilet. How could this be? Tallulah's body was supposed to stay hidden forever. What did this mean for Calder? Is this why he'd vanished?

I rinsed my mouth and staggered to my room. Rain splattered on the window, leaving long-fingered patterns behind. Outside, the sky seemed to pull me from the house, like a black hole, endless and unforgiving.

There was a flash of lightning, and—happy to do anything that would get my mind off Tallulah—I began to count for the center of the storm. *One Mississippi. Two Mississippi. Three Mississippi.* At three seconds, the house rattled with thunder. "Three miles away," I whispered to myself.

The storm was getting closer and Calder was out there—*somewhere.* I wanted desperately to reach him, for him to tell me nothing would change, that the discovery of Tallulah meant nothing. That everything would be okay. That he was coming soon.

I lay my palm flat against the window pane. Down below, something moved in the darkness. I threw open the sash and leaned out into the rain. My hair plastered to my face and shoulders. My vision distorted. I curled my arm across my forehead to shield my eyes. It seemed the whole world was underwater.

Another flash of lightning illuminated the street in a vibrant blue. I sucked in my breath, certain I must be dreaming, because in that flash I saw him, standing between the parked cars, looking up at me. His sad eyes pleading.

"Calder!" I called, reaching for him. At the sound of his name in the air, electricity surged not from the sky, but up from where he stood on the street. It blazed through my bloodstream. And everything went dark.

4

CHICKEN

I didn't remember getting into bed, but that was where I woke up. In my pajamas, no less, and I didn't remember putting them on, either. My head pounded, and I reached behind me. An enormous, throbbing egg was growing out of the back of my skull. *When did that happen?*

The storm had marched on, leaving shards of bright light streaming through my window. I groaned, rolling away and making my pillow crackle.

I slipped my hand to the cold side of the pillow and felt a piece of paper, folded in half, at the edge of the mattress.

I dropped the note on the floor and threw back the covers. My hair hung wild and tangled in my face, and I blew a few tousled waves out of my eyes. Jules cracked open my door.

"How you doing?" she asked. The way she said it made me feel ridiculous. Maybe she knew how I got the goose egg.

"Not sure," I said, my voice froggy.

"You freaked everyone out last night."

"I did?"

"When you didn't come back downstairs, Robby got worried."

I must have frowned, because Jules reproached me with a look that said I could be a little more appreciative of the fact he'd been paying attention. She was right, of course. He was only looking out for me.

"So we came up to check on you," she said. "You had the window open and you were lying on the floor in about a quarter inch of water."

"I don't remember opening the window," I said, more to myself than to Jules.

"Your dad was all freaked out. Thought maybe you'd been hit by lightning."

"Was I?" My body did feel a little tingly.

"Judging by the fact that you're talking to me, I'm going to go with no. But you did get pretty soaked."

I glanced at the floor. It was dry. My mind flooded with light, over and over like the flash on a camera. A silhouetted figure filled the lens.

"Robby and I soaked it up with bath towels. Don't worry. My mom never saw it. You really don't remember anything?"

"Is *my* mom okay? She's not worried, is she?"

"No, not once we got you in bed. I mean . . . you *are* okay, aren't you? Because Zach got his mom's van; he's picking us up in about twenty minutes."

My expression must have reflected my general bleariness.

"Beach?" Jules asked. "Remember? You and me . . . breaking some hearts this summer?"

The paper chain hung from my bedpost, as if wondering whether I'd add a thirty-second link. After last night's hallucination, it looked even more pathetic than it had in days past. I could see it for what it was now: an anchor, holding me back. Jules was right. I'd let my fantasies get out of control. Leaning out into an electrical storm was just plain stupid. If Calder White wanted to be with me, there was nothing stopping him. Enough was enough. It was time for me to move on.

We didn't get up to Square Lake until eleven, and by that time the beach was already crowded. Jules and Colleen lugged the cooler down the hill from the parking lot, while Sophie pulled an inflatable raft behind her. The boys carried armfuls of towels and dumped them in a heap on the sand before taking off running into the lake. Colleen managed to claim the last picnic table, but it had a broken bench and it was covered in sticky pine sap. Out in the water, the boys were already tossing their football back and forth.

I hadn't been in the water since that disastrous day in

May. Now that I knew my father was a merman, I didn't know what my half nature would mean.

The lake sparkled with sunlight. It was beautiful, but I hung back and adjusted the straps on my vintage bathing suit.

So what? I thought. So what that I'd never transformed into a mermaid in all the times I'd swum in Lake Superior. Maybe it was like bee stings, building up in your system over time until one day you're stung and your throat swells shut. Maybe, with me, it would just take one more trip into the water before genetics would catch up with me. Would I really want it to happen here? Now? In front of my friends and a beach full of strangers? That would be my luck. Why did I agree to come again?

Of course, Calder would say I was being ridiculous on all accounts. But then, he wasn't here to tell me that, now, was he? *Moving on,* I reminded myself.

"Coming in, Lily?" Rob called.

I cupped my hand to my mouth and yelled back, "In a sec."

I'd been stupid last night, thinking I'd seen Calder below my window. If it had really been him, he would have waved. He might have even rung the doorbell. Out of the corner of my eye, I saw a brown oval spiraling toward my face.

"Heads up!" someone called.

I managed to catch the football between my elbow and my ear. "Thanks, guys. That's awesome. Hysterical."

Rob was there a second later, laughing and apologizing and dragging me into the water. I protested, pushing at his chest and trying to sit down so he couldn't budge me. I grabbed at his biceps. He wrapped his arms around my hips. I was waist deep before I knew it and tingling from toe to hairline.

It was too late now. Whatever was going to happen, was going to happen. I dunked under, conscious of the muffled voices above me and the rush of churning water around me. The soft sound of *leh, lee, leh, lee* and then my name called out. "Lily."

I resurfaced with my chin up, my wet hair dragging down my back. A feathery touch glanced across my foot, and then someone was prying my legs apart and swimming through. My feet left the ground as I rose, involuntarily, out of the water, astride Robby's broad shoulders. He started walking toward Scott while I struggled to keep my balance.

"Chicken!" Colleen yelled as she scrambled onto Scott's shoulders.

Ah, crap, I hate this game. I'd had enough water wrestling for one lifetime—that was for sure. But before I could say no, Colleen and Scott were coming at me with better motivation than I could muster. Even though Scott could barely see without his glasses, he was taller than Rob so they had the advantage, and Colleen's hands were like chicken claws, clenching and unclenching.

"You're going down, Hancock," Scott said.

No doubt.

Colleen's fingers laced through mine and her wrists bent to get better leverage.

"Come on, Lily. You can take her," grunted Rob from below. He held my feet like stirrups and tried to push me up to get the better of Colleen. All I could think about was how clumsy and awkward I felt with Rob struggling beneath me.

31

Colleen rammed into me, and Rob staggered. The world pitched at a forty-five-degree angle and hung suspended for a second before I splashed into the lake, now deeper. Iron and silt tinted the dark water. The soft *leh, lee, leh, lee* filled my ears.

"Again," said Rob, but I backed away, treading water.

"I don't think Chicken is my game," I said.

"We don't have to play, then," Rob said. "Let's do something else."

I sputtered water from my lips and pushed my hair off my face. "What exactly did you have in mind?"

He put both hands on my arms and gave me a look that said something I didn't want to hear. *Oh, no. Oh, no no no.* I turned one shoulder into his chest, laughing so I wouldn't offend him. I looked to Colleen for support, but she and Scott had not-so-subtly turned their backs and were focusing on each other.

"Listen, Lily, I was thinking—"

"I already have a boyfriend," I said, hoping it wasn't a lie, hoping I wasn't embarrassing myself by misreading where this was going. I turned toward the beach and swam until it was shallow enough to stand.

Rob was still right there, but at least now it was his turn to look awkward. His cheeks flushed as the sun reflected off the water and up at his face. "That guy from up north?"

"Jules told you?"

"Yeah, but I guess I thought you were making him up."

"Oh, c'mon, Robby. Why would I do that?"

"Well, you never dated anyone around here, and you weren't up there for that long; I thought maybe you were only saying that because I hadn't asked you. . . ."

"My ego isn't that fragile," I said.

"Oh, I know, I didn't mean . . ." His hand was back on my arm.

"Whatever." I kept moving.

"Don't be like that. We'd be great together."

"Don't be like *what?*" I asked, spinning on him. "Reasonable? Not idiotic? We're friends." This would have been embarrassing if it weren't so maddening. What was wrong with guys? It must by the Y chromosome. Even if this made sense, we were leaving for college in ten weeks.

"Right! Friends!" said Rob. "We already like each other."

"I don't want to ruin our friendship."

Rob rolled his eyes. "Are you kidding me?" He plucked at my bathing-suit strap, and I slapped his hand away.

"What's that supposed to mean?"

"God, Lily, you are such a tease."

His words punched the wind out of me. "Take. That. Back."

"No," he said, folding his arms across his chest. "I won't."

"What have I ever done to you?"

"Exactly my point," he said, his face turning smug.

"Are you for real? Since when did you become such an ass?" I turned and slogged through the water, then marched up to the picnic table. Jules and Colleen were fighting over a chip bag. Sophie was nearby, burying herself in the sand. By the time I'd squeezed the water out of my hair, Scott, Zach, and Rob had resumed their football game, although I noticed Rob throw a few furtive looks my way, too.

Stupid, stupid, stupid boys. Ruining everything with their stupid assumptions and stupid hands and stupid promises to come back for me. I wrapped my towel around me like a sarong. I needed a few minutes to myself. When no one was looking, I stole away, following a line of oak trees thirty feet from the shore, north toward a wobbly boat dock. There were three aluminum rowboats on the shore, turned on their sides. A perfect, shady place to sit. And hide. And wait for it to be time to go home. *Home.* Wherever that was these days.

I drummed my fingers on the first metal hull, which rang hollow. Same with the second. The bow of the third rowboat rested against the dock. As I prepared to sit beneath its shade, a hand shot out and grabbed my ankle.

5

REUNION

I stifled a shriek and hit the sand as another hand reached around my waist and pulled me under the small metal boat.

For a moment all we did was stare. His green eyes brooding, yet as frightened as my own. His wet hair hanging in dark, twisted ropes against his olive-tanned face. His soaking-wet board shorts pressing against my thighs.

The hull closed in on us from all sides, and the small confines amplified my senses. Even the silence bounced around, echoing in my ears. The smell of patchouli hung heavy in the air. Heat licked up at us from the sand, and his breath was hot against my face.

"Look at you," he said, and his voice was disappointed.

I pulled the towel closer around me, but he yanked it off–his hands shaking–pressing his lips to my neck, trailing my collarbone. He pulled back and studied me with as much distance as the boat would allow. I counted to five before he let out a small groan, saying, "There. That's better. It's killing me to look at you, but I've really missed that color. Nobody lights up like you do."

Instinctively, I pushed him away. How dare he show up, out of the blue, without so much as a lame excuse for his silence. More than that, a shiver of fear raised the hair on my arms. Was he working up my emotions just so I'd be a more satisfying absorption?

I was ashamed of myself for even thinking it–Calder had worked hard to overcome the merfolk's naturally gloomy disposition and his craving for human emotion–but from the way his hands were shaking, it was clear our separation had set him back a few steps. How far back I wasn't sure I wanted to find out.

"Definitely better," he said.

I laughed nervously, wondering what color I might have been when he first grabbed me. Based on the flash of terror I'd had, it must have been pretty awful. Now, despite my attempt to stay mad, he was stoking me into euphoria with his touch. I could only imagine the temptation my emotions presented. Two deep breaths and I hoped I could subdue it, but he trailed his finger across my lips and then put it to his own so I knew I'd have to work harder on that.

"Man, you look beautiful." His voice was deep and rich like a riverbed.

"Where have you been?" I demanded.

"Around," he said, combing his fingers through my hair, fixing his warm gaze on my narrowed eyes, drawing me into his spell against my will.

"Yeah?" I said, doing my best to at least keep my tone sharp. I wasn't doing as well controlling my hands, which lay flat against his hip bones but no longer pushed him away. His long legs tangled with mine. "That's all you've got? *Around*? How's the fasting going?"

A rush of blood flooded his cheeks, making him look, if it were possible, even more gorgeous. "Don't be mean, Lily."

"*Mean?* You think *I'm* mean?"

"Of course it's been harder without you," he said. "A few close calls, but I've held it together."

"Could have fooled me. What were you doing grabbing me like that? I could have been anybody." As soon as I said it, I wished I hadn't. It probably *hadn't* mattered to him who it was. I probably was just anybody. "Close calls"? I didn't want to think what that implied.

"You're right," he said, drawing his fingers down my sternum. "It could have been somebody who bathed in orange juice this morning. I really should be more careful." He brushed a strand of hair off my face. "Hmmm. You look confused. I guess I never told you that," he said. "You smell like oranges."

He twisted my long hair several times around his hand and held it in a knot at the back of my neck while my hands came up to lie limply against his bare chest. A familiar silver band faded around his neck.

I sighed, giving in to the inevitable. Now that he was here, it was too much work to stay mad. And I didn't want to be mad. I wanted him. I wanted all of him. All the time.

"You were in the lake?" I asked. My fingers traced the topography of scars that crisscrossed his back and shoulders, my soft stomach pressed against his solid one.

"So were you," he said.

"You could have been seen."

"Not likely," he said, his voice blasé but gaining in intensity. "But I saw you."

His eyes turned a dark jade green as I tried to remember what should make him sound so accusatory. I might have been able to come up with a good comeback if he'd given me more time.

"Who is he?" he asked.

Crap. "A boy from school," I said. "An old friend." I choked on the last word.

"Didn't look like just a friend."

For some reason, that really ticked me off. If he cared so much, why hadn't he come sooner? My anger returned, and I let my words fly at him like hungry birds. "And what does it matter to you? Where have you been for the last thirty-two days? Probably traipsing—"

"I never traipse."

"—all over God knows where. Meeting up with other mermaids. Or maybe human girls. Pulling a Pavati, I suppose?" It was a low blow, suggesting he was capable of matching his sister's careless, cruel affairs with humans.

"I've been nowhere of importance."

"Nowhere with a phone?"

"Don't be mad, Lil," he said, stroking my arms in long, smooth movements. "You're muddying up on me."

"I'm not mad," I said. It was impossible to stay mad now that he was finally here. I struggled to even muster up a frown. "I'm not mad, but why didn't you call as soon as you heard?"

"Heard what?" he said, his lips moving up and down my neck.

"About Tallulah."

He pulled back and his expression was unreadable.

"Tallulah's body," I said. "It washed up onshore."

He shook his head infinitesimally.

"You didn't know?" I asked.

"That's impossible," he whispered.

"It's true. It even made the local news."

His face darkened so much I was convinced I could see the color in him. "Oh, God," he moaned. "Lulah."

"She was badly decomposed." I didn't realize how ugly the words sounded until I heard myself speak them aloud. I'd meant to be reassuring. Only Jack Pettit knew that the remains were those of a mermaid. "Do you think your sisters have heard?" I asked.

"How should I know?" he snapped. "I got my wish. Even if I were at the lake, our minds aren't connected anymore. I have no way of knowing what they're thinking or what they've heard. Not anymore."

"Couldn't you talk to them? Find out?"

"I'm not going back there, Lily. I can't."

I hadn't planned on this. I had no choice but to return. If Sophie was right, I needed to be there for Dad when he discovered the truth. "Well, I'm going home," I said.

"Lily, no. *Please* don't make me go back there."

"I'm not making you."

"If you go, I'll have no choice."

His words were delicious. I wanted him to repeat them over and over, but rather than ask I said, "I can't let my dad go back to Bayfield without me."

"You overestimate your ability to protect him from Maris."

I blinked. Confused. "This isn't about protecting him from Maris. I paid my dad's debt. You said—"

"That will change when they find out you're not really dead. Going back puts everyone in danger. I don't blame you for wanting to be with your family, but can't you make your dad stay here?" he asked.

"He has a job up there."

"Lily, I won't let you go."

"Like hell you won't." I rolled over to escape the boat, but he pulled me back.

"Okay, okay, settle down," he said, his voice soft in my ear. "I don't want to fight."

He buried his forehead against my chest. "This is my fault. I didn't think even a storm could shake her loose, but clearly I didn't do a good enough job of hiding her body."

"No one will come to the mermaid conclusion," I said, trying my best to put his mind at ease.

"Maris will hear of it. If it's making the news, it's only a

matter of time. They'll want to finish what Tallulah started."
Calder grimaced. "Going back is a bad idea."

"Dad is on the verge of experimenting. He's still trying to resist, but he's going in the lake soon. I don't think he should transform . . . accidentally . . . without any warning."

"I was afraid of that."

"It's time to tell him," I said.

Calder drew his eyebrows together, knitting them into an inverted V. "Again. Bad idea."

"Why?"

"Remember what I told you. Once I changed, I wrote off my entire family. Once he transforms, he won't be the same."

"You were only three. That won't happen with my dad. Besides, not telling him isn't an option anymore."

"You're not seeing the big picture here, Lily."

"I need to fix this."

"Fix this? What needs fixing? Quit thinking you can fix everything. I need you to stop and listen to me."

"Not on this." Muffled sounds from the beach reminded me of where I was. I kissed him once more. "I'm glad you came back. I thought maybe you changed your mind about me."

"You should know by now, I never break my promises."

He was very serious, but I grinned broadly. "I was counting on that. Let me go check on Sophie. You stay here."

Carefully, ducking my head, I rolled out from under the metal hull. The sun blinded me for a second so I didn't immediately recognize the dark, silhouetted figure surrounded by sun spots.

"Lily?" Jules asked. She grabbed my shoulders and shook me until my teeth rattled. "Haven't you heard us calling for you? We've been going crazy. The lifeguard has everyone in a line, doing a freakin' body search of the lake. I thought I was going to puke thinking I'd be the one to step on you. Sophie is bawling! God, Lily, I thought you were dead. I could *kill* you right now!"

I looked past her shoulder to the people linked at their elbows, shuffling through the water as a single unit. Most of them I'd never seen before. "I'm sorry, Jules. I really am."

"What were you doing under that boat?" she demanded. Seriously pissed.

"I, uh . . ."

"Sorry," Calder said, and crawled out from under the hull. The muscles in his chest and shoulders flexed as he pushed himself to his feet. "It's my fault."

"Oh, man," Jules said.

My sentiments exactly. "Um . . . Jules, this is Calder White. Calder, this is my best friend, Jules Badzin." Calder stuck out his hand, and I didn't have to look at him to know what he was doing. Jules wasn't blinking, and Calder's projections were readable in the air. At least to me. Jules, poor thing, was sinking like a stone. How well did I know how *that* felt. I jabbed Calder hard in the ribs.

"So glad to finally meet you," Jules said, pushing her hair behind one ear.

Oh, brother.

Walking with Calder back toward the picnic table was a surreal experience. It was like two universes colliding: On my left walked my past, steadfast and normal. On my right walked my hoped-for future, less certain and one hundred and eighty degrees removed from normal. I wondered which one would implode from the pressure of the other. I couldn't help but notice Jules stealing sideways glances at Calder. I knew what she was thinking without being telepathic.

"Quit having impure thoughts," I whispered in her ear.

"Oh. My. Goodness," she said through her teeth.

Calder squeezed my hand. Of course he heard every word. He probably could have heard it from across the parking lot.

Jules ran ahead to tell the lifeguard I was safe. I almost wished I was hurt. It would make this so much less embarrassing if I was bleeding. Maybe I could fake a head injury.

The lifeguard blew his whistle in three sharp bursts and a collective groan came up from the shore. Rob came running, his face pale and sickly.

"Geez, Lily, where were you?" Then he noticed Calder. "Who's this?"

"The figment of my imagination," I said, more coolly than he deserved.

Rob pulled me from Calder's side and nearly suffocated me in a hug. "I thought you were dead," he said. "Don't do that again."

"Yeah, okay. Fine," I said, laughing a little. "I'm sorry. I should have told someone I was going for a walk." I pushed Rob off while electricity fizzed in the air behind me.

Rob let me go and stuck his hand out toward Calder, who hesitated and blew a long stream of air from his lungs before taking Rob's hand.

"Thanks for bringing her back safe," Rob said.

"I can take care of myself," I said, which made Calder wince, though I wasn't sure why.

Scott carried Sophie up the beach toward me, cradling her body in his arms. Her face was red and blotchy, making me feel my guilt more intensely than anything else.

"Honey," I said as she reached toward me. She was too heavy, and we collapsed on the sand.

"Hi, Calder," Sophie whimpered, without really looking at him, as if she expected nothing less than to see him walking me home.

"I think I've had enough sun," Colleen said. "Maybe we should call it a day."

Calder picked Sophie out of my lap and slung her onto his back without any effort. Together we climbed the hill toward the parking lot, dragging our coolers and towels with less finesse than we had hours earlier.

"I don't think we have room for you in the van," Rob said to Calder.

"That's okay. I've got a car."

I looked around for the Impala but I didn't see it anywhere.

Calder asked, "Ride with me, Lil? Sophie, too?"

I took his hand, and Rob jogged to Zach's van a little faster than normal.

"There's something not right with that guy," Calder said.

I laughed, looping my arm through his. "Yeah, all right. Remind me to tell you the one about the pot and the kettle."

"Robby's sad and kind of confused," Sophie said, watching him climb into Zach's van.

"Oh yeah?" I laughed. "And what do you know about it?"

Sophie shrugged. "You just have to look at him."

Calder gave Sophie a funny look, then ruffled her hair with his hand. "Get in the car, kiddo." He held the door open, and she slid into the backseat of a rusty black Buick. I got in the front and sat as close as I could to Calder.

"You look very pretty, Lily," Sophie said as she drifted off to sleep.

Calder's gaze went to the rearview mirror; then he raised his eyebrows at me. I felt the blood rush into my cheeks. "She probably has heatstroke," I said.

6

TRUTH

The motel where Mom and Dad were staying was a one-story structure with an enormous peak over the entrance still strung with sagging Christmas lights. Calder pulled into a spot alongside the pool but near my parents' room. The brass number 12 hung askew above the peephole in their door.

Sophie peeled her sweaty legs off the vinyl seat with a ripping sound and climbed out. She ran to the motel room door and knocked. In the brief second it was open, I saw Mom packing and the blue flicker of the television reflected in a mirror.

"I'm telling him now," I said. "Before they leave. Maybe you'll get your wish and he'll change his mind about going back."

"Please rethink this, Lil. He's gone his whole life not knowing."

"You probably don't need to worry so much," I said with a sigh. "I doubt he's going to believe me."

"That's not what I'm saying," Calder said. His hand came to rest on my knee. I could feel the tingle of electricity in his fingertips, stimulating my muscles, making them jump. "He'll believe you. You can trust me on that."

I turned away from the door to look squarely at him. He brought his arm back to the steering wheel. "Why are you so sure?" I asked.

"Not believing you and not *wanting* to believe you are two different things. As soon as you start explaining, he'll believe you. In his heart, he might already know."

"You're sure?" I turned back to stare at Number 12.

"Without a doubt." He stroked my hair now and my confidence grew exponentially.

"Okay," I said, releasing all the air from my lungs. "How do we do this?"

"You mean how do *you* do this. I told you what I think. This is all on you. Besides, having me there isn't going to make him any more receptive."

"I need you there with me. To explain," I said.

He picked at the peeling rubber around the steering wheel. "I'll wait in the car."

"You seriously aren't going to help me?"

He took a deep breath and slowly turned to face me. "What exactly are you going to say?"

"I'm going to start at the beginning. And then I'll end by explaining about Tallulah, and her being found, and what it might mean for the future."

"As if we knew," he said, his tone scoffing.

"Are you going to be a jerk about this?" I stared at him, giving him the few seconds he obviously needed to think clearly, but he didn't budge. He stared at his hands on the wheel.

"Fine," I said. "I'll tell him on my own. But don't go anywhere."

"I won't."

I unbuckled and kicked open the car door, which creaked on its hinges. When I slammed it shut, shards of rust sprinkled to the blacktop like glitter.

I knocked, and Sophie opened the door. Mom and Dad were already standing right behind her, apparently clued in to another one of my near-death experiences. How many did that make? Three, counting last night. This time I hadn't even gotten wet.

"Mom. Dad," I said, for lack of a better introduction.

"What's going on, Lily?" Dad asked. "Are you trying to make us prematurely gray? Sophie said you almost drowned?"

"Hardly. Can I talk to you outside, Dad?" My voice was a thin wavering line.

Mom gave him a look and turned her wheelchair back toward the suitcases. Dad stepped out and closed the door quietly behind him.

"What's going on?" he asked. "Are you feeling okay? We shouldn't have let you go to the beach."

"Dad, we need to talk." He narrowed his eyes and followed

unwillingly. I led him to one of the white plastic table-and-chair settings that were placed around the swimming pool. It didn't escape my notice that he walked barefoot through every puddle on the pool deck.

The chairs scraped on the concrete as we pulled them up to the table. Dad's face was pale, his blue eyes slightly sunken. His lips chapped and cracking at the corners of his mouth. Again I wished Calder had come with me. There were too many details I still didn't fully understand.

"Okay. I know what you're going to say, Lil, and I've already talked it over with your mom."

"You talked to *her* about this?"

Dad looked at me with a puzzled expression. "Of course. She wants you to come home, and I don't have any great excuse for keeping you away anymore. Heck, Lil, I want you to be with us. I've missed you. More than you know.

"And since I haven't seen any sign of . . . *him* . . . Don't look at me like that, you know who I mean. I don't think we'll have any more–"

"Dad, this isn't about begging to come home, although I'm really glad you want me to. Really. But what I want to talk about . . . well, it is kind of related to that."

"Related to what?"

"Home. I know you haven't been feeling yourself lately."

He looked at me intently then.

"And I think I know why." I waited for him to give me permission to go on. He didn't say anything more, though, so I faltered. "Um . . . so yeah. Well . . . Maybe I should tell you a story."

Dad ran his fingers through his hair. "Is this about what happened last month? Because I don't–"

"Sure, Dad. But that's where the story ends. It's not the beginning."

I watched the replay of last month's events in his eyes, the panic of seeing me in the water, the terror of seeing the monster his dad had warned him about, the uncertainty of not knowing what to do. "Do I want to hear this?" he asked.

"I'm hoping you already know what I'm going to tell you."

He shook his head and started to stand up. "Your mother needs some help packing. We want to leave by five."

I caught his hand when he was halfway up. "Sit down, Dad. This is important. You need to hear this before you leave."

He collapsed with a sigh into his chair and ran his finger up and down one of the grooves in the white plastic table. "Fine, Lily. You talk. But I can't promise to listen."

I pulled my chair up to his, bringing our knees together. The skin on his hands was dry and cracked. I rubbed my finger over my own knuckles a few times, looking for the words to start. "Okay, so, once upon a time . . ."

He raised his eyebrows, and I looked into his eyes. How many times had this situation been reversed? Him reading me a bedtime story that began exactly this way. My story wasn't starting the way he expected.

"There was a woman named Nadia. She lived on Lake Superior, or I should say, she lived in the lake."

His lips tightened in response.

"Dad, remember that story Jack told us around the

campfire? The one about the mermaids who walked around like regular people?"

"That's just a story, Lily."

"That was Nadia," I said. "Nadia had children. Three daughters. And a son."

Dad closed his eyes and sighed in resignation. "You're right, Lily. I do know what you're telling me. I saw it. And him. That boy. That . . . *thing*. Calder." He said his name like a curse. "Is that what you're trying to tell me? Calder is this Nadia's son?" He shook his head to clear the impossible image of the mermaids from his memory.

"No, Dad. Not Calder. *You*. You are Nadia's son."

The words hung there. In the air. Hovering. Like a soap bubble waiting to pop.

"No," he said.

"Dad, just listen to what I'm—"

"*No,*" he said again. This time louder. He nearly growled. "I know who my mother was."

I nodded and bowed my head. I'd always known Grandma would be the biggest obstacle to making him believe. "Dad, I don't know what Grandpa told Grandma, but after what you saw last month, you have to realize that Grandpa wasn't crazy after all. He kept the truth a secret from you because he must have thought he was protecting you."

Dad pressed his fists against his forehead. "You're being preposterous."

I could tell it was just as Calder had predicted: Not believing and not wanting to believe *were* two different things, and in that moment they were battling to the death in my dad's head.

For a second, I wished I'd taken Calder's advice. Maybe I shouldn't have told Dad. He'd gone all this time not knowing and things had been fine. Well, maybe not fine, but he'd managed. Still, I couldn't shake the thought of him giving in to temptation, jumping into the lake, the full transformation happening without any warning or explanation.

A family with three shrieking children arrived at the pool. The oldest did a cannonball, drenching his dad, who shook the water from his magazine.

I pressed on. "The way I understand it, Grandpa was supposed to give you back to Nadia when you turned one, but he refused."

"Stop it, Lily," Dad said.

"Think about it. He kept you from the water. He refused to ever go back to the lake. Didn't you yourself say that you always felt the pull?"

Dad stood up fast, and his chair toppled over behind him. "I've been losing my mind. You have no idea what I've been suffering."

He was pacing now. "You have no idea. I've been insane with worry, thinking I'm going crazy just like him. Seeing mermaids. My God, what next? And what about your mother? If I lose it, how am I supposed to take care of her? How can I take care of her when I'm falling apart?"

I glanced over at the other father at the pool and caught him watching us. He quickly looked away and turned back to his magazine.

"Dad, sit."

"Gah!" He righted his chair and sat down, his head dropping to his chest. His face, pale with exhaustion. "What am I supposed to tell your mother?"

"Nothing! Don't tell her a thing. She couldn't handle this."

The next time he spoke, his voice was barely a whisper. "Why is it so much worse for me now?"

"I'm not sure," I said. I turned around, hoping Calder would come help—he had to be able to hear everything being said—but the landscaped shrubs surrounding the pool were too thick for me to see him. "I have a theory."

"What?"

"When you jumped in after me that day. That day you saw the mermaid. And Calder. You started to change. I saw the first sign. A silver ring. Right there." I touched my finger gingerly to his throat. "But you didn't make the full transformation. I think your body has tasted a bit of it. You're craving the water. Your body wants it."

"It's always been like that. It's only worse now."

"That's what I'm saying," I said.

"Why are you telling me this?"

Again, the doubt weighed down on me, crushing me. "The mermaid, Dad. The one Jack shot? She washed up onshore. If Calder's other sisters find out she's dead, he thinks they'll come after you."

"Me? Why–? Wait, have you been in contact with that . . . that . . . ? You know I told you to–"

"Calm down, Dad. Focus on what's important here." I launched into the rest of the story: How Nadia had grieved for him after he was taken from her. How she suffered when he didn't return. How she died. How Maris and Pavati blamed him for her death.

"I was a baby!" he protested.

I went on to explain how Calder had come to join the mermaid family and how my attempt to save my family

53

had all gone terribly wrong, though Dad had been there for that part.

"You're saying that . . . that was my sister in the water with you," he said, slowly accepting the truth. "It wasn't me. I didn't kill her."

"No," I said. "But Maris and Pavati don't know the truth, and they won't believe Calder if he tells them."

"Why not?"

"That's a longer story, Dad."

He stared straight ahead at the motel swimming pool, and I could guess where his thoughts were going.

Dad opened his mouth, then closed it. Then opened it again and asked, "If I dove into that pool, would I turn into a mermaid?"

"Mer*man*," Calder said, coming up behind me.

I spun around in my chair.

"And you don't want to do that in chlorine. It's a nasty business."

7

NEGOTIATION

"**Y**ou!" Dad exclaimed, rising from his chair. He recoiled in disgust, and a vein popped down the center of his forehead. "What are you doing here?" Dad threw out an arm as if to shield me from Calder, and the other father at the pool gathered his children closer to his lounge chair.

"I'm here to help Lily," Calder said. "That's all I've ever wanted to do."

"Help," Dad sneered. "You weren't much help when she was nearly drowned by that . . . that . . ." It looked like it was going to be a long time before Dad was comfortable with the word.

Calder ground his teeth and looked sideways at me. If that look was meant to remind me that he thought this conversation was a bad idea, and that he wasn't pleased about being dragged into it, well, yeah, I figured that much out for myself, thank you.

"I know how you feel about me, Mr. Hancock," Calder said. "You don't have to like me, but you do have to believe Lily."

When I turned to Dad to see his reaction, it looked as if he was trying to grind his knuckles into his forehead.

"And," Calder added, "I would be negligent if I didn't explain the rest before setting you loose on the world."

"No," Dad said, backtracking on whatever progress I'd made with him. "You can't expect me to believe any of this."

"I do, and you will," Calder said, dropping his voice lower. "You owe it to your daughter for what she did for you last month."

Dad's face paled. He didn't look at me when he said, "Do me a favor, Lil. Go to the lobby. Get me a coffee."

Calder nodded at me and I stood up reluctantly, leaving them alone by the pool.

The shabby motel lobby featured several outdated arcade games and an electric fireplace. Beside the check-in counter there was a low table with a grimy coffeemaker and a stack of Styrofoam cups. I filled one and stirred in powdered cream before hustling back to the pool. I didn't want to miss anything.

One of the little water-winged kids ran in front of me, and I had to stop short. Half the coffee sloshed onto the concrete deck, not to mention burning my wrist.

When I got back to the table, Dad had his fingers laced behind his neck and his head bent low over his knees. I could tell by his posture that he was done being angry and the truth had finally settled in.

Calder was already into his lesson. I pulled in close, irritated that he'd started without me. I set the coffee down in front of Dad, but he never touched it.

"Ideally, you'd stay here," Calder said.

"But I have a job. I can't lose my job."

Calder nodded. "I understand obligations. If you have to go back, there's no reason you can't teach in the fall. When you feel the need to swim, do it as soon as it's practical."

"Practical," Dad said, repeating the word like it was a bad joke. "What about this winter?"

"You'll start to dry out. More than before. More quickly, too. But you do have some options. After the channel between Madeline Island and the mainland freezes, get wet however you can, whenever you can. A tub. A sink. It's only a temporary fix, but no one will think anything of it. And then it'll be spring again. Trust me."

Trusting Calder looked like something my dad was going to struggle with for a while. "What about your sisters?" Dad asked, sitting up.

"*Your* sisters," corrected Calder. "I'm not blood related to any of you. And you're right—Maris and Pavati are going to be a problem. See, they think Lily is dead."

Dad turned a strange shade of green. I started to protest, but Calder gave me a look that silenced me.

Dad pulled his chair in closer. "What does any of this have to do with Lily?"

"If they discover Lily is alive, they'll still need retribution for our mother's death. For all I know, they'll want two lives. One for Mother. One for Tallulah. The only thing I can predict is that they'll be unpredictable."

"Lily, if you're in any danger, I'm afraid Calder is right," Dad said. "You're going to have to stay in Minneapolis. We'll make something up to tell your mom. Maybe you could get a job at the U for the summer."

"Uh-uh," I said. "No way. If you think I'm going to stay locked up in Mrs. Badzin's guest room like some fairy-tale princess for the next ten weeks—"

"Actually," Calder said, "now that I'm not compelled to stay up north, I was thinking of going back to the Bahamas early. I thought maybe you'd go with me, Lily."

My mouth popped open, and for a second any thought about protecting Dad disappeared. *The Bahamas with Calder? That could work.*

"Wait," Dad said. "What? No. Definitely not. Lily's staying with her family."

Calder shrugged. "That's fine as long as you're not going back to the lake. In fact, I don't know why I didn't think about this before, but given that you're related to Maris, I bet she'll be able to read your thoughts. If there's any hint in your mind that Lily survived . . . I'm sorry," Calder said, shaking his head. "I won't allow it."

"You won't allow it?" Dad asked scornfully. "You don't even know for sure that this Maris person can hear my thoughts."

"You already told him that part?" I asked. "What else did I miss?"

Neither of them acknowledged my questions.

"The other option isn't any better," Calder said. "If she _can't_ hear you, your silent approach will mean only one thing to her: that you've come to avenge Lily's death. Maris will understand that. She knows revenge. But how do you think that confrontation is going to end for you?"

"I told you," Dad said. "I have no choice but to go back, and I can't allow Lily to go anywhere with you."

It didn't seem like Calder was listening to my dad. He was staring down at the table, deep in thought. "I need Lily with me," he said. "She's the only thing keeping me . . ."

Calder hesitated and looked up at Dad. There was a lot more he needed to explain about what Dad's new merman nature might mean. Neither of us knew what forty years of being landlocked would do to his psyche. Maybe Dad would never suffer emotionally, like other merpeople did. I took Calder's second of hesitation and made my move.

"Then it's settled," I said. Mentally, I licked my finger and made a hash mark in the air. Score: Annoying mermen, zero. Mutant girl, one. "Dad's going back to Bayfield. He won't let me go to the Bahamas, and I refuse to stay in Minneapolis. You won't go anywhere without me. We're all going back to the lake!"

"This is insanity," Dad muttered under his breath. "All of it. But Lily's right, we're going back. To the Hancocks', that is. If you intend to join us, Calder, that will be your choice to make."

Calder scowled at the table and after a few long seconds said, "If you refuse to listen to reason, then you're not giving me much choice. But, Lily . . . I'm sorry, but if you insist on going, you have to do something for me."

"Anything," I said.

He looked up at me as if he didn't believe I could do what he was asking. "You have to promise to stay out of the water and close to the house. That is nonnegotiable."

Dad shook his head slowly, his neck bent toward the table. "Are there any more secrets I should know about? I'd like to get everything out in the open all at once."

I looked at Calder, whose eyes sparkled with good humor that felt completely out of place. He said, "Maybe now's a good time to tell your dad about that tattoo."

8

BAYFIELD

Shortly after we left the pool, Dad developed a sudden and alarming stomachache, so my parents ended up staying in Minneapolis an extra night, which gave me time to pack and say goodbye to Jules and her family.

The next morning, Calder asked if I'd ride with him on the trip north. But when Dad learned how Calder had come by the Buick, he made him put it back where he found it. Immediately.

There was a lot of protesting, bargaining, and attempts to justify the situation. It was actually hilarious. No matter how skilled Calder might think he was in the art of persuasion, he'd be the first guy in the history of the world to convince a dad that felony theft was a good idea.

"If you're going to be part of this family," Dad finally said, "there'll be no more thievery."

I'm not sure if he picked his words on purpose, but I could see what they meant to Calder, having no family of his own. Ultimately, Calder promised to try.

Unlike Dad, Mom was pleasantly surprised to hear about our meet-up with Calder. I thought she'd have more questions. I mean, it was all a little too serendipitous, wasn't it? But Calder worked his charms on her better than he'd managed with Dad. No surprise that she was *only too happy* to have him ride with us up to Bayfield.

The only bad part about the trip was that the backseat was cramped with Sophie, Calder, and me squeezed together, and Dad had his rearview mirror focused on Calder, rather than the road.

Calder's decision to come back with us had triggered a lovely father-daughter chat the night before. "We've got to set some ground rules," Dad had said.

I hadn't really cared too much what they were. For me, I was glad to obey as long as I wasn't in exile anymore, and rules had never mattered much to Calder. I'd leave any rule breaking up to him.

A couple of hours out of the Twin Cities, towns made way for pine trees and the air temperature dropped. Calder rolled his window down all the way, and my hair whipped around my face until I was able to find an elastic band tucked under the floor mat. I looped my hair into a messy bun, exposing my neck. Calder's fingers were quick to find it, and his fingers worked out the tension knots in my neck and shoulders. I caught my dad watching in the mirror.

To my left, Sophie scribbled on a crossword puzzle balanced on her knees; she sang aloud to whatever she was listening to on her MP3 player, off-key and perfect all at the same time. Some eighties hair band belted out a ballad from the front-seat speakers. Dad held the steering wheel in a white-knuckled death grip. Mom buried her nose in a book.

I reached down to the floor to pull *MY SCRIBBLINGS* from my backpack. As I did, my new beach-glass pendant fell to the outside of my shirt.

Calder lifted the pendant gently in his fingers. "Where'd you get this?" he asked. "I haven't seen you wear it before."

"It was a graduation present from my parents."

His brow furrowed, and he turned the pendant over a few times before letting it fall against my chest. I could feel the heat of his fingers, absorbed in the glass, warming my skin.

Calder turned back to the window, throwing his left arm around my shoulders. Dad's eyes were in the mirror again, but I didn't care. I snuggled against Calder's chest. The whole car was perfumed with patchouli.

Trees and convenience stores flew by the window in an amazing blur of shape and color, and in a few hours, the lake appeared like blue chips of paint through the dense tree line. Five minutes later, the trees fell apart, the road cut to the edge of the bank, and the wide expanse of blue welcomed us home. My voice rose above the car radio, "We're here!"

Sophie yanked the earbuds from her ears and looked out

Calder's window. Dad and Calder kept their eyes straight ahead, but I guess they could smell the lake long before I saw it. We all inhaled, holding our collective breath before simultaneously exhaling. Something about the smell tugged at my heart, which beat madly beneath my pendant.

Pulling through town, past the bookstore, Big Mo's Pizzeria, the IGA, and the Blue Moon Café, I felt a twinge of guilt at having left Mrs. Boyd in the lurch. I supposed by now she'd hired our replacement baristas. I slunk low in my seat in case she saw me as we passed.

Mom turned around and said, "Leaving a job is not a capital offense, Lily. My goodness, how did I raise a child with such an inflated sense of guilt? Quit worrying. We gave Mrs. Boyd your notice."

"She probably hates me," I moped.

"Oh, for crying out loud, she's not mad at you."

Calder looked quizzically at me and then at the café storefront. By the look on his face, it had never occurred to him we'd been irresponsible. He was probably used to taking off without notice. Clearly, he hadn't given Mrs. Boyd a second thought.

We pulled north out of town, finding the driveway more easily than the day we first moved in. This time when we unpacked it wasn't such an ordeal. Dad helped Mom into the house, and Calder grabbed my parents' and Sophie's suitcases at once.

I had somewhat more than the others, having moved most of my things back to Minneapolis. I carried my biggest suitcase up the porch steps, thankful for their welcoming lean under my feet. Seagulls squawked overhead, saying they remembered me. Or at least, that was the way I saw it. I was home.

Even if Calder insisted I be landlocked, the proximity of the lake brought me a comfort I hadn't realized I'd been missing.

Mom went into the kitchen to check the answering machine. "Sounds like the Pettits got your message, Jason. Martin's offering to bring dinner over if we want. They're such a nice family. Should I call them back?"

Calder followed me upstairs and dropped Sophie's suitcase in her room. "Oh," he said, sighing and closing his eyes. "That's what it is." He inhaled deeply, savoring the air.

"That's what *what* is?" I asked. All I could smell were mothballs.

"Mother. She was here."

"I think you're imagining that."

"No. It's her. I smelled it before, back when I first moved Sophie's things into this room. It didn't make sense to me then, but her scent is in the paneling. She must have spent a lot of time in here."

"It could have been Dad's nursery, but if she was that close, why wouldn't she have just taken him?"

The floorboards creaked in the hall, and I looked up in time to see the back of Dad's shirt pull away.

"Let's not talk about this now," Calder said, and I could see there was still a lot of sadness there.

He took my suitcase from me and followed me into my room. Once inside, he said, "So, this is your room." He trailed his hand along my patchy, homemade wallpaper. Before I'd left, I covered nearly half a wall with dead poet portraits, pages from *Sonnets from the Portuguese,* friends' school photos, and magazine cutouts.

I opened the window to let in some fresh air while Calder yanked Robby Hache's picture off the wall and slipped it into his pocket. He didn't think I noticed, and I didn't let on that I had. He could have it if he wanted.

When I came back to Calder's side, he pulled me onto the bed with such force I bit my tongue and the box spring slipped off the frame, crashing onto the floor. "Geez, what are you doing? Do you want my dad to come running? I doubt this falls within his ground rules."

His hand slipped behind my neck and held my face to his. My insides liquefied at his kiss, his fingers skimming the waist of my pants, his breath on my face, as he said, "I'll be a safe distance away before his feet hit the stairs."

"Yeah, okay" was all I managed to say. My fingers explored his face, the straight nose and square jaw, a slightly crooked tooth; I took a risk and stared straight into his eyes. *Fascination*, I thought. That was at least one thing I felt for Calder White. Pure and utter fascination. I couldn't get enough.

"Besides, he has to know I'm perfect for you," Calder said. "What other guy is going to put up with your mess of a family?"

He had an excellent point there.

Ultimately, it wasn't Dad's feet that pulled Calder away from me. It was the sound of tires crunching on the gravel below my window. We both went to look down on the driveway.

"And here come the Pettits," he said. "Their timing is always amazing." I watched Calder closely. Mixed emotions played in his eyes: malice, gratitude, disgust, fear. Sure, Jack might have saved me, but he was also Tallulah's murderer, and there was something else in Calder's eyes, too. Jealousy?

"I hate that that bastard gets credit for saving you," Calder said. "It should have been me."

"You're being stupid," I said, resting my head on his shoulder.

"Doesn't matter how stupid it is. I'll never forgive myself."

The Pettits climbed out of their van. Gabby had chopped ten inches off her hair, leaving it edgy and blunt. Jack was barely recognizable. His shirt hung crookedly across his sunken chest, and his overgrown hair stood out in odd angles around his face, as if he hadn't showered in weeks. A black stubble covered his face. Mr. Pettit and an older-looking woman followed them.

Calder grimaced and turned away from the window with a growl low in his throat. "What is wrong with that Jack Pettit? I've never seen anyone put off colors like that. He looks putrid."

Dad leaned in my doorway. "Jack came, too," he said. "Maybe you should make yourself scarce, son." Then his feet clomped down the stairs.

Calder blinked a few times and said, "Your dad's probably right. I don't think I could stomach being within six feet of him."

"Good, because I kind of like the idea of you being trapped in my bedroom."

He looked at the floor and said, "I've been trapped in worse."

"I'm going to have to go down and be social."

"Not too social," he teased.

"No, not too," I said.

I followed Dad downstairs. Mom greeted the Pettits in the doorway.

"This is so nice of you guys," she said. "Jason! Martin's here."

Dad grasped Mr. Pettit's hand, avoiding eye contact with Jack.

"My wife, Margaret," Mr. Pettit said, introducing her. Mrs. Pettit was a tall, thin woman, prematurely gray. She and Gabby carried two foil-wrapped pans of hotdish with globs of burned cream of mushroom soup clinging to the sides. My stomach growled.

Jack pulled around his dad. Sophie took one look at him, yelped, and ran up the stairs. I thought at the very least he'd say hi to Dad, who had been at the top of the cliff with him. Instead, he charged at me like a bull and jerked his head toward the back room. What could I do but follow?

He wheeled around and grabbed my arm in a too-tight grasp.

"Hey!" I said, prying his fingers loose.

"How come you never answered my texts?" he asked, shaking me.

"Texts? That was you? You're my unknown caller?"

He tossed my arm, and I staggered back. "Who did you *think* it was?" he hissed through his teeth. "I figured once you saw the picture you'd know it was me."

"What picture?"

He rolled his eyes and put his hands to his greasy hair. "The link to the photo I sent. The one of that beached bitch who tried to kill you."

I felt sick and dropped down onto a chair. "Why would you take a picture?"

"Proof!" He slapped his hand flat against the wall to accentuate the word. "I wanted you to know she was really dead. I thought if you knew, you wouldn't have to be afraid anymore. Then you'd come back." He lowered his voice and whispered, "I thought you'd want to help me."

"I wasn't afraid, Jack. And I already knew she was dead. I was there. Remember?"

"Yeah. I remember," he said. "Apparently better than you do." He seethed. "They tried to kill you, Lily."

"No," I said, as calmly as I could. "*They* didn't. Only one did, and you only know half the story."

"I know all I need to know. You're brainwashed enough to let one of them keep hanging around. I suppose it's *him?*"

"Who?"

"Don't play me, Lily. This place reeks of incense."

There didn't seem to be much point in lying, so I shot back, "Why do you sound so surprised?"

"Me? Don't *you* be surprised. Don't come crying to me when your precious merman takes off for good. I warned you. That's what they do. He'll mess with your head. Then he'll be gone."

When he said it like that, it resurrected the old fears I'd had during my exile. I tried to muffle those doubts by re-membering what Calder had said at the pool: *I need her, I need her, I need her.* Of course, that didn't negate what Jack was saying. I supposed there could come a day when Calder didn't need me anymore. And I couldn't deny that his need hadn't meant anything over the thirty-two days he'd been gone, without a word to me.

"I thought you liked the mermaids," I said. "I thought you *loved* Pavati. You told me once you secretly hoped you were one of them."

Jack laughed darkly and it raised the hair on my arms.

"Funny thing happened on the way to a cliff last May. I finally grew up. I realized what a fool I'd been to think Pavati cared about me.

"Mermaids are only in it for themselves. They take, take, take. If they give us anything, it's only a tease so we stick around long enough for them to take some more. They don't care about us, Lily. And they're all the same. Don't. Trust. Mermaids."

Dad and Mr. Pettit came into the back room as Jack's last word dropped to the floor. Gabby followed, looking embarrassed and like she wished she'd found something better to do tonight.

Fortunately, both our moms were busy in the kitchen talking hotdish recipes, so they were oblivious when Mr. Pettit reproached Jack, saying, "Oh, for Pete's sake, would you shut up? This is getting ridiculous."

"What's it to you?" snapped Jack.

"Dad, Jack, please don't," Gabby said.

"If you want to make a fool out of yourself," Mr. Pettit said, "talking to news reporters, spouting your mouth off to the *police,* for God's sake, that's one thing, but when people start asking *me* about it, when you start embarrassing the family, pushing this nonsense on *these good people,* it's gone too far."

"I was only talking to Lily," Jack said. "You're the one making this a bigger thing than it needs to be. And I've probably got a much more receptive audience in 'these good people' than I'll ever get from you."

Dad silenced Jack with a look.

"Excuse me," I said. I pushed around Jack and ran for the

stairs. When I got to my room, the box spring and mattress had been made right. Calder was gone. The vacancy took my breath away.

Gabby followed me up. "Hey, um, I'm sorry about that." She gestured behind her toward the stairs just as the front door slammed. "We should have left Jack at home. He is seriously messed up. Even more than before." She tried to laugh, but failed.

"No more than usual," I said. I opened my closet door to see if Calder was hiding inside, but it was empty save for a musty cardboard box full of vintage band T-shirts. I noticed that someone had pulled my Lady of Shalott dress off its hanger and thrown it in the wastebasket. Apparently, the dress raised too many painful memories for Calder. As much as I wanted to keep it, and as much as I didn't like people telling me what to do, I left it where it lay. It was a small price to pay.

"It's been coming on slowly all year," Gabby said. "Dad was pissed enough when Jack didn't go on to college last fall . . . spending all day on the lake . . . but the last couple of months have been bad. At first, I thought it was because all his friends had moved on while he stayed back. But that was his choice, right? That shouldn't make him act so crazy. Then I thought it was because you left. I thought maybe he liked you even more than I thought."

"Yeah, that's not it," I said. "He's just being stupid."

"No, I know it's not you now," Gabby said. "It's this mermaid obsession. It used to be kind of quirky. Now it's getting embarrassing. Did you hear my dad say that Jack went to the police?"

"What for?"

"He told them the town needed to set up a night-watch group." She paused, waiting for me to catch up, but I was already two steps ahead.

"An armed patrol." She lowered her voice. "He's telling anyone who will listen that mermaids are killing people out on the lake."

That's rich, I thought. *Apparently he's forgotten that the last kill on the lake was at* his *hands.* I got down on my knees and looked under the bed.

"Jack refused to leave the station until someone took him seriously. They had to call my dad to come down and get him. Chief Eaton is one of my dad's best friends. Super embarrassing. What are you looking for?"

"Oh, um, I lost something," I said. "An earring."

"Let me help you. Was it special?"

"Very," I said, noticing for the first time that the screen was off the window.

Later that night, rain splattered against my open windowsill. Calder was out there somewhere. I wondered if he was cold. I wondered if he'd found shelter for the night. Dad came into my darkened room and stood by the side of my bed. I pretended to be asleep, but he knew I was faking.

"Lily, we need to talk to you."

We? I turned over quickly to find Calder standing in the dark, behind my dad's shoulder, staring down at me with serious eyes. I pulled the blankets tight around me.

"I'm going to give this a go," Dad said. "See if there's any truth to what you've told me."

"Yeah, Dad. Okay."

"Tonight," he said.

"Wait? What? Without me?"

"Lily," Calder said, drawing closer. "Is that really something you want to watch?"

When he said it like that, when I thought about *all* that a transformation would require, I cringed. No. He was right. I didn't need to see that.

"Our first step," Calder said, "is to see if Jason can, in fact, transform."

So it's Jason now?

He glanced at my dad. "If he can—and I don't doubt that for a second—then we'll have to start training right away. He needs to know how to scramble his thoughts if Maris and Pavati can hear him, and he needs to know how to defend himself if they can't. Well, he should really know how to do that either way. He's not going to be able to stay out of the water—like you are." He looked at me hard to remind me of my promise. "So we're going to start training immediately."

"Train?" My voice was a whisper. "How long will you be gone?" I asked, dreading where this was going. The feeling of abandonment trickled through my chest, and I braced myself against their answer.

Dad paced back and forth at the end of my bed. "I can't stand it any longer, not knowing. I've got to stretch my . . . I've got to go. For just a little while."

"Tell me how long you're going to be gone," I demanded.

"It's just for a little while," Calder said.

"But I haven't seen you in over a month!" I hated how hysterical I sounded, but I couldn't help it. This was unfair, and Calder didn't seem to care at all.

"Lil," he said, bowing his head.

Dad stepped closer again. "I told your mom the college was sending my whole department to a conference and that I'd be home on Sunday."

"But that's *three days*!"

"Shhhh," Dad said, tamping down my volume with his hands. "It'll probably take me at least that long to learn what I need to know."

Dad looked at Calder and tipped his head toward the door. Calder took the hint and said, "Good night, Lily." He hung in my doorway for a second before slipping away like a shadow.

I watched the hall for a few more moments, in the hope that he'd come back. When he didn't, I set my jaw and flopped back on my pillow. I turned away from Dad to hide my face. He put his hand on my shoulder and rolled me back toward him. My cheeks were already wet.

"So it's that way? You'll miss him that much?"

"Every minute."

"Remember you'll be leaving for college soon, Lily. It's not a good time for you to get so involved." He brushed my long bangs off my forehead.

"You know what? I wish I'd never told you about any of this. This was my secret. I shared it with you, but now you're taking it from me."

"Lily, I'm not taking anything from you. Frankly, I don't want any of it."

I wiped my face on my pillow. Dad headed for the door, then he stopped and turned at the threshold. "You're too young to feel so strongly about someone."

I almost smiled. "Maybe you're too old to remember."

He smiled, and for a second, he was just my dad again. Normal Dad. The dad I wanted to remember. "Touché, sweet girl. I'll be as quick a study as I can. I'll have him back soon."

"Promise?" I asked, wondering if he was enough of a merman that I could bind him to his word. But he wouldn't take the bait, and my door closed softly behind him, without an answer.

I flipped on my light and pulled *MY SCRIBBLINGS* out from under my mattress. I bit down hard on my pencil to keep from crying. Within seconds, the loneliness I felt poured out of my heart and onto the page.

I almost missed the sound of one clean dive, followed by the sound of a second body convulsing in the water.

MY SCRIBBLINGS

The Fool Hearty

You left me where you found me,
A buzzing
early summer morning with the newborn honeybee
and the hatching bird.
The wind ~~slaps~~ slapped my face for my impertinence
in thinking you were mine to keep.
And mushrooms
like bald-capped actors memorizing ~~their~~ lines
gathered 'round the spot where ~~last you~~ you last stood
and promised me your love, still
wet with dew.
Not yet burned by the rising sun.

                    —Lily Hancock (Bayfield, Wisconsin)

9

SERIOUS

I fell asleep with *MY SCRIBBLINGS* still in my hands. Sometime after two a.m., the rain stopped and the silence woke me.
Moon shadows flickered across my walls. June bugs bounced
against the window screen. Restless and lonely, I tiptoed down
the stairs and out the door, closing it gently, resisting the pull
of the springs that wanted to snap it shut. The porch steps
creaked, but I didn't think the noise was enough to wake Mom.

I walked halfway across the yard and peered out toward
the islands, wondering where Dad and Calder were now.
"Calder," I said, under my breath.

"What are you doing, Lily? I told you to stay away from the water." I turned and saw a dark shape sit up in the hammock under the trees.

"Calder? You're back? Already? What are you doing in the hammock?"

He answered my questions in succession. "Yes. Clearly. For now. And trying to sleep. You've been tossing and turning all night."

"Why didn't you tell me you were out here?"

"Jason told me not to."

"And you listened?"

"Of course I did. I want to stay close to you, and he wasn't about to let me sleep in the house. How could he explain that to your mom? I'm supposed to be on Madeline, living on my parents' sailboat. Remember?"

"Yeah, but he's making you sleep outside?"

"I always sleep outside. Don't be mad at him. I promised I'd behave, and I want to stay on his good side."

"So . . . ?" I asked. "How did it go?"

Calder smiled in the darkness. "He transformed, all right. He's a natural." His eyes tightened on the last word. "Better than me when I was new."

"Where is he now?" I asked.

"In the house, hopefully sleeping. The transformation back to legs took a lot out of him. He was puking for a good half hour."

I bit my lip and turned to look at the house. "Are you sure he's okay? Maybe I should go check on him."

"Relax, Lily. This went much better than either of us expected. Something about science types, they find this whole thing more fascinating than horrifying. That must be why Mother sought them out."

I groaned in disgust.

"Hey," Calder said. "Don't forget this was your idea. We're heading out again at sunrise."

I climbed into the hammock alongside Calder. His muscular arms enveloped me, warming me against the night air. Then his fingers lifted the beach-glass pendant off my chest and turned it around in his fingers, just as he had once before.

"What is it?" I asked.

"That's what I'm trying to figure out. There's something different about you. The last couple of days, it's like your colors are changing. I can see them even in the dark."

I shifted uncomfortably in his arms. "Well, I *have* been under a little stress."

"I know what stress looks like and, yes, I can see that, too, but that's not what I'm talking about."

"Well, do I look different *good* or different *bad?*"

"Neither. Just different. You said your parents gave this to you?" he asked, still studying the pendant.

"It was a family heirloom from my grandpa," I said, gently taking his hands from the necklace.

"Tom Hancock?" he asked, his voice raising.

"*Shush.* Geez, relax."

"You're right. You're right," he said, stroking my hair. "I'm sorry. Old prejudices die hard. Still, could you take it off for a second?"

"Why?"

"Just curious." He reached behind my neck with both hands and undid the clasp, releasing the chain around my neck. I took it from him and slipped it into the pocket of my sweatpants.

"Better," he said. "You look more like you again. I wonder why that is."

We lay in silence, the night pressing in on us, as I convinced myself that any kind of different would mean *different-bad* to Calder. When the silence grew to an uncomfortable length, I broke it.

"It's killing me to think about you and Dad out there when I can't come with." My lips brushed against his shoulder as I spoke. A strange bitterness percolated in my gut.

"I know it is. I can *see* that, too—probably more clearly than you'd like to let on."

"I never thought I'd have to be jealous of my dad. Other girls, sure, but—"

"Don't be ridiculous," he said, his hand slipping under my shirt, his long fingers encircling my waist.

"Did you ever think what would have happened if Dad hadn't been there to pull me out?"

"I try not to."

I pressed my nose to his neck, behind his ear, and breathed in the heady scent of him. I whispered, "If Dad hadn't pulled me out of the water, I would have died."

I felt a shiver run through him, and I cherished the confirmation that changing colors apparently didn't change how he felt about me. "You said you would have reinvigorated me and made me a mermaid."

"Those were desperate times. Desperate thoughts. It wouldn't have worked. I told you before, only a mer*maid* can reinvigorate."

I ignored him. "Then *I'd* be the one swimming with you this summer, instead of being on house arrest."

"A part of me does wish you could come with us."

"Then bring me," I said, tracing the contours of his lips and then kissing them softly.

He pulled away, saying, "Please take this seriously. It's important. You don't want to undo everything we've worked for. Your dad without a target on his back. My freedom. Your safety."

His words slowed to a deep, rhythmic pulse. Like blood through a vein. Like salmon pushing upstream against the current. I stared into his eyes and found my mind adopting the same steady pulse as his words, until my thoughts slowed to a stop, incomplete and lost. Just as a brilliant counterargument would occur to me, it would dissipate in the night.

"Go to sleep, Lily," he said, and although I protested with my words, my mind was in complete agreement. I closed my eyes for only a second. That was my first mistake, because when I opened them again, it was morning. It was raining. And Calder was gone.

I did my best to follow Calder's house-arrest orders. Honest truth. The first day, I folded everyone's laundry and did the dishes for Mom. I dusted; I vacuumed; I alphabetized the CD rack, then the spice rack—pretty much did anything I could think of to kill time.

But by the second day there was nothing left to clean. I stared into my closet, wondering if I could color-code it, but the whole thing was getting ridiculous. Screw it. I needed air, at least air that didn't smell like Pine-Sol.

Outside, a storm front was rolling in. It was the kind of weather that made me feel boxed in. I pulled on my running shoes and ran out the front door and up the berm on the far side of the road, through the pine forest, and along a well-worn deer path. There wasn't any harm in this. It wasn't like I was going to run into a mermaid out here. I wasn't breaking any of Calder's rules.

I picked up my pace, reveling in the feel of the wind against my face, until the path dipped into a mud-slick ravine and slowed me down. I crept down the steep slope, carefully inching my way along the edge, clinging to pine branches to keep my shoes semi-clean. I thought I was past the worst of it when I slipped on a patch of loose pine needles and had to catch myself against the trunk of a tree. A layer of amber-colored tree sap smeared against my palm.

As I looked for something to wipe my hands on, my eye caught a movement on the path ahead. I watched as a guy dressed in a dirty baseball uniform approached. He didn't see me. His eyes were on his shoes as he kept track of his footing. Baseball cleats hung around his neck. He was about my age and not much taller than me, stocky, with brown, shiny skin—like an acorn—and gelled, spiky black hair.

He held his expression in a serious scowl, and when he got ten feet from me, he inhaled sharply and looked up with a panicked expression. Surprisingly, his wide, frightened eyes were a pale sky blue.

He said, "Whoa! You're a long way from home."

"I'm sorry," I said. "Do I know you?"

He gave me a puzzled look. "Huh. Guess not. Thought you looked familiar for a second." His face fell back into its serious frown, and he looked over his shoulder as if he were being followed. "What are you doing out here?" he asked.

I wanted to retort with *It's a free country,* but just because he was impolite didn't mean *I* had to be. "I thought I'd get some exercise. Go for a run. But the path's a mess."

The serious boy laughed, startling me with his volume, like I'd said the funniest thing he'd ever heard. I took a step closer, but my foot caught on a tree root, and I stumbled forward. I reached out to catch myself on him, but he leaned back, letting me fall in the mud.

"Careful!" he said. "Don't touch me."

"Geez, what's your problem? Ah, *crap,* these are newish pants!"

"Listen." He looked over his shoulder again, as I got back on my feet. "I'm not supposed to be talking to you anymore."

"Anymore?"

"You know what I mean."

Behind him, the muffled sound of voices grew louder. Then he whispered, "I gotta go. Do us both a favor and hide behind that tree. I don't need my brothers to see you. They wouldn't like it if they caught us talking."

The approaching voices rose and fell with bits of laughter. "But–"

"Go on," said Serious Boy. "Hide."

I ducked behind a massive cedar, muttering, "Whatever." As ridiculous as I felt, something made me take Serious Boy's advice. From my hiding spot, I watched as several boys with baseball bags slung over their shoulders made their way up

83

the path. Their once-white pants were pulled up to their grass-stained knees.

"Too good to walk with us?" yelled one.

"That's right," said Serious Boy.

I peeked around the side of the tree and swiped at a bee that buzzed by my head. One of the boys turned around to look, and I ducked back before he saw me.

"What's wrong, G?" Serious Boy asked.

"Nothing," said the other. "Thought I heard something."

"Quit being so jumpy. Maybe if you got your nerves under control, you'd stand a better chance of hitting the strike zone."

"That's big talk from Mr. Oh for Three."

I listened as their feet sloshed away through the pine needles and last year's leaves. When I thought it was safe, I snuck another peek, and found Serious Boy walking backward, thirty yards ahead but still looking at me. He shook his head and gave me a patronizing look; then he turned, talking loudly and forcing a laugh.

I watched until they were out of sight. After they were gone, I stood–baffled–behind the tree, wondering why I was hiding and why a gangly bunch of ballplayers posed any kind of threat. I bet the boy was having a good laugh at how gullible I'd been to listen to him.

I took my time walking back to the house. If I couldn't even manage a run in the woods without paranoia setting in, this summer was going to totally suck. I left my muddy sneakers outside and threw my pants in the laundry before running up to my room.

There was a pink envelope on my bed. I broke the seal

and pulled out a grocery store greeting card with a picture of a droopy-eyed basset hound. *I'm Sorry,* it said on the front. The handwriting inside was unfamiliar.

Dear Lily,

You probably think I'm the biggest prick ever. And maybe I am. I'm sorry I was so angry at you last night. I've made stupid decisions. You're entitled to make your own. But I really do need you to back me up on this. So call me ok so we can talk it through.

Jack

I dropped the card in the wastebasket and walked down the hall to the bathroom. I stared at the face in the mirror. Dark circles lurked under my eyes like lazy purple moons. I splashed water on my face and leaned my forehead against the glass.

I wondered what color I'd look to Calder right now. I bent low and drank from the faucet, swishing the water around in my mouth and spitting every lonely thought down the drain.

10

DEFIANCE

After three days' absence, Dad made it back in time to go to Mass with us, but it wasn't until we got home from church that Calder knocked on our door.

"Good morning, Lancelot," I said, thinking it would at least get a smile out of him, but no such luck. Looked like our Lady of Shalott days were behind us.

He dropped his gaze once more to the beach-glass pendant around my neck and asked if Dad was ready to go.

"What do you mean *go*? You just got back. I've barely seen you!"

"This is important," he said. "Jason insisted on coming back to go to church with you, but I'm teaching him how to navigate the lake today. You wouldn't want him to get lost out there, would you?"

"I'll buy him a compass."

"You're a riot, Lil."

"I thought you wanted to protect me," I said, playing the only card I had. "How are you going to pull that off when you're miles away?" Calder pulled back, shaming me with a disappointed look.

"Are you planning on doing any more secret negotiations with your aunties?"

"Of course not," I said.

"Planning another virgin sacrifice?"

I crossed my arms. "No."

"Then you'll be perfectly safe until we get back." He lifted my chin and tapped the end of my nose.

Dad came down the stairs, pulling a T-shirt over his head. "Tell your mom I'll be in Duluth for most of the day." Then he ran out the door, and I had to call him back.

"Maybe you should at least make it look good, Dad. Take the car and park it somewhere." I tossed him his car keys. "It'll be hard to believe you're in Duluth with the car sitting in the driveway."

"Good call, Lily. You're a natural at this."

Yeah, right, I thought. *Natural what?* And then they were gone, leaving a cloud of dust in their wake.

A half hour later, Mom came out of her bedroom, changed into painting clothes. "Where's your dad?" she asked.

"He said he was going to Duluth."

"Duluth? Did he say anything about taking Sophie to her Girl Scout retreat?"

"No."

Mom groaned and fished her cell out of her purse. She dialed Dad's number, and his cell phone rang in the kitchen.

"Are you kidding me?" she said. "He's been so spacey lately." Then she was calling around for a ride for Sophie.

I grabbed an apple and headed down to the water. I was still in the yard . . . practically. I wasn't breaking any rules . . . not really. Technically, I was staying close to home, but halfway across the yard I stopped.

A dark spot bobbed on the water. A head? No, only a loon. I was being paranoid. But it scared me enough that Calder's warning echoed in my head. "I should go back to the house," I whispered to myself. I didn't want to make Calder mad.

But the water looked so inviting. Intoxicating. I rocked back and forth from my heels to the balls of my feet. This was stupid. I should listen to Calder. But, as melodramatic as it sounds, the lake called to me.

My pendant hung heavy and hot against my chest. The spot of heat spread through my skin to my heart, drawing me closer to the water as if reeling me in. I struggled to remember why I was supposed to stay on land. My head and my heart felt detached from each other.

Maybe I'll dip my toes. That was hardly dangerous. Then I'd be a good girl and go back to the house. Calder and Dad would never have to know.

I hiked up my long skirt and wetted my toes on the sandy shore. After a few seconds, I waded in—just up to my shins—then sat down on the soft sand. I leaned back, letting the cold water break across my thighs, flexing and curling my toes, digging my heels into the sand.

Closing my eyes, I imagined the feel of my legs blending into one. I could almost feel the heat, the burn, the knitting of bones. Somewhere out there, Calder and Dad were circling sunken ships, sweeping underwater sand dunes. But here on the beach it was only me and my imagination, and if I closed my eyes, it was almost as good. I snorted. *Yeah, right.*

The sound of a boat engine broke through the daydream, and I wish I could say I was surprised to see Jack out in the Sun Sport. The boat was close enough for me to see the light glinting off his mirrored sunglasses. If he saw me, he didn't acknowledge it. The ever-present binoculars hung around his neck.

I wondered when Pavati would make good on her promise from last May to visit Jack and, when she did, if he would call a truce. It was painful to watch him suffer like this. Even if Pavati didn't want to be with him anymore, the least she could do was tell him why.

I took off my skirt and inched out farther. I lay down flat, letting my hair fan out around me. The waterline pulsed at my temples. Metallic humming filled my ears, numbing my brain. I quoted T. S. Eliot under my breath.

"Let us go then, you and I,
When the evening is spread out against the sky
Like a patient etherized upon a table."

I wasn't surprised not to be cold. What I couldn't get over was the sensation of heat. It started in my toes, and then the soft spot behind my knees. My thighs burned as if I'd climbed a hundred stairs. And then there were whispers.

I turned over onto my belly and pulled myself out deeper with my hands flat on the sand until the ground dropped off below me, and I was swimming. I breached, gulping at the air, then dove, moving my body like a dolphin, savoring the oxygen like an expensive delicacy.

"To wonder, 'Do I dare?' and, 'Do I dare?'"

Did I dare to discover what my birthright could mean? When I came up for air—somewhat disappointed that I still required it—I was surprised by how far out I'd gone. It was way beyond what I could justify to Calder, so I quickly tucked and rolled in a somersault, turning back for shore, swimming underwater.

Small, delicate whispers, like feathers, brushed against each other, slipping together, blending into the next. I tried to listen harder as I quieted my thoughts and disturbed the water as little as possible. Now and then, if the sounds were hard or crisp—a *keh* or a *teh*, sometimes a *deh*—I could almost make out a whole word. I imagined they were calling, whispering, "Come to me." But then the whisper was a shout. Then the shout was a screech.

I broke through the surface, flinging water from my hair, and Maris was rising out of the water, staring down at me, violence in her silver eyes, her face radiant with fury.

She dove, and bone-cold fingers clamped down on my ankles, pulling me deeper. My body bucked and twisted as I tried to climb my way back toward the shore. I had been here before, locked in a mermaid's embrace. But being there by choice was so much different than now. I grabbed Maris's corn-silk hair and pulled. I slashed at her face. For a second, she loosened her grip, and I kicked furiously for the surface, only to get pulled back down.

And then there was another set of arms, and I was being yanked apart. My skin stretched and joints popped. I thought I might transform, that perhaps the adrenaline of the moment would be the catalyst for a metamorphosis. But today was not the day.

I was being torn in two—fought over by two emotionally ravenous creatures tearing me apart, like lions fighting over prey. I'd heard Calder talk about the mermaid's need for human energy. *Absorption,* he'd called it. It always sounded so much more gentle than this.

My mind was blank—just a buzzing sound. I couldn't think what to do or where to go or how to do any of it if I could. And then one thought came screaming into my head: *Stop!*

There was great jerk and thrust and one set of arms let go. I rushed for the surface. Gasping, I crawled through the water, frantically kicking at whatever creature was still close.

The screeching sound was now in the air, along with another voice, grim and unforgiving.

"Maris," Calder said, his voice stern with warning, his arms stretched wide as if he could defend the whole lakeshore, his muscles tense and flexing. He must have heard me open my mouth to speak, because he shushed me with a backward flick of his hand.

"Why is she alive?" Maris asked, her voice like a rake scraping my ears.

Pavati emerged from the water, perfectly formed, more beautiful than I remembered.

"And Hancock lives, too?" Maris asked.

"Don't do this," Calder said. Long red gouges ran down his arms and back where she had torn his skin. Blood dripped from the wounds.

Behind him, I dragged oxygen from the air in ragged breaths. I tried to swim backward, to reclaim the shore. Somewhere in the back of my mind I remembered Calder saying they wouldn't kill on land. But I couldn't make any progress; my fingers could not find purchase.

"You know Jason is one of us," Calder continued. His words were a calming rhythm. "Now he knows it, too."

Maris sneered at Calder's familiarity with the man who had once been their target. "A little too late to do us any good. I will have my justice." Her glaring gaze pierced me to the core.

"You have no right to retribution," Calder said. "Lily paid her father's price. She fulfilled the promise."

"How can you say that?" shrieked Maris, the whites of her eyes showing all around the irises. Pavati laid her hand on Maris's shoulder, but Maris snarled and Pavati withdrew.

Calder reached toward Maris, palms out. "She promised to sacrifice herself to Tallulah in her father's place. She didn't back out. You saw that much for yourself. The debt is satisfied."

A sharp slap of her tail on the water might as well have been a slap across the face. She said, "I don't see it like that."

Pavati drifted closer, smoothly, as if being pulled on a line.

Calder continued with his argument. "Lily did all she could do when she jumped. It's not her fault she lived."

"Let me speak to Tallulah. I want to hear her side," Maris demanded.

Calder's voice dropped an octave. "You can't."

Maris froze for just a second, the waves sloshing against her shoulders. "She isn't with you?"

"No," Calder said.

"She followed you when you left. I haven't heard from her in weeks. What did you say to her?"

"Nothing," he said.

Pavati tried again to enter the conversation. Once again, she laid her hand gently on Maris's shoulder. "You might not be able to hear his thoughts, but read our dear brother's face. Don't you see it?"

Maris studied Calder, and my heart trembled as she learned the truth. His face was always so easy to read. Calder couldn't look Maris in the eye. Grief weighted his eyes, pulled at the corners of his mouth. When he tried to speak, nothing came out.

"No," Maris said. "I don't believe it."

"A man," Calder said, doing his best to protect Jack from the penance they would demand. "With a gun. He must have thought he was helping."

Maris threw her head back and howled; the sound filled the sky, ruffled the trees. She covered her face, and then wrenched handfuls of hair from her head. I had a strange yearning to comfort her.

"A man with a gun?" Pavati asked. "Took quite a chance, didn't he? He could have shot the girl by mistake."

That had never occurred to me. I had already been so close to death, a bullet was nothing. What had Jack been thinking? Or hadn't he cared?

Maris wailed. The sound would have broken anyone's heart. It was the wind in the trees, the crash of breakers on the rocks, the cry of the gulls. It was all that wound into one.

She pointed at me, saying, "This is your fault. Why is my family shrinking while the Hancocks all remain?"

"I–"

Calder quieted me again with a sharp twitch of his head.

"Watch your back," Maris said. "You will pay. You will all pay." Then she shot from the water, arching with a black flash of her tail, and was gone.

"Pavati," Calder said. "Tell her. Convince her I'm right. The debt has been paid."

Pavati didn't respond. She slinked into the water, her eyes never leaving Calder's face.

When she was gone, Calder didn't say a word to me. He merely wrapped an arm around my body and swam me back to shore.

"I can explain," I said.

He stared straight ahead, his full lips drawn thin and tight. "I doubt it" was all he said.

11

NAKED

When my feet hit the shore, I pushed Calder's arms off me and staggered to the house. My legs shook under me, and I tripped as I ran up the stairs to the bathroom. I flung open the door, locked it, then filled the tub with hot water until the mirror and the windows fogged over. I emptied what was left of Sophie's bubble bath into the tub, sure that Calder was outside apprising my dad, telling him how childish and impulsive and reckless I'd been. How I couldn't be trusted. How I should be sent back to the cities without a chance for appeal.

How much time did I have? Still shaking, I stepped into the tub and slipped under the mountain of bubbles. Maybe if I promised to never go near the water ever again, they'd let me stay. I was glad Mom had gone with Sophie to the Girl Scout retreat. Neither I nor Dad would want to explain this one, not that he'd been there to see. For a second, I wondered why that was, but of course Calder would never have let him get so close to Maris, so soon.

There was a soft knock on the bathroom door. Through the sound of running water, a muffled voice said, "Lily?"

"G-go away!" I yelled. "You can't say anything I don't already know."

The handle jiggled against the lock. "I thought you agreed to stay in the house."

I cranked off the tub faucet. "If you're trying to make me feel better, you're going to have to work a little harder."

"Tell me you're okay," the voice said.

"I'm not okay."

There was a *click, chick, chick* from the hallway, and then the bathroom door slowly opened. Calder slipped inside and dropped my wet skirt on the bathroom floor.

"Geez!" I grabbed at the bubbles, trying to strategically place them. Sure, he might have been used to nudity, but I wasn't. He kept his eyes on me but, for all it mattered, I could have been wearing a burka. He was irritatingly blasé about this. Yeah, I knew I was nothing to look at compared to a mermaid's physical perfection, but he could at least pretend to be interested. I looked over the edge of the tub for a towel.

"Where's Dad?" I asked.

"Outside, watching the lake."

If not for the fading silver line around Calder's neck, I would have never suspected he'd just come from the lake himself. He was completely, and infuriatingly, self-composed.

"Now tell me what happened today," he said, his voice flat and parental.

I closed my eyes. I couldn't look at him and try to explain myself. Instead, I said, "Did I ever tell you I'm allergic to bees?"

"What does that have to do—"

"They always know where to find me. There could be ten of us, sitting side by side on a porch, minding our own business. If a bee came by, I'd be the one it would sting." I looked up at the ceiling above the tub. A long jagged crack ran from the corner.

"Bees have those special eyes," he said. "Maybe they're seeing the same thing in you that I do."

"My mom says I'm too willing to open a vein for whoever comes along."

"Is this how you're answering me? You went into the lake because you wanted to 'open a vein'?"

"I was . . ." How was I supposed to explain? It sounded so pathetic. I'd opened myself up to the danger—risked everything—because the lake begged for me. Because I couldn't say no to it when it asked. Because every cell in my body wanted to be what, somehow, it couldn't make itself be.

Without warning, I was crying. I pulled up my knees to bury my head.

Calder dropped to the pink bathroom tile, grabbing my hand out of the water. Soapsuds slid down his arm. He pressed my palm to his lips, but I pulled back, sloshing water on the floor.

This was so humiliating. In so many, many ways. I wished I could make myself shut up, but the words slipped out. "I miss you," I said.

"This is my fault," he said. "Lily, listen."

But there were things I needed to say. "Those four weeks we were apart were hard for me. I understand it wasn't the same for you. I'm okay with that. You finally had your freedom. I expected you to go out and enjoy it."

"Lily . . ."

"Close your eyes," I demanded. When he complied with an exasperated sigh, I climbed out of the tub and wrapped a towel around myself, stomping off for my room and leaving wet footprints behind. I slammed my bedroom door and kicked through a pile of clothes, eventually finding a pair of shorts and a fluffy, oversized sweater. I finished getting dressed a split second before Calder let himself in.

"I wasn't having fun being away from you, Lily. Being on my own was awful. I basically borrowed a car and drove. I got as far as Moorhead when I saw a bumper sticker that sidetracked me."

I kept my eyes wide open, staring at the wall, refusing to blink and let more tears fall.

"It was a red maple leaf," he said. "I'd been trying to remember the name on my parents' boat for so long, I'd forgotten about the flag. When I saw that bumper sticker, it clicked. I remembered."

"The Canadian flag."

"Exactly."

"You went to Canada."

He sat down on the edge of my bed and leaned back on his elbows. "Actually, I went to a library. I got on a Canadian transportation site and searched for vessels with names that started with *K* or *R*. Guess how many."

I crossed my arms. "How many?"

"Together, about four thousand."

"That's a lot to weed through. Did you think about cross-checking against stories about kids who drowned?" The moment I asked the question, I wished I hadn't. He took on such a sad countenance that I wanted to take him into my lap and rock him like a child. Instead, I said, "You already thought of that, didn't you. So? What happened? Did you find your parents?"

He shook his head. "There are too many drowned children . . . or children reported as drowned. . . . I couldn't bring myself to read those stories. I did narrow the search to Thunder Bay. That would have been their most likely port. It's close.

"And what would it matter even if I did find my parents? They've probably forgotten all about me." I tried to interrupt, but he touched his finger to my lips. "Even if they haven't, what are the chances they'd believe me if I told them who I was? I wouldn't look old enough to them. I don't even know my given name. They'd think I was a con artist or something. But what does any of that matter now?"

"I don't understand."

"Your dad and I had the most amazing day today, right up until . . . well . . . did you know your dad played three varsity sports?"

I wasn't following his train of thought. "So?"

He shook his head, as if he were trying to explain astrophysics to a toddler. "He's backpacked on five continents. He knows the lyrics to every Queen song ever written."

I covered my eyes with my hand. "Please tell me he didn't sing them for you."

"He was all caught up in some ancient mythology about merfolk being fantastic singers."

"I take it there's been no improvement."

"Terrible. Absolutely tone-deaf. But now I know all the words to 'Bohemian Rhapsody.' "

"Geez."

"Jason's done things. He's seen things. He's really lived. Don't you understand? Being with Jason is like having a real dad. Your dad *is* like family. Better than that. He's family who needs my help. *That's* why I'm spending so much time with him, Lily. Can you understand this? I wish I'd found him years ago."

"Yeah? Well, I'm glad you didn't."

He sat up and leaned toward me, taking my hand. "Why would you say that?"

"If you'd found him when I was Sophie's age, I doubt things would have worked out the same way. First off, my dad would probably be dead by now, and I wouldn't have you." *If I have you.* No matter what he said, his actions spoke louder. There was no denying he was spending far more time with Dad than he was with me. I couldn't make eye contact anymore.

"You know how much I need you," he said.

"It's stupid—with everything else going on—to feel this way."

"What way?"

"Like you've traded me in for my dad."

Calder tipped my chin and kissed me. "I know you just got dry, but how 'bout I show you something. It will do a better job of explaining than I can."

"You don't mean we're going swimming. What about Maris?" A chill ran down my arms.

"I was thinking more like a *virtual* swim." He sat down on the floor and he pulled me down. I straddled his lap, facing him, and wrapped my arms around his shoulders. He fixed my sweater so it didn't bunch up between us.

"Now," he said, adjusting my weight on his legs. "I know, in the past, you've preferred to resist this, but let me have my way with you, just this once?"

My cheeks burned. "I thought you said something about a *virtual swim?*"

"Look into my eyes, Lily. Relax. I want to show you something. Some*one,* actually. I want you to understand why I'm spending so much time with your dad. It's more than just needing to train him, and I don't want you to be anxious anymore."

I exhaled slowly, releasing the tension in my shoulders. I leaned in, staring into his beautifully clear green eyes. "Where are we going?" I asked, as they intensified in color.

He didn't blink. His irises burned with an inner fire I'd allowed myself to see only a few times before. His pupils dilated and, involuntarily, I leaned in farther. I felt myself falling into him, but my forehead never bumped against his.

His fingers trailed up my spine, and although a part of me knew I was still sitting in his lap and in my bedroom, another part of me was giving way to his hypnosis and equally convinced I was underwater.

Instinctively, I held my breath. Calder's lips were on mine, filling me with air. A cold burn flashed along my arms.

He made me believe he was swimming me deeper, farther into the lake, past the southern tip of Madeline Island, through surprising patches of warmer water. We dodged lake trout and whitefish, swatted at loons as they dove for prey. The low, muted bumps and high, metallic clinks of the marina faded behind us. They were soon replaced by an unfamiliar vibration that trilled along the lengths of my arms.

Calder responded to the change in sound with a change in direction. He tucked me gently under his arm and bore southeast. Eventually, we surfaced in an unfamiliar spot. The lake was calm with only a washboard ripple of waves across the surface.

"Cold?" he asked, his voice a soft murmur, his eyes still piercing my own.

"No," I said. "I'm a mutant, remember?" He rolled like a seal in the surf, pulling me on top of him. His heart beat against my chest.

"Well, c'mon, you creepy mutant."

I gulped another lungful of air before he rolled and dove, bringing me down to depths I didn't think I should go. Leaving the security of the air, I waited for the pressure to crush my lungs, but I never felt more than a firmness about me—like the water was holding me—my mind let go of earthly concerns, leaving the world behind, my thoughts slipped to the Lady of Shalott:

She left the web, she left the loom,
She made three paces thro' the room,
She saw the water-lily bloom . . .

This is it, I thought. The pressure on my body made me believe I was about to turn. Every thirty seconds, Calder sealed his mouth on mine. I searched ahead, following the line of his arm, which stretched out in front of us like a prow as he swam. Eventually, a dark spot took shape, growing as we drew closer, until it became a crumpled mass of dark, splintered oak, a broken mast, vacant portholes staring out at us like a many-eyed sea creature. The name *J. P. Brodie* was written in large script across the stern. Calder pulled me along to the starboard side, to the third porthole. On the other side of the glass, I could see part of a black coat and a button decorated with an anchor. Calder gestured for me to come closer.

I smiled, accepting his invitation, and peered through the window. A second passed, and then a dead man's pasty face bobbed ghoulishly across the porthole. My stomach hit my throat.

I scrambled out of Calder's arms to find myself standing in my bedroom—dry and disoriented and gasping for breath. "What the hell was *that*?"

Calder smiled impishly up at me from the floor. "*That* was Joe. He never changes. We can thank the lake's cold temperatures for that. Nothing bloats or rots."

"That's disgusting!"

Calder shrugged, surprised by my revulsion. "I found Joe in '74. I visited him regularly after that."

"Why?" I was going to have nightmares for sure. It was going to take a lot to erase the pasty-faced corpse from my memory, and I already had plenty of nightmares to deal with.

"He's a good listener. Maris wasn't what you'd call the nurturing type. Do you understand what I'm telling you now? Up until I met your dad, Joe was who I turned to. He was the closest thing I ever had to a father."

Compassion tugged at my heart. How selfish I'd been. "I'm sorry. I take back everything I said before. Have as much time as you want with my dad."

"No. I get it, Lily. I need to find some balance. You are the most important thing to me. Don't ever doubt that. You saved me from hell. I don't ever want you to feel left behind."

"Does that mean you're not taking my dad out again tomorrow?"

His ears flushed, and he looked away. "I'm afraid I have to. Now that Maris knows Tallulah is dead and you're, well— *not*—we'll need to be extra vigilant."

"Do you think she'll buy your argument, that the debt has been paid?"

"I hadn't considered it before, but judging by what I saw of Pavati today, she's had a taste of life without Maris's Hancock obsession. She doesn't want to go back to living with that. I'm hoping she'll convince Maris that it's time to move on. Right now, I'm more afraid of Maris's grief than retribution."

"I don't get that."

"If Maris's grief becomes too unbearable, if she loses control of her emotions, it's not just *you* who should stay off the water. Despair will take over her mind, and she'll go on a binge.

The lake will turn into an all-night buffet. That's what I mean about vigilance. We'll need to keep tabs on her. Pavati, too. She's no less dangerous. We don't need any more surprises."

There was something I'd been thinking about since getting Jack's card, something that would have been impossible before. But if Calder was switching gears from avoiding Maris to actively *looking* for her . . . "Calder, I think you should warn Maris and Pavati about Jack."

"Warn them?"

"He's trying to expose them. If they go on a killing spree"– I shuddered at the thought of all those helpless, unsuspecting people–"they'll be playing right into his hands."

"You might be right about that."

"If you can find Maris, do you think warning her will even make a difference in their attack rate? They'll still be mourning."

"Maybe. If they've retained any concern for self-preservation."

I bit my lip. There was one more thing I wanted to tell him, or not tell him, I wasn't sure which. The former won out, and I spoke quickly before I changed my mind. "If you need help finding Maris . . . um . . . When I was lying in the water . . . For a second, I thought I could–"

"Don't," he said.

"But–"

"Be careful what you wish for, Lily."

"I just–"

"Listen, I've been thinking, I should take you on a date."

The non sequitur caught me off guard. "A date? I thought we were talking about–"

"A date. Like a real couple. We can't sneak around forever."

That made me laugh, and it felt good. "I didn't think we were sneaking."

With his index finger, he tucked my hair behind my ears. "Your bedroom isn't exactly the social epicenter of Bayfield, Wisconsin."

"I didn't realize Bayfield had a social epicenter."

"Absolutely. Every summer the town does 'Summer Tuesdays.' They show movies on the side of Oleson's barn. The whole town goes."

"O-kay-ee." I dragged the word out into three syllables, wondering what Jules would have to say about this.

"So, movie on Tuesday?" he asked.

"I guess I could stand a little normalcy."

"Exactly my thought. Only one problem. They've got a theme going. Each Tuesday is a movie from a different decade. They've already done *Rebel Without a Cause* and *Beach Blanket Bingo.*"

"So it's the seventies?" I ran through a list of possibilities in my head. "*Saturday Night Fever?*"

"As if we had that kind of luck. They're showing *Jaws.*"

I squirmed as the iconic cello and bass played the E-F notes in my head: *da-dum, da-dum, da-dum.*

Calder read my apprehension easily. "Maybe we should postpone the date. Next week it's *Ghostbusters.*"

I laced my fingers through his. "Nope. This will be perfect. Deadly sea creatures are my favorites."

"Oh, right. I knew that," he said, and he pulled me under the waves again.

12

DATE NIGHT

Two days later, just after dinner, I stood in the upstairs hallway, wondering what smelled so rank. From the top of the stairs I could see my room and bedding strewn across the floor. Laundry–dirty and clean all mixed together–lay in heaps among books and crumpled paper balls. Although I didn't want to admit it, I thought I'd found the source.

"Are you going to strip your sheets?" Mom called up the stairs. "I'll do a load if you bring it down."

"Maybe we should burn it all," I yelled back, entering the pit of shame.

"Don't be so dramatic. If you want new bedding when you leave for college, we can think about a bonfire then."

College. Right. It was the furthest thing from my mind. I'd bought the obligatory U of M sweatshirt six months ago, as soon as I got my acceptance letter. That was about the extent of my planning.

I bent over and searched under the bed. *Ah, the source of the stank.* "Who left a tuna fish sandwich under my bed? Sophie?"

"Not me," she yelled from her room. "I don't like tuna fish."

"That's disgusting, Lily! Bring it down to the kitchen. I just finished scraping the dinner dishes. I'll take the trash out."

"No, I got it, Mom." I carried the plate to the kitchen, dumped the sandwich in the trash, and sealed the bag, holding my breath the whole time.

"Well, there go my plans for tomorrow," Mom said from the living room.

I dropped the plastic bag outside on the porch.

"What's that?"

Mom put her phone on the coffee table. "Sophie's Girl Scout leader just called to cancel our swim outing for tomorrow. Apparently they're reporting more rip currents. Nearly drowned another kayaker. That's two this week."

I stared at her wordlessly. Two kayak accidents? How had I not heard that? Calder was probably just sparing me the guilt trip. If Maris was starting a binge already, it was my fault. If I'd done what I was told and stuck to the house . . . Or maybe Calder didn't know. We hadn't seen much of him or Dad since they started looking for Maris. Obviously they hadn't found her yet.

"They're sure it's just rip currents?" I asked, working to keep my voice calm.

"*Just?* Isn't that bad enough? I want you to tell your friends to stay off the water. What's so funny? I'm serious."

"If you haven't noticed, Mom, I'm not exactly deep in friends here. Second, we live on a freakin' lake."

"Watch your language."

"Gabrielle's here," Sophie yelled from upstairs.

"Did you know she was coming?" I asked Mom.

She shrugged. "Guess you've got a friend after all. Tell her to stay off the lake."

Gabby knocked at the door by kicking it with her foot. I opened it for her, and she came in—arms loaded with a pink, plastic toolbox and an overflowing shopping bag. "Ready?" she asked.

"Ready for what?"

Gabby jerked her head in the direction of the stairs, and I followed her up to my room. She dropped her bag on my bedroom floor and turned. "Humor me. I need a serious distraction from my nightmare of a brother."

"Yeah, but—"

"It's Summer Tuesdays, which is cool by itself, but it's your first real date with the hottest guy in town. I'm here to help." Gabby went to my tiny closet and started digging.

"Who told you tha–?"

"You can't wear just anything," Gabby said, "and if I recall . . . yep, there's nothing in here that's going to work." She didn't mask her disgust. "God, where do you shop?"

"Minneapolis," I said, "and I can guarantee you there are more options there than up here."

"Duh. That's my point. You lived in a shopping Mecca your whole life, and this is what you came up with? It looks like you raided the Goodwill bin."

"Some of it," I said with a shrug.

Gabby groaned. "Other people wore this stuff? Do you have any idea how many pounds of dead skin cells you're dealing with?"

"It's all been washed," I said, ripping my army jacket out of her hands.

"And don't get me going on other people's sweat stains."

"I only buy the good pieces."

She ignored me. "Don't worry. I'll figure something out for you. If all else fails you can borrow something of mine."

Now I was worried. I glanced at her shopping bag and noted several pieces of lace and Lycra. "I don't know, Gabby. All those Pettit skin cells . . ."

"Shut up." She dug deep into the back of the closet and popped open the cardboard box I kept there. "What's this?" she asked.

"Vintage band tees," I said. "I found them in the attic when we first moved here. They must have been my grandpa's, because they're all from the sixties and early seventies."

She pulled one out and held it up to read. "Who's Jefferson Airplane?" she asked. "Never mind." She returned to the clothes on hangers. "Don't you have *anything* sexy?"

"I can barely say that word out loud."

"Are you kidding me? Do you know how many girls would kill to have curves like you? Not that *I* need help in that department . . . and your hair totally rocks. Okay, what about this?"

She pulled a cream-colored blouse out of the back. "It goes off the shoulder, right?"

"I wear it pulled up. With a scarf. What about a Santana T-shirt? Santana's sexy."

"Uh-uh. Not tonight. Tonight I'm dressing you."

"I don't know if Calder really likes the girly-girl kind of thing."

"He'll love it. At the very least, you'll have everyone else's attention. Nothing piques a guy's interest like thinking he's got competition."

I rolled my eyes. "There's no competition."

"Of course there isn't, but keep that to yourself. He doesn't have to know. Do you have any other jewelry?"

"I'm not taking off my necklace," I said. The beach-glass pendant was a permanent accessory by now. I couldn't imagine being without it.

My phone vibrated on the bed, and I slid it open.

JULES: Whatcha doin?
LILY: Being tortured.

Gabby threw the silky blouse on the bed, then a few more odds and ends, followed by a pair of jeans from my bottom drawer. They were from last year and way too tight.

111

JULES: By Calder? Sounds fun.
LILY: I wish. What are you doing tonight?

"Come here," Gabby said. "Let me do your makeup." She yanked me off the bed toward the bathroom.

JULES: Promise not to be mad?
LILY: Why would I be mad?

Gabby closed my phone and tossed it on the bed.
"Hey! Why'd you–?"
"I demand your full attention," she said. "How do you feel about red lipstick?"
"*That* I can do."
By the time Gabby was done with me, my hair was teased and rumpled to look like I'd spent the last three days in bed. She dusted my bare shoulders with something shimmery called Roller Derby Princess. I pulled the neckline of my blouse up over my shoulders, and Gabby yanked it back down.
"It won't kill you to show some skin," Gabby said, whining a little.
"I'm worried about mosquitos."
Gabby made a *psssh* sound and experimented with piling my hair up on top of my head, then stood back to appraise her work. "If you're lucky, it won't be just mosquitos biting you tonight."
"Geez, Gabby!" I swung at her, and she ducked out of the way, letting my hair fall heavy on my back.

Tires crunched on the gravel driveway, turning both our attentions to the window.

"Looks like Calder's got new wheels," she said.

I went to the window to look. It was a 1980s brown sedan—about as nondescript as a car could be. It wasn't going to get much attention around here even if someone was looking for it, which, knowing Calder, was doubtful. By now, the owner had probably forgotten he even had a car. Chances were he was touting the benefits of "going green" and telling his neighbor how much he enjoys walking everywhere. I guess Dad's No Thievery rule was out the window. That, or Dad wasn't going to be around enough to care.

"It's a total shitmobile," Gabby said, "but at least *he's* fine. I can see his six pack right through his shirt, or is that twelve? And, seriously, that's the most rock-solid ass I've ever—"

"Please don't ogle my boyfriend."

"Well." She dragged me toward the bedroom door as I dug in my heels, feeling completely ridiculous. "If you can't appreciate what you've got, I'm happy to take over."

"Stop pulling my arm," I said. "I'm coming."

"Fine. I'll see you up at the barn. Oh, I almost forgot." She pulled a faded quilt out of her bag. "You can use this. It's my lucky blanket."

"Ewww. I don't think I want to know."

"You can thank me later," she said as she ran down the stairs. I heard her open the door and say, "Well, hell-o, Calder. Lily's all ready for you."

I took a deep breath and exhaled slowly. When I came downstairs, my cheeks burning, Calder's eyebrows rose to his hairline and his pupils dilated. He stuck out his hand and said, "Hello, gorgeous. My name is Calder White. I don't think we've been formally introduced."

I grabbed his elbow and dragged him across the porch. "You're hilarious. Let's go."

13

FIGHT

We were some of the last to arrive at Oleson's barn. I recognized a few faces from the party I'd gone to at the Pettits' awhile back. I also saw the parish priest, Father Hoole, and a bit later, Mrs. Boyd, with whom I tried not to make eye contact. Jack made it to the movie, too, though he was clearly there against his will. He scowled at the ground and leaned against an outbuilding that looked as beaten down as he did.

Practically the whole town turned out. Multiple generations gathered together, talking, laughing, turning bratwursts on a grill. I tried to ignore the strange looks and turning heads or, when that failed, hoped they were gawking at Calder's usual conversation-stopping good looks and not at me.

I smiled nervously at several mothers who were spreading out their family blankets, overlapping theirs with friends' to create large, quilted continents. We'd have to act quickly to claim our territory; the center areas had already been staked out.

"Why are there so many little kids here?" I asked. "It's an R-rated movie."

"They're just here for the ice cream," said Calder. "They'll all be asleep before it's dark enough to start the movie. Okay, over here." He towed me to an open patch of lawn in a circle of light cast by a floodlight that was mounted on a pole and swarmed by moths. The side of the barn was covered in king-sized white bedsheets, sewn together and stretched taut. I chewed my lip.

"Are you nervous being here with me?" Calder asked, taking Gabby's quilt from my arms and laying it flat on the lawn. "It's okay if you are," he said. "I'm kind of nervous, too."

"What are you nervous about?" I asked.

"Crowds give me a headache. If it wasn't going to be dark soon I wouldn't bother to come. Besides, don't you feel like the whole world is looking at us?"

"*Ugh*. If they are, I hope they're focused on you. I look ridiculous."

"You are intoxicating."

I blushed and buried my head in my hands. "It's Gabby's fault."

"She did a good job," he said, uncovering my face, "although I do miss your style."

"Are you talking about the clothes, or am I not my normal color again?"

"Now that you mention it, both."

I didn't know what to say to that, particularly because he frowned when I mentioned the changes he saw in me. We sat in awkward silence for what seemed like hours. Alone, I could have told him almost anything, but I couldn't put two words together when I felt so on display.

Thankfully, it wasn't long before someone decided it was dark enough to start the movie and killed the outdoor lights. The town took their seats and obediently fell silent, with the exception of someone's baby. The little kids were already sleeping. The air was thick with bug spray. The movie projector flickered, then projected the image of a young girl onto the side of the barn.

I watched as the girl made the rookie horror-movie mistake of separating herself from the group. She ran by a dark, weather-worn fence that looked strangely like the skeletal remains of a large fish. A boy chased her, and she teased, stripping off her clothes—piece by piece. *I'm going swimming,* she said. Normally, I'd make some crack about *How stupid can you get?* But considering my recent run-in with Maris, I was in no place to judge.

The girl swam naked out into the ocean, too far from shore, the *da-dum* music working its way into the audience's collective psyche. I wished the girl could hear the music. Maybe she'd turn back.

Calder sighed. I glanced over to see if he was all right. His profile was a beautiful line that I wanted to run my finger along, letting it bump over his lips, which were slightly parted now. Maybe he would slip his hand behind me. He could lean in and kiss me. I imagined his hand going to my neck, and then my sigh as he lay me back on the lucky blanket, his weight pressing down on me, his knee between my legs. The crowd disappearing . . .

I bit down on my bottom lip and imagined its softness between his teeth.

But Calder paid no attention to me. He was focused on the swimming girl, watching her warily, holding his breath. The shark jerked her under. The audience screamed. The girl's eyes grew wide. And then she was pulled again. She rang the bell on the buoy. A flash of the shark. And she was gone. The water stilled. The boyfriend lay passed out on the beach.

Calder groaned. "That's so fake. A great white would never act like that. They're normally very sweet."

"I think I'd need more convincing," I said. "Those are some seriously scary teeth."

He slipped behind me, letting me recline against his chest, and pulled the neckline of my blouse up, over my shoulders. "Teeth are the least scary thing out there," he said, wrapping his arms tight around my waist, squeezing a little to make a point. The strength in his arms was sure and comforting.

"Terrifying," I said as I settled in.

Sitting in the dark made me feel brave and excited. I wanted to test the boundaries. I wished Calder would. He couldn't have thought I would push him away if he tried. But neither of us moved.

Calder's legs flanked mine, which tingled at the contact, all my cells fizzing like mist on a power line. At first I thought my toes were falling asleep, so I adjusted my position, and bright white sparks snapped in the small spaces between us.

I leaned to my left so I could see his face and found him staring at me with those eyes that nearly glowed and drew me closer, those eyes that scared me a little because of what they confessed of his heart.

"Stay still," he warned. "Or maybe a little distance would be better. It's harder to control the electrical impulses when you're close."

"No, this is good," I said. "Please stay."

He pulled back anyway and flipped over to lie on his stomach. I followed his example, lying alongside him, my head resting on my arms. He wove our hands together, and the tingling that had once been in my toes bounced between my fingers.

"Sorry," he said. "I hope that doesn't hurt you."

I shrugged. I'd always heard about sparks flying between people. With us it was a literal thing, and I didn't mind that one bit. I kissed Calder's fingers and looked up at the screen. The colored shapes of people moving across the side of the barn were like the inside of a kaleidoscope. The dialogue sounded like the inside of a seashell. I didn't know if I was just that tired or if it was too much of a strain on my eyes to watch the movie from that angle, but I soon drifted off, dreaming about a boat loaded with friends as a bloodthirsty monster circled us.

Someone screamed. My dream? Somewhere else? The monster threw one black arm over the stern and slunk over the rail, slipping like an enormous leech onto the floor of the boat. I jumped back while someone braver than me pushed the long hair from the monster's face: My face. Pale and freckled. Another, more beautiful, face pressed close, saying my name.

"Lily?"

I woke with a gasp as the credits ran and the outdoor lights flicked on. I'd missed the end. Had the monster eaten everyone? Did the hero kill the shark? Who was the hero again? Around me the whole town gathered up its lawn chairs and blankets, coolers and bug spray.

"It's over," Calder said. "You were really quiet. Did you fall asleep?"

"No," I said unconvincingly. "It was great."

"Definitely an unfortunate choice. A movie like that could really hurt tourism."

Before I could respond to his joke, a cacophony of young, male voices erupted from behind the Porta-Potties. Calder glanced over and grimaced. "Oh! Oh, man. Come on. Let's go." He jumped to his feet and yanked at the corner of the blanket.

"What is it?" I asked, getting to my knees. I toppled over as he pulled the blanket out from under me.

"I got to get out of here," he said. "Are you coming with me?" He grabbed my hand and pulled me up so fast my feet left the ground.

"Of course I'm going with you. What's the hurry? What's going on?" My mind was still groggy from my dream, and the ground seemed to shift and sway under my feet.

"Jack." Calder pulled desperately at my arm, dragging me toward the car. He practically threw me into the passenger seat.

I turned around to look out the back window. I could see Jack. A group of guys I didn't recognize surrounded him in a circle. One guy pushed Jack, and he staggered backward into the arms of another, who shoved him again. Jack spun around and threw the first punch. And then everyone was yelling and piling on top of Jack, who disappeared into the scrum. A couple of men came running up and pulled the pile apart.

"What's going on?" I demanded of Calder. "What are they saying?"

Calder threw the car in reverse and peeled out of the gravel parking lot.

"That Pettit kid is getting on my last nerve," he said through his teeth, his back hunched over the steering wheel. Despite everything Jack had done, that didn't seem fair. He was the one getting his ass kicked.

Calder was still ranting. "He can't keep his mouth shut. He's going to start naming names. With me making such a public appearance, guess whose name will come up first."

"No way," I said, wondering what he'd heard that I'd missed. "Jack's messed up, but he's not sadistic."

Calder shot me a scandalized look, and I thought of Tallulah.

"That was different," I whispered. He took a corner too fast, and I fell against the window. "So you're running away from Jack Pettit?"

Veins bulged in Calder's temples, and his face flushed. "I'm not running!"

I tugged my seat belt tighter. "Okay. You're not running. What's Jack fighting with those guys about?"

"Same thing as before. The two kayak accidents from this week–"

"So you *did* hear about the kayakers."

"How could I not?" he asked with an exasperated sigh. "Both of them reported seeing a dark shadow in the water and then *bam,* their kayaks turned over and they were pulled out. I expected Maris and Pavati to hunt, and I worried their grief would cause them to take too many lives in too short a time, but letting two kayakers *get away?*"

"I don't understand. That's a good thing, right?"

"Wrong," Calder said. "The worst thing. Letting a target escape is sheer negligence."

"You think because those kayakers have told their stories, Jack will have more fuel for his anti-mermaid crusade?"

Calder's fingers gripped the steering wheel tightly. "That's part of it. For now the other guys are still giving him crap. They're calling him a freak back there. That's what started the fight."

"That's good, then," I said.

"For whom?" he asked, looking quickly at me, then back at the road.

That was a question I couldn't answer. "You just said no one believes Jack."

"Not yet, but it will take only one to get it started. It'll be like before. At first, it'll be curiosity. Some adventure seeker will come searching the caves. Then they'll come with underwater cameras and sonar."

"Be serious."

Calder yanked the steering wheel hard to the right and hit the brakes. I fell forward into my seat belt, and my hand hit the dashboard.

"I couldn't be any more serious. How can you ignore the facts?"

"Maybe life is better for me if I do," I said grimly.

His eyes flashed emerald. "Don't be a fool."

"Don't call me a fool!"

"We should have never come back to Bayfield," Calder growled.

"*You* didn't have to."

His face darkened, and his eyes turned more menacing than I'd ever seen them before. For the first time, I could see the bleakness of his soul. It coiled and curled like smoke and eels in his darkening eyes. How was it that his mind could spiral into misery so quickly? It scared me that I wasn't proving an effective talisman against his despair. Not now, anyway.

What scared me even more was the strange heat that pulsed through my own chest. I might not have been able to see the colors, but I could feel the burning, mustard-colored haze that hummed around the outline of my body. It didn't surprise me at all when Calder recoiled at the sight of me. If I didn't have enough control over my own emotions, how could I bring him back to himself?

"I need a fix," he snarled. "I've pushed this abstinence long enough. I've been kidding myself. If Jack wants a monster, he's *got* one!" Calder hazarded another glance my way and snapped, "Because you're certainly not helping me any."

I sucked in my breath and stared straight ahead while Calder added, "What is *wrong* with you? Take that necklace off."

I wheeled around on him and slapped my hands down

on the cracked vinyl seat. "Why is this my fault? Why do I have to be the one to make everything all better for you. For Dad? For *everyone?*"

"No one asked you to."

My mouth popped open to give him the best retort I could muster, but nothing came.

"God, Lily, you're impossible."

I turned toward the window and yanked my blouse back over my shoulders. "Take me home," I said, folding my arms across my chest.

Calder threw the car back in gear, muttering "Gladly." A few minutes later he pulled into my driveway. He didn't say good night. I didn't either. I slammed the car door and ran up the porch steps.

"How was the movie?" Mom asked.

"Awesome. I'm going to bed," I said as my feet hit the stairs.

"Lily?"

"Good night." I slammed my bedroom door with enough force that our family portrait, which hung on the other side of the wall, slipped off its nail and crashed to the floor.

14

DISCOVERY

The next morning, I stood in the middle of my bedroom, still dressed in my clothes from the disastrous Date Night. The house seemed smaller, and that was saying something. Even alone in my room, the place was too crowded. Though everyone was asleep, the house was loud. The walls pressed in on me until I had no choice but to crawl out onto the porch roof for some air.

Waves sloshed gently against the smooth gray stones on the beach and made sucking sounds under the dock. I crept to the edge of the roof and dropped silently to the ground, just in case Calder was in the hammock. I didn't want to fight, and I didn't think I was the one who should apologize. As it turned out, it didn't matter. Calder wasn't there. Of course he wasn't. He was probably still pissed, too. He was probably out with Dad. Maybe they hadn't slept here at all.

It was still so early that the sun barely peeked above the trees on Madeline Island. I peeled off my too-tight jeans, hopping from one foot to the other, until I was down to my underwear. The blouse Gabby had picked out for me hung crooked across my body, the neckline draping halfway down one arm. The water stretched out before me like a blue blanket. It waited for me, and my body tingled with longing for it.

This was stupid. I was stupid.

I touched my fingers to the beach glass hanging around my neck, feeling its warmth on my skin. Problem was, when it came to the lake, I couldn't help myself.

Despite what Calder said about his sisters never attacking onshore, land was where I felt more unsure of myself. Only in the water did my tensions dissolve. I had no fear. I felt lighter, smarter, braver. I belonged in the lake.

"Stupid," I said, this time out loud. But there was no convincing myself. Try as I might, I couldn't ignore the instinct to dive simply because I was afraid of the consequences.

I kissed my pendant for good luck and dove, reveling in the crushing rush in my ears. I wouldn't go far. I promised myself that much.

The water combed through my hair and caressed my cheek. It pulled along my legs, making them seem longer than before. I kicked and propelled myself away from shore, skirting the surface, pretending I was a real mermaid, that I could keep up with Calder and Dad.

Reaching forward, I pulled myself through the water stroke after stroke, stroke after stroke, feeling the remaining bits of my rage dissipate. I turned a somersault. And then another. Twisting in the water. Startling a lake trout that came up to investigate. It made me want to laugh, and I surfaced so I could. I made no gasp at the air. It was all too easy. So very easy.

When the air hit my face, I turned in a quick circle, completely disoriented. The dock was gone. The willow tree was gone. I turned again to look for the scattering of islands and realized I was at least a quarter mile north of our dock. How long had I been underwater? Or was it a matter of speed? No. That couldn't be it. My body was nothing more than human. I hadn't suddenly broken out with a tail. I would have noticed that. Still, I couldn't help but look. Nope. Two legs.

I turned south and filled my lungs to capacity, submerging and swimming underwater as I had before—though this time without fooling around. I counted in my head, *One Mississippi. Two Mississippi* . . . When I hit sixty, I started to panic, but not in the normal way. My lungs didn't burn with their pending collapse. I had no need to scramble toward the surface. This time, the panic came from not *needing* to breathe. At least, not yet.

Two hundred Mississippi. Two hundred one . . .

Familiar voices filled my head. The higher-pitched ones were muffled and far away. The lower ones were closer, south of the ferry route. There were no distinct words; instead, they hummed and blended into a kind of melody, an eerie harmony, like wind over an empty bottle.

The lake floor sloped up to meet me. I reached forward, my hands hitting the slippery timber-and-boulder foundation of our dock. I threw one arm up on the deck, and the sun hit my face, unnaturally hot, burning my skin, like someone was staring at me.

"Have a nice swim?" Sophie asked. She was sitting cross-legged at the end of the dock, drawing in a sketchbook with one of Mom's charcoal pencils.

"Yeah," I said. How long had she been there? What had she seen? "Thanks, Soph. Can you go grab me a towel?"

"You're done already?" She rubbed her pencil furiously over the page.

"Um, yeah. Think so." I stared at her, waiting for her to look up from her drawing, wondering how to interpret her words, but she just kept scribbling. "No, I'm good," I said, finally giving up.

"Okay." She set the sketchbook down, saying, "Back in a sec," and she ran for the house.

I pulled myself out and sat on the edge of the dock. Four minutes. I'd held my breath for four freakin' minutes. Without really trying. That was seriously messed up. More amazing: I'd only come to the surface because I'd reached the dock. How much longer could I have gone? I'd find out tomorrow.

I dripped water on Sophie's sketchbook, leaving dime-sized circles that bled into quarters. When I picked up the book, I saw a picture of myself. But this time the metamorphosis was complete. She'd drawn me with a tail.

I turned around and watched Sophie come skipping across the lawn, whipping the towel over her head like a lasso. When she got to the end of the dock, she tried to snap it at me, but I grabbed it out of her hand and wrapped it around my shoulders.

We sat in silence, staring out across the lake. Dad and Calder were out there somewhere. Did Sophie know that? I sincerely hoped I was reading too much into her drawing, but I had to ask.

"What's with the picture, Sophie?"

"You don't like it?" she asked, her lips pursed.

"Who's that supposed to be?" I asked, tapping the picture with my fingers.

"It's *supposed* to be you," she said. "Is it bad?" She held the picture closer to her face, scrutinizing the details.

"No, not at all," I said. I put an arm around her shoulders. "It's just that the last time I checked, anyway, I didn't have a tail."

"No," she agreed, still sounding disappointed. "But it's pretty, don't you think?"

"I didn't know you were into mermaids," I said casually.

"They're pretty," she said. She picked up her things and stood. Before she left me she said, "Mom's making blueberry pancakes. Are you coming?"

"Yeah, I'll be up in a bit."

Sophie stared at me for a few seconds, then said, "Don't skip out."

"I won't. I said I'd be up."

Sophie chewed on her lip and stared at her feet. "Mom looks weird. Kind of sad. So be really nice to her."

"I'm always nice."

"And be nice to Calder. You weren't nice to him last night."

Before I could retort, Sophie stole the towel from around my shoulders and ran back to the house chanting, "Lily's in her un-der-wear! Lily's in her un-der-wear!"

MY SCRIBBLINGS

A Lake Superior Haiku

Cold lake consumes me
as if it were the one who
needed me to live.
                    —Lily Hancock

MERMAID STATS as of today

Swim Time: 4 min. 17 secs
Hearing Voices?
Tail: None

15

HAMMOCK

Thursday dinner went by, still without any word from Calder and only an email from Dad, which was sent from another fictitious teachers' conference sponsored by the so-called *Midwest Ecology Review*. All I could think was *M.E.R.?* Was that supposed to be funny? Mom didn't seem to think so, either, although not for the same reasons.

Sometime around three in the morning on Friday, I woke up shaking. I'd left my window open. Cold lake air filtered in, and my teeth chattered uncontrollably, threatening to shatter like glass. There was an extra blanket in my closet, but I was too cold to leave my bed to get it. Same was true for shutting the window. For a second I wondered if I could telepathically close the window from where I lay. If I thought about it hard enough. Long enough. *Harder.* Nope. Not going to happen.

The tree branches creaked and dragged wooden fingers across the roof. No matter how cold I was, it shamed me to think Calder was somewhere out in that wind with nothing more than the trees to cover him. No matter how mad I'd been, no one deserved that.

I pulled myself from the sheets and, just in case Calder was there, gathered what he might need. I found him shivering in the hammock outside.

"How have you survived all these years living outside?" I asked.

"It's warmer underwater, or by a campfire. I'm not used to so much wind. What you got there? Sleeping bag?"

He rolled out of the hammock, and I handed it to him. He wrestled it flat and, finding the opening, crawled inside. "Very roomy."

"I zipped two of them together."

His green eyes glowed in the darkness. "Does this mean we're not fighting anymore?"

"Sophie says I have to be nice to you. Besides, I like my fish fresh, not frozen."

He laughed warmly and held the bag open for me to climb in. I snuggled into his chest, and he pulled me up so our faces were even. Gabby was wrong. I appreciated every inch of him. And not just the parts I could see, but the way he made me feel when he looked at me like this—like I filled some hollowed-out part of his heart.

"You're in a better mood," I said, zipping the bag closed around us.

He winced. "Marginally. But don't worry. It's not because I took someone last night." He sounded ashamed, even though he was telling me he had nothing to be ashamed of. "I mean, if you were wondering about that. You look nervous. I'm guessing that's it? I didn't really think I would—take someone, I mean. At least, I was pretty sure I wouldn't. Jack set me off, and then you . . . well . . . you scared me . . . the way you looked. Something's changing with you, Lily. I wish you'd tell me. I promise I won't be mad."

"You can't promise that."

"Okay, I will *try very hard* not to be mad. But I will promise you this: I won't ever try to guilt you again. I was wrong the other night. If, for some reason, I was to slip, it wouldn't be your fault. It would never be your fault. You're still all I want."

I ignored the contradiction in his words. I couldn't take my eyes off his lips as he spoke. I put my finger against them and lied, "I never thought you'd slip."

"Then tell me what's bothering you."

I took his bottom lip between my teeth, tasting the sweetness. He inhaled sharply and pulled me so close I imagined what it would feel like to be absorbed, to be soaked into his skin as pure emotion, to be but one body. My heart flip-flopped between us as his fingertips pressed my lower back toward him. I slipped my hand inside the back of his shorts, feeling his muscles tense.

"Lily, are you sure?" he asked, his breath hot in my ear. His hand slid over my hip, then up my waist to my rib cage. He threw one leg over mine and waited for my response.

He was right. I wasn't sure.

Desire turned to fear, which—no doubt—he could see on me, too. He groaned and rolled away from me.

"Wake me up before my dad finds me out here," I whispered.

He shook his head and said, "I don't think that'll be a problem."

"Which part? The waking or the finding?"

"Shhh."

Something about the way he dismissed my question put my mind on red alert. "He's barely been home since we got back to the lake."

"I know," Calder said. "He's having a hard time adjusting. I'm trying to help."

"Please tell me you've at least made some progress in finding Maris and Pavati. Has Dad been able to hear either one of them?"

Calder closed his eyes. Two vertical lines formed between his eyebrows. The hammock swung gently, and I watched as Calder gathered his thoughts and rolled back to face me. "Is this *really* what you want to talk about?" he asked, kissing my eyelids and then my nose. "Your dad?"

"Yes. No," I said, my mind addled. *What did I ask?*

"The answer to your question is no, not yet. And no, he hasn't been able to hear them, either, but I'm working on a theory."

"Tell me."

"He's never heard their voices before. On land, I mean. Maybe he *is* hearing them, but he doesn't recognize the sounds for what they are."

"That's possible." It occurred to me that I was in a unique

position. Dad, Maris, Pavati—even Calder—were all family to me, by blood or by choice. I knew all their voices on land. I'd heard Maris's screeching accusations and Pavati's seductive murmurs. I knew Calder's, of course, and Dad's best of all.

Although I'd heard no distinct words in the water before, only muffled sounds, I was convinced it had been all four of them I'd heard the other day.

"That's my theory," Calder said. "The other option is that they're a million miles away. They *feel* like a million miles away. Especially now, when you're here with me. And we're not fighting. Now, can we talk about something else?"

"Are you and Dad going out again tomorrow?"

He sighed. "He wants me to, but after how Tuesday night ended, I told him I still needed to recharge, that I needed to spend some concentrated time with you."

I choked on my words as I asked how my dad reacted to *that.* "Yeah," Calder said, laughing a little. "That might have been more than he wanted to hear."

"Don't worry about me," I said. "It's okay if you need to go."

Calder pulled back so he could see me fully. His eyes narrowed as he scrutinized my face, his nose twitched at whatever he was seeing.

I scrambled to put his mind at ease. The last thing I wanted to do was tell him about my experiments and apparently I was unable to disguise them completely. "I've got . . . things . . . I'm working on. If you and Dad need more time to train . . . I don't want you to think I'm moping around. I got on fine before I met you. That was only a couple of months ago. I think I can figure out how to fill my day."

"You don't need to use reverse psychology on me. When

I say I need to spend time with you, I mean it." He placed his finger on the end of my nose and drew it over my lips, my chin, down my neck to my belly button. He grinned, then swallowed hard, his eyes closing.

I molded my body to his, feeling his muscles flex against me and his skin flushed with heat. I traced circles in his hair, lightly across his temples, watching his eyes flicker, then close. His muscles relaxed, and he sank heavier into the hammock, which barely swayed with his changing weight. His skin was smooth, taut, and packed with muscles and sinew and bone. I drew my finger along a pattern of scars on his shoulders, feeling his exhaustion, but also his contentment.

"Go with Dad," I said. "When you get back, I'll be here waiting for you."

While I was generally oblivious to the light he saw in me, I could sometimes see traces of it on him. For instance, right then, I could have sworn the inside of the sleeping bag shimmered like the northern lights.

MY SCRIBBLINGS

Missed Opportunities

I am worth
y
and skilled
a force
you must reckon
with honey
and sweet wine is yours
for the taking
if you only knew
to ask.

TO DO:
Try to listen for Maris
Goal: 5-minute swim

16

NEWS

As soon as Calder got back from his morning expedition with Dad, he suggested we finally pay Mrs. Boyd a visit at the Blue Moon Café. I wished we hadn't put it off because it felt awkward now that we'd been back for two weeks. Calder and I walked to the café hand in hand; he grinned, while I struggled to come up with several well-phrased apologies for having left her so abruptly. But when the bell over the door rang out and Mrs. Boyd looked up, I forgot every one of them.

"Hmph. 'Bout time," she said, wiping the marble countertop. "I wondered when you'd have the audacity to show your face again."

Calder said, "Sorry, Mrs. Boyd," before I could muster up any spit in my mouth.

"Sorry's not going to cut it, mister. You left me high and dry. This place won't run itself, y'know."

She didn't seem to be too upset with my desertion. I guess Mom had made a good enough excuse for me.

"It was rude of me to go without telling you," Calder said.

"Rude? Rude is forgetting to flush. What you did was irresponsible."

Calder led me forward across the black-and-white checkered floor. I guess I was dragging my feet because his pressure on my wrist increased. I looked sideways and saw the intensity in his face. His eyes trained on Mrs. Boyd's. What was he doing? We weren't here to reapply.

Mrs. Boyd stammered and lost her train of thought. Her fingers shook and went to her silver-streaked hair pulled back into a loose knot. "I suppose you'll be wanting your job back," she said as her pupils dilated. "And I would be a fool to give it to you."

I jabbed Calder hard in the ribs, but he didn't break eye contact with her. "Not me. But Lily's feeling better now. She's got the whole summer, and she needs to make some money for school."

"We're just here as customers," I said.

Mrs. Boyd noticed me for the first time. "That's good. I've been shorthanded. You're all better, Lily?"

"Much, but . . ."

"You can start back up tomorrow."

"Lily would love that," Calder said.

What the heck? Was he trying to keep me busy and out of trouble? Didn't I tell him I had things I was working on?

139

"For now, you two go sit down," Mrs. Boyd said. "I'll make you your usuals. Caramel mocha latte and a double espresso?"

"Perfect," Calder said as he turned me toward the multicolored tables and chairs. We took our seats by the window.

I scowled at him and hissed, "I don't need a job."

His eyes sparkled with suppressed laughter as he picked up a copy of the *Ashland Gazette* that lay on the windowsill. With his other hand he fiddled with the purple fringe on the scarf I'd tied around my waist.

When Mrs. Boyd returned with our drinks, he was already finished with the cover story, and his mood had obviously dampened.

"Rip current, my ass," he said flipping the newspaper over to read the conclusion on the back page.

"What is it?"

"Two more. This time kids on WaveRunners."

I scooted my chair around and read over his arm. "Why are they always so young?" I asked.

"Listen." Calder read aloud. *"Marie Bauer and Elly Cook, recent graduates of Washburn High School, were out in Chequamegon Bay Wednesday afternoon with a group of friends when they were knocked off their WaveRunners. The girls were saved by a vigilant family who was watching from the beach. It is believed that rip currents, which have been persistent risks over the last few weeks, were the cause of the accident. The students, however, claimed to have seen a dark shape in the water shortly before, and they believe they were the victims of an animal attack, raising questions of other large fish in the lake like the specimen found weeks ago."*

Calder crumpled the newspaper and pushed it away. "I guess I was wrong. Maris and Pavati aren't a million miles away after all."

"You don't know that," I said. "It could've really been a rip current."

"Chequamegon Bay is Maris's favorite hunting grounds."

"But I still don't understand. If it's Maris and Pavati, why are all these people getting away?"

Calder looked over at me, and I could tell he was wondering how much he should say.

"I'm in this," I said, my voice rising. "Don't keep secrets from me."

"Lily, I don't want to fight." He pressed his fingers to his temples.

"Why are they all getting away?" I said softly, taking his hands in mine.

He exhaled. "Maris and Pavati's attacks are coming too close together. That's bad. But now they've let four escape? That's really, really bad."

That still seemed backward to me, but this time I didn't interrupt him when he tried to explain.

"They've gone too long without a kill and it's throwing their timing off. They're slow and . . . Back when . . . back when your dad was the target . . . Maris had us on strict instructions to pace ourselves. I was already at the end of my line when I started stalking–" He cut himself short and made an apologetic face. "Pavati slipped once. But as far as I know, Maris has had only one kill since the migration. She's got to be seriously depleted.

"Now you add to that Tallulah's death, and . . . Lily, I've

seen Maris miserable, enraged, manic even, but the other day on your beach—that was full-on despair."

"Yeah, but, Calder, I still don't understand. Even if their timing is off, they still managed to pull those people out of their kayaks and off WaveRunners. Why didn't they finish the job?"

"That's what I'm trying to explain. Their timing is off from lack of practice and because their minds are overwhelmed by despair and grief. Bad timing equals a bad kill."

"A bad kill?" I asked. It seemed a little redundant.

"If they can't make the kill quick enough, their prey sees what's coming. If the target gets scared, its emotions sour."

"And absorbing negative emotion . . . ," I said.

"Panic, fear, God forbid, *terror* . . . when you're already in the emotional toilet. . . . They're not 'finishing the job,' so to speak, because a bad kill will only make things worse for them. Trouble is, the longer this goes on, the deeper they're going to sink. The depression will get worse. In the end, they won't be able to see straight. They won't be able to eat. Or sleep. They'll keep making more and more desperate attempts."

What he'd been trying to tell me after the movie slowly sank in. It wasn't just about getting Maris and Pavati's grief under control, or warning them about Jack's campaign to "out" them. It was much bigger than that. Maris and Pavati's carelessness could affect us all.

Calder nodded, seeing the realization in my eyes. "Yes. Too many accidents and people *will* come looking for the cause," he said. "We'll all be in danger. Maris. Pavati. What if they find me? Or your dad? If they find your dad out there, what will they make of you? Or Sophie?"

Thinking of Sophie in some scientist's lab, being tested, poked, and probed, sent an icy shiver down my arms. "Maybe the city will put up caution signs. That should keep people out of the water."

"Yeah, come up to the lake for your vacation, but don't go in the water. I don't think that's going to sell."

"Could we patrol the beach?" I asked.

Calder looked out the window and stood up quickly. "There's over twenty-seven hundred miles of lakeshore, Lily. Think of something else. I've got to go."

"Wait? What? Where are you going?"

He kissed me quickly on the cheek and exited through the back of the café as I watched slack-jawed. Mrs. Boyd mumbled something about someone acting like he owned the place, just as I saw the reason for Calder's exodus.

The bell rang, and Gabby walked in. Jack shuffled behind her, his bangs hanging in his eyes, a dark blue hoodie pulled over his head doing little to hide the bruise around his eye or the cut on his lip. He'd really taken a beating the other night.

Jack didn't sit with us but dropped into a chair in the corner, a surly expression on his face.

"What's with him?" I whispered to Gabby. "He looks like the Unabomber."

"That would be a serious PR improvement." Gabby glanced at the two cups on the table in front of me. "Double-fisting it?"

I tried to laugh. "Yeah, feeling a little sluggish lately. Why don't you take that one. It's still fresh. I haven't touched it." I doubted Calder was coming back.

"Give it to Jack," she said. "I'm getting a smoothie."

I didn't really want to sit with Jack. I couldn't think of anything worse than pretending to have a normal conversation with him in front of Gabby, when both of us were having a very different conversation in our heads. Plus, his gloomy disposition looked contagious.

I got up anyway and crossed the room, sliding him the coffee. He glowered at me and sank farther into his chair and deeper into his hood.

The bell rang out again, and a huge guy in a red UW sweatshirt walked in. He glanced at me, and then at Jack. He never finished his trip to the counter. "Whoa. Is that who I think it is?" he asked.

"Give it a rest, man," Jack said, his voice like gravel.

The guy rubbed his eyes in an exaggerated way, as if he didn't believe what he was seeing. "Is it? It is! Jack Pettit! Did you know they're calling you Aquaman over at Big Mo's?"

"They can call me whatever they want," Jack said.

"Mm-hmm. So you seen any mermaids lately?"

Gabby arrived with her drink and swallowed (as I judged by her expression) a headache-inducing gulp of smoothie. "You got balls, Peterman. Lay off!"

Jack sat up a little straighter. "Shut up, Gabrielle. I don't need your help."

The guy laughed and shrugged. "Aw, I'm kidding. It's good to see you guys. Who's your friend?"

"Lily," I said.

"Brady," he said, and he shook my hand, holding on to it a few seconds longer than necessary.

Jack made a *pssh* sound.

"Hey, a bunch of us are going camping on Manitou Island tonight," said Brady. "You girls up for it?"

Gabby said, "Absolutely! Jack, you'll take us?"

"Yeah, Jack. You should come, too," Brady said.

Jack said, "I've got plans."

"What plans?" Gabby asked. "You never want to do anything fun anymore. What about you, Lily? Would your parents let you go?"

"I'd have to check," I said. The last time I'd gone to a party with the Pettits, it hadn't turned out so great.

"Well, check," Gabby said. "You've never been to Manitou, and it's always a good time."

"Yeah. I'll ask," I said as memories of mine and Calder's day on Manitou flooded my mind. That was the day he'd let me into his world.

"So what've you been up to, Jack?" Brady asked. "Besides the obvious. Nice shiner, by the way. Just bumming around town?"

"I guess."

"I'm telling you. You should have come to Madison with us. College is awesome. Change of scenery, if you know what I mean." He waggled his eyebrows in a way that made it clear he wasn't talking about rocks and trees. Jack made another *pssh* sound under his breath.

"Don't mind Jack," Gabby said. "He hasn't had his coffee yet this morning."

Jack backhanded the cup I'd given to him, and we all flinched as it flew across the table, the cover snapping off and creamy liquid splashing across the table.

"Oh, c'mon," Mrs. Boyd said. "Guess who's got to clean that up?"

I got up out of habit and snagged a rag from the bleach bucket and wiped up the spill. "How 'bout I start work today instead?" I asked.

Mrs. Boyd stared at me, confused, and I felt like a complete idiot. Apparently Calder's hypnotic abilities had a time limit.

"What?" she asked. "Oh, Lily, I'm sorry. I don't have any openings right now. But if you want an assignment, how about you get those friends of yours out of here before they make a real mess."

17

PREPARATION

I came through the front door of the house, wondering what Mom and Dad would say about the camping trip. I didn't think camping on an island was going to sound like a good idea to Dad. That is, if he was home to cast a vote. Either way, Mom was my best bet. If she said yes, Dad wouldn't rule against her. He couldn't afford to get on her bad side any more than he already was.

"Mom?" I called, letting the screen door slam behind me.

"Back here, hon." Her voice traveled through the house, sounding garbled.

I found her in the back room. She'd pulled her wheelchair up to a giant canvas, which was set on one of several easels. Her mangled tubes of paint and various-sized brushes were arranged on a TV tray to her right.

Instantly, I saw why her voice sounded weird. She was holding her paintbrush in her mouth and leaning forward into the canvas. The sight choked up a strangled sob in my throat. When had the MS got so bad that she couldn't hold a brush? Had she been doing this for a while? Why hadn't I noticed?

"Mom?" I asked, my voice wobbling.

She reached up and retrieved the paintbrush from her mouth and dabbed it in a glob of burnt sienna.

"What's up?" she asked.

"Your hands?" I asked, hoping she understood the question without me saying more.

She looked at her paintbrush, then looked at me. "Oh, honey, they're fine. I was experimenting."

"Why?" I asked, with barely any sound.

"Just in case I need some options later," she said. "It's good to be prepared."

I wanted to crawl into her lap. I wondered if I could make myself fit. I wondered if she'd let me try. She laid her brush down on the palette and swiveled her wheelchair away from the easel.

"What's wrong, baby?"

"You scared me. I don't want you not to be able to paint."

She laughed. "Me neither, which is why I was practicing with a new technique before I really need it." She gave me a sympathetic look and wheeled closer. I knelt in front of her and she brushed my hair with her hand.

"Life's short, babe. If I want something, I make it happen. You should, too. How's your poetry coming? You haven't shared any with me in a while."

"Jules says there's no money in poetry."

"Jules is probably right, but why should that stop you? I'm just saying when you figure out what you want to be, go for it. Carpe diem and all that."

"I'm going to be a scientist," Sophie said, sneaking in behind me. "And a fashion designer."

"You see," Mom said.

"And a bareback rider in the Shrine Circus?" I asked her.

"Maybe," Sophie said. "But only if you'll be my horse."

I dropped to my hands and knees. Sophie climbed onto my back.

"Well," Mom said, "I meant it when I said be whatever you want to be, but I think you'll have to draw the line at switching species."

That pulled me up short, and Sophie tumbled off me.

Mom laughed and went back to her painting. "Okay, fine. I'll stick to what I said, but you'll have to work especially hard if you want to be a horse when you grow up."

"Hey, Mom, would it be okay if I went camping with Gabby tonight?"

"Gabby camps?" With the paintbrush held between her teeth, she dabbed the bristles against the canvas. "She doesn't strike me as the camping type."

"Some of her friends are going, too," I said.

Mom turned back to face me, the paintbrush dangling

from the corner of her mouth like a long cigarette. "Friends as in boys?"

I twisted a lock of hair around my finger and examined it for split ends. "Some of her friends might be boys."

She took the paintbrush from her mouth and pointed it at me. "Have you asked your dad about it?"

"I haven't seen him. Not for a while, actually." I wished I could take it back. Mom's look of surprise turned to pain. Silently counting out the days in my head, I tried to remember when I'd seen Dad last. Five days ago? A week? I smiled weakly. "So can I go?"

She sighed and refocused on her painting. "If Martin's letting Gabby go, I guess it's okay."

"Thanks, Mom." I pecked her cheek and ran for the front door. I found Calder sitting at the end of our dock.

"Hey, you!" I called. He turned and waved. "You never got your coffee this morning."

"Professional hazard," he said. "Unexpected exits."

"Were you going to let me know you were out here?" I asked, taking a seat beside him on the dock.

"I'm watching your dad. He's truly amazing. I don't think there's anything more for me to teach him. See?" He pointed and I caught the flash of a dark shape in the water. You had to know what you were looking for to see it. I wondered if Jack was out there right now, looking.

I waved at Dad in a big sweeping, overhead gesture. He stared at me blankly, then dove.

"A black tail?" I asked. I don't know why, but I assumed he'd be silver like Calder.

"Same as Maris's," he said. "He's just as fast, too. He takes off on me all the time, and unless he stops, I have no chance of catching up. He's good at this, Lily. Maybe too good."

"What's that supposed to mean?"

"It's getting harder and harder to convince him the day is over. You said he's barely been home? When's the last time you talked to him?"

I didn't answer and Calder nodded, saying, "That's what I thought. So, I'm still planning on that concentrated time together that we talked about, but first, I promised him we'd take another stab at finding Maris."

A few days ago, this news would have thrown me into a solid funk. But things had changed. Although the idea of Maris and Dad in close proximity still made my heart race, I was actually excited for some more private time to continue my breath control experiments. So far I'd succeeded in holding my breath for a solid four minutes, but I was pretty sure I could make it to five.

"That's probably smart," I said. "Judging by Jack this morning, he's not doing any better."

"Yeah." Calder picked at some loose strings on the edge of his shorts. "You're doing it again, y'know."

"Doing what?"

"Giving a chameleon a helluva run for his money. You're changing colors as fast as someone flipping through a book."

"Shut up."

He glanced at me, and the bridge of his nose crinkled. "Excitement, anxiety, excitement, anxiety, back and forth, back and forth. I could handle that, except for the little bit of fear that keeps leaking in."

"You have a very, very active imagination." I gave him a shove. He didn't budge.

"I'll miss you," he said. "Don't forget that. I'll be thinking about you every minute I'm gone."

"Good," I said, smiling encouragingly. "Now go. Dad's waiting. And tell him it wouldn't hurt to spend some more time around the house. For Mom."

"You know I have been. But there's something more you wanted to tell me?"

I'd almost forgotten. "I'm going camping on Manitou Island tonight, and I have no idea what kind of trouble I'm going to get into."

"None," he said. "I'll see you there." Then he pulled away, a worried expression still playing in his eyes.

"Go," I said, standing up. "I promise I'll be good."

"Just stay on land," he said.

I gave him a salute and clicked my heels. He shook his head and dove.

When Calder and Dad disappeared from view, I turned back toward the house. Sophie was watching from her bedroom window, looking down at me. I waved feebly. Had she seen Dad?

I didn't take the time to find out. I ran to the house and dug in the kitchen junk drawer until I came up with an old stopwatch Dad used back when he used to coach track. It was pretty basic by today's standards. But it would do the trick.

I had my own training to do.

18

CAMPING

Later that afternoon, Gabby, Jack, and I threw our camping gear into the Pettits' Sun Sport. I found a seat at the stern. The only reason I was excited to go was that Calder had promised to meet me there, although I couldn't imagine how that was going to work. There was no way he'd sit around a campfire with Jack—even if it was easier to stomach Jack's moods in the dark—and we couldn't risk Jack publicly accusing Calder of being a merman.

Gabby untied the bowline knot and held the line as Jack backed their boat away from the slip. At the last possible moment, Gabby stepped from the dock onto the side rail as Jack shifted from reverse to forward, and we pulled away from the marina.

I watched uselessly as Gabby scampered around the deck, pulling in the white rubber bumpers, and tightening this or loosening that. She gestured for me to stand and she lifted the lid of my bench seat, exposing a deep storage unit. She dropped two bumpers inside the compartment and was about to close the lid when she paused.

She reached inside and pulled out the sleeve of a jet-black wet suit. She tapped Jack on the shoulder and showed it to him, yelling over the engine, "Why is Dad's old wet suit in here?"

Jack shrugged and furrowed his brow. He left the wheel for a second to stuff the rubber suit back into storage. He closed the lid and jerked his head at me to sit down again. Which I did gladly, because the boat was rising and falling over the ferry's wake in spine-crushing jolts.

Jack threw the throttle into a higher gear and raced the twelve miles to Manitou Island, cutting the lake between Madeline and Basswood. I wanted so desperately to see if I could catch a glimpse of Maris and Pavati's campsite on Basswood, but I didn't dare look.

Jack wanted to get up to Manitou fast. He said he didn't want to set up camp in the dark. I wondered if he just wanted to get there in time to make an appearance and then ditch us first chance he got. I mentioned that theory to Gabby. She only said, "So what if he does? At least we got a ride out."

By the time we arrived, a dozen people were there. Blue

and green tents spotted the campground. Two other boats were anchored offshore. Jack killed the engine and pocketed the key. He opened another storage unit and pulled out a cinder block with a long heavy chain.

"What's that?" Gabby asked, reaching for it.

Jack knocked her hand away. "I lost the anchor," Jack said. "I had to make a homemade one. Don't tell Dad." He glanced furtively at us as he attached the chain to a metal loop at the back of the boat and dropped the block, which made a deep sucking sound as it went under.

Gabby pulled off her sweatshirt and stuffed it in her duffel bag.

"So we swim the rest of the way in?" I asked.

"Go for it, if you don't mind hypothermia," she said, "but I'm catching a ride." She pointed toward shore. Brady Peterman was rowing out to us in a dinghy.

By the time the sun set, there were around twenty kids in the campground. Most of them had graduated from Bayfield High School with Jack, although a few were from Cornucopia, including one whom I recognized as Serious Boy from the woods. I didn't have to wonder if the recognition was mutual. He sat directly opposite me across the campfire, and he fixed his eyes on me, following my every move. It was like those creepy portraits in haunted houses with the eyes that shifted. I leaned left, his eyes went right. I leaned right, he narrowed his eyes and whispered to his friend.

I tried to end the war of stares by moving my chair closer,

but it didn't help. "Stay away from him," the other Cornucopia boy said. I wondered if he had been one of the other baseball players I'd seen in the woods with Serious Boy, but I couldn't recall his face.

"Excuse me?" I asked.

"You heard me," said the boy.

"No, I've got this," said Serious Boy.

"Lily," I said, extending my hand. Serious Boy looked at my hand without taking it. He stood up quickly and walked away from the circle. The other boy followed, putting his hand on Serious Boy's shoulder.

I moved back to my original spot and listened while Jack's former classmates traded stories about their freshman years at UW and Marquette and Notre Dame. Jack poked at the fire with a long stick, now charred and smoking. When Serious Boy returned, Jack and he exchanged a few words. Serious Boy's friend decided to cozy up to Gabby. So now there was no one for me to talk to.

Over the din of other conversations, I heard Serious Boy ask Jack, "Did she come with you?" He tipped his head in my direction. Jack looked up from the fire and met my eyes.

"Yeah. Guess so."

"Do you think that's smart?" Serious Boy asked.

"Probably not," Jack said, smirking, "but I don't think people expect that much from me anymore." He jabbed at the coals, sending a shower of sparks into the air.

I pretended not to be able to hear. They didn't seem to think I could. Was this another mermaid stat to add to my list? Was my hearing really keener than before?

I yawned and removed a poncho from my bag, pulling

it over my head. It was a nonchalant thing to do; hopefully, they wouldn't realize I was paying such close attention to their conversation.

"Yeah, we've heard about that," said Serious Boy, and Jack looked at him sharply to see if he was picking a fight. "Hey, no worries, man. We believe you."

Jack and I both waited for the punch line, but it didn't come. My heart pounded furiously in my chest. Calder had said it would only take one to believe Jack.

"No one else will, though," Serious Boy said, passing a bag of chips that was making its way around the circle.

"I'll just have to try harder," Jack said. He sounded confident, but across the circle I could see Jack's sad eyes glistening in the firelight.

After that, they had nothing more to say to each other, and I grew impatient with the other conversations around the campfire.

A golden retriever lay under one guy's chair. Now and then the dog lifted her head and sniffed the air, piquing her ears. Then she'd lay her head back down on her feet. I watched her closely. When Calder arrived, she'd be the first to know.

The campfire danced in the darkness, and as the wind switched, we'd get up and shuffle our chairs around the circle to avoid the smoke. Someone would say, "Rabbit, rabbit, rabbit," to dispel the fumy cloud—which didn't really work. By midnight, our game of musical chairs had me sitting by a guy named Connor.

"Who are you looking for?" Connor asked. "You keep looking around like you're expecting someone."

"Oh, no," I said. "Not really."

"I don't really know anyone here either. I came up to visit my college roommate. That's him there." Connor pointed toward the tents where a group of guys were talking and shoving each other. "His name's Erik. He graduated from Bayfield."

Connor was smaller than the rest of the Bayfield crew: a tennis player, not football. After our initial introductions, he didn't say much, which I appreciated, but he laughed too loud, and he rarely distinguished between what was truly funny and what was just plain stupid. He was harmless, but after a while, it got on my nerves. I got up to leave.

Serious Boy watched me stand and asked, "Going somewhere?"

"Do you have a problem with that?" I asked.

Gabby pulled away from the other boy long enough to ask if I wanted her to come with me and guard the outhouse door.

"No need," I said.

"Take this," Connor said, and he handed me his flashlight. "It's pretty dark once you get away from the campfire."

"At least there's one gentleman in the group," I said, and I think Serious Boy got the hint.

In the dark, the ground seemed more uneven than it did in the daylight. I staggered a little as I walked, sending beams of light zigzagging off the canopy of trees like a laser light show. A jar light mounted at the peak of the outhouse roof lit the way and kept me on course. A swarm of moths competed for the light. I was nearly there when a pale arm darted out from the trees and yanked me into the woods.

"Would you *please* stop doing that!" I whined. "That is so annoying. How long have you been out here?"

"Since sunset," Calder said.

"I've been waiting all night for you," I said curtly. "Maybe you should try being a little less antisocial."

"No, I'm good." He took me into an embrace, curling me up in his lap between a moss-covered rock, and a shaggy cedar tree. He touched his lips gently to mine, and the tingle of electricity off him felt like humming through a comb.

"Someone will come looking for me if I don't get back soon," I said, although I didn't really believe it.

"Not for a while," he whispered; then his lips were at my ear. "Who are you sharing a tent with?"

"Gabby, of course."

"I've got another option, if you're interested."

"I'm interested."

He leaned back and admired whatever colors I was putting off. They must have been bright because it was enough to attract a trio of white moths that flew halos above my head.

"But I *do* have a reputation to maintain," I said.

"What's that?" he asked, smirking. "Moody city girl? Or were you going for the less emo, artistic out-of-towner? I've been listening for hours, and you've barely said two words since dinner. And who wears a . . . what is this?"

"It's a poncho. It's chenille."

Calder shook his head. "Who wears a chenille poncho on a camping trip?" He took two fingers and flipped the pompon ties that hung under my chin.

"The wind is cold," I said.

159

"I didn't think the cold ever bothered you."

"That only applies to the lake, and it's easier to stay warm when you're around, *but since you weren't* . . . I guess I had to resort to inappropriate outerwear."

He kissed me quiet. "When everyone else goes to bed, you go, too. I'll come wake you later."

It was harder to pay attention to the campfire banter after that. Serious Boy had grown quiet, and he was the only one I was interested in hearing from anyway. Once or twice he looked at me with a strange wistfulness that made me squirm in my chair.

As the night drew on and people got tired, the conversation slowed. Some people seemed to be asleep in their chairs. Others got up and quietly retreated to their tents. Gabby snuck off with Serious Boy's friend. Looked like I was going to have the tent to myself.

Before I had time to consider what that might mean, Brady broke the long silence with a sentence that brought everyone back from the dead: "So how goes the mermaid hunt, Jack?"

Serious Boy looked up quickly, his eyes wide and intent, first on me and then on Jack. There was a beat of silence, then the fire cracked on a pine log. Connor looked around the circle. "What's this?" he asked.

"Jack here thinks we should spray mermaid repellant around our campsite," said Brady. Connor snorted, then— when he noticed Jack's serious expression—laughed so hard he fell out of his chair.

Jack glared at him in the darkness, vitriol in his eyes.

19

CONCENTRATED TIME

My dad always said if anything good was going to happen, it would happen before midnight. That was the rationale for my twelve o'clock curfew back when we lived in Minneapolis. Of course, he was wrong. Dead wrong. Even when I was in junior high, slumber party conversations didn't get deep and interesting until after one. The same was true with dating a merman. Nothing compared to a midnight swim—our first real swim, alone, since returning to the lake. If this was what Calder meant by "concentrated time," he could have it whenever he wanted.

"I thought you didn't want me in the water," I said when he brought me up for air.

"Just this once," he said. "For old time's sake."

The Big and Little Dippers filled the sky with a light that held its own against the pale disk of the moon and stirred the lake into a rich navy, with black ripples, like a Van Gogh painting. The only other light was the reflection of the silver-sequined tail that propelled us forward and kept us buoyant when we stopped to appreciate the time alone together. When the moon hit it, a dazzling spray of twinkly lights scattered across the surface of the water. It was like dancing under a disco ball, and it was like choreography, slow and twirling.

Calder would extend his arm, letting me out as far as I could go while maintaining contact, and then he'd pull me in so close his heart pounded in my ears. He circled me over and twisted me down. Sometimes I wondered if he was reliving the experience of taking a life. I didn't like to think of another girl in this dance with him. But I could at least revel in the knowledge that he got more from our dance than he had from any other. For now, Calder still found all his happiness in me–and he didn't have to kill me to get it.

At one point I heard the soft sound of the letter *L* lilting under the water. Like a song: *luh, luh, luh.* And then the word *love.* It startled me because I didn't know where the thought came from: him or me?

"I've missed this," he said.

"You don't have to," I responded, impressed that the most perfect words came to mind in time to speak them. Usually they came to me in the middle of the night, allowing me to only wish I'd said them.

"I guess I don't," he said, and we dove, his mouth on mine as we serpentined the rocks and sandbars. I accepted the air I didn't really need and kept my eyes closed so I wouldn't betray my secret.

It was too dark to see anyway, and Calder seemed to navigate more by sound than sight. I imagined I could almost hear the vibrations and tinny nuances of the varying topographies of the lake. The pictures played on my mind like a sonar image, but I didn't open my eyes to verify whether there was any truth to my imagination. I would have been too disappointed to find out I was wrong. Pretending was so much better.

An hour or two later, Calder brought us back to a small strip of sand not far from the campsite. I let go of him and swam up to the shore, walking the last few feet, my clothes saturated and plastered to my body.

"Hurry back," I whisper-yelled as Calder swam away, and he must have heard me, because a silver tail breached the surface and hit the water with a gentle *thwap*. *Someday*, I thought. *Someday that will be me.*

Minutes later, Calder returned and led me to a small, moss-lined cave cut into the side of the hill. It was warm there, maybe even more comfortable than the tent. I was so tired I could have slept standing up, and I took no time curling into Calder's arms. My wet clothes clung to me, and I shivered in the night air. He pulled a quilt from deeper in the cave. When I looked at him questioningly, he shrugged. "I borrowed it from Gabby's tent. I doubt she'll miss it."

"I don't know. It's her lucky blanket."

He ran his thumb over my fingertips. "We swam for a long time. Shouldn't your skin be pruney?"

"Hmm?" I mumbled, already half asleep. I thought he said something more, but I wasn't sure what.

When the first pink and orange strains of Saturday morning laced across the horizon, I couldn't help feeling sad that the night was coming to an end. The morning was already turning humid and the air in the cave was suffocating. I peeled myself out of Calder's arms and wandered the beach, pocketing a few pieces of beach glass that caught my eye: two whites and a brown.

A buzzing noise broke my concentration, and within seconds it was all around me. It was all I could hear. Out of nowhere, Calder's hand came down on my shoulder, but I brushed it off. He couldn't startle me anymore. I turned to silently ask him if he heard it, too. His face was tense with concentration, and his nostrils flared as flies buzzed past our heads.

I took one cautious step toward the swarm of insects. My feet sank into the soft sand, slipping under me as I tried to climb the bank to investigate.

"Lily, no," Calder said. "Stay back." But my feet kept moving. There was something half buried in the sand. Something big. Not a log or a rock. Goose bumps rose on my arms.

As I got closer, I saw toes. Then bare legs. Blood pooled inside the still body. Milky eyes stared up at the sky. Flies crawled in and out of slack jaws. A scream ripped through my chest, but Calder slapped his hand over my mouth before I made a sound. He pulled me back as I gasped for breath through his fingers, forgetting to exhale in between.

"Maris," I finally whispered as bile rose in my throat. Blood rushed away from my head, and I swayed. For a moment I thought I was in a slow-motion fall and I wondered, as the sand came up to meet me, how I could avoid falling on top of the body. Calder supported me as my legs gave way.

I knelt in the sand, Calder's breath hot on my neck. I couldn't look away from the gruesome scene. I'd never seen a dead body before. It repelled as much as it compelled me to draw closer.

Connor, the laughing boy from the night before, lay in the sand, staring blankly up at me. Red stripes lashed across his bare chest. His shorts, once wet, were caked with drying sand.

Would Maris have dragged him from his tent? I couldn't picture that. Had she lured him out into the water? That seemed more likely.

"I'm sorry," said Calder. "I am. Be glad it's only one."

"Glad?" I pulled away from him. How he could he minimize this?

He leaned forward and carefully closed Connor's eyelids. "Clearly, Maris is in bad shape. It could have been much worse."

I couldn't see how.

"Letting targets escape is a bad sign, but *this*? They've lost complete control of their senses. Leaving a dead body on land . . . it's completely reckless. We're lucky they didn't wipe out the whole campground. This is insanity."

"Really, Calder?" My tone was scathing. "Tell me what a *sane* murder looks like."

He gritted his teeth until bands of muscle jumped in his jaw. "That's just it. A *sane* murder wouldn't look like anything.

You'd never see it. They'd hide the bodies underwater. They'd be inconspicuous. This is anything but."

I waved the flies away from Connor's face. They swarmed around me before settling back on his corpse. "Such a waste," I said, waving them away again. I reached toward his face and tried to close his jaw—I couldn't let the flies have their way with him—but it was locked in place. "Can we move him?"

"Best that we leave the body alone."

"Then let's go," I said. "There's a radio on Jack's boat. We can call the Coast Guard."

"No, Lily. We can't."

"Obviously we won't tell them the truth, but we can't let Connor rot out here. And the others are going to wonder where he is."

"You're right," he said, hanging his head. "Of course, you're right. I wasn't thinking."

But I wasn't paying attention. I already knew I was right, and I was distracted. Someone was crying. First, low snuffling, followed by deep gasps at the air. Someone was crying and trying to hide it. It was coming from the woods, farther up the embankment.

I climbed after the noise. Calder held me up when my feet slipped in the loose sand. We made our way over the rocks and up the bluff and into the trees. Below a white pine, a dark, hooded figure sat curled into a ball, a blanket bunched in his arms.

Jack Pettit looked up, his face wet with ugly red blotches. He quickly wiped his nose, and his expression darkened. Hatred burned in his eyes when he saw Calder behind me. "Did you see?" he asked.

I opened my mouth, but nothing came out.

"*You* did this," Jack said, glaring at Calder.

"Of course he didn't!" I cried. "Why would you *say* something like that? Besides, he was with me the whole night."

Jack snorted in disgust. "Then another one of your kind."

Calder's silence was his affirmation.

Jack choked on the air and his face contorted with pain. "This should have never happened. It wasn't supposed to be like this."

"She's grieving," Calder said, and I recognized his effort to physically restrain himself. "We did lose a sister. Perhaps you remember."

"*She's* grieving," Jack scoffed. "So she gets a pass on murder? What about the rest of us? What about *him*?" Jack couldn't bring himself to look toward the body. "Where is she? Where's Pavati?" Jack was yelling now. "Tell me where your sister is!"

"Jack," I said, trying to calm him. "You can't tell anyone what happened here."

He laughed one short, humorless laugh. "People need to pay attention." His words bit at the air between us. "If this keeps up, everyone will have to listen to me. It'll be like '67."

"Then let me handle it," Calder said, and his voice was rigid.

"Yeah, you go ahead and *handle* it," Jack said. "You're a real pro at that, aren't you? You did an awesome job protecting Lily from them. If it wasn't for me, she'd be no better off than this kid."

Calder was as much bird as fish. He flew through the air

at Jack, tackling him to the ground. Sand spit up in all directions before Jack was skittering out of the way and yelling, "Get off me! Get off me, you freak!"

"Stay away from Lily, and stay away from me. Don't think I don't know who killed Tallulah. You set this ball rolling. This boy's death is as much your fault as theirs."

Jack's face burned red, and he looked nervously at the body. "I acted in defense. In defense of Lily. What they do . . . it's disgusting."

"Yeah, but you didn't always think so, did you?" Calder's voice rose above Jack's, and Jack cowered back into the trees. "You were all right with it when you thought Pavati was yours forever."

"Shut up!" yelled Jack, covering his ears. He turned away from us and banged his forehead against a tree.

The sound of voices coming up the beach pulled us out of the trees, back toward the spot where Connor lay.

"What's this? Hey, guys," said Brady Peterman. Three people followed, including Connor's roommate, Eric, and Serious Boy. "What's going on? Has anyone seen–"

Brady froze and put his arms out to stop the others from going any farther. I watched as his mind worked to come to terms with what he was seeing.

I stepped in before Jack could say anything more. "I found him here," I said.

Serious Boy trained his eyes on me.

"How did he get here?" asked Brady. "What the hell happened?" Eric covered his mouth to hold back the dry heaves.

"I warned you about this," Jack said, wiping the remaining tears from his cheeks. Bits of pine bark clung to his sweaty face.

"Shut up, Jack," Brady said. "Bear, maybe? I told him not to have snacks in the tent."

"Oh, wake up!" Jack said. "The body's too clean for a bear."

"Show some respect," Brady said. "You've got a lot of nerve." He looked over his shoulder at a tall blond guy in a Marquette sweatshirt. "Get on the radio, Mick. Call the Coast Guard. Jack, give me that blanket of yours. We need to cover him up."

Jack handed off the blanket and stalked down the beach. I watched him go and saw, beyond him, my father's face barely above the waterline, watching from the dark water. "Calder," I said, turning, but he'd disappeared, leaving just as silently as he'd arrived.

Over the next few minutes, the rest of the campground was alerted and gathered solemnly on the beach. The other kids displayed a combination of fear and curiosity. No one knew Connor well enough to cry; rather, ashen expressions were the norm. Eric, Connor's roommate, sat beside the body until the Coast Guard arrived.

Serious Boy kept his distance from me, just as he had the night before, but his pale blue eyes never left my face. That is, until the other Cornucopia boy dragged him away, saying, "Let it be. One should be enough," and giving me an icy glare that froze me to the core.

20

FATHER'S DAY

The next day after Mass, Calder and I sat in a sunny park across the street from the Bayfield Police Station. It was quiet here, and I was glad for that. Early-morning sun streamed through the trees. Two coffee cups stood in the grass between us. This morning I'd opted for Calder's double espresso in lieu of my usual caramel mocha latte. Calder read to me from my anthology of Victorian poets, trying to distract me from morbid thoughts, but it was tough going considering the material he was working with.

After a few minutes, he turned the page and began to

recite from one of my favorites–the one that always made him roll his eyes. This time he used a funny voice, mugging and preening, as he read Tennyson's "The Merman":

I would be a merman bold,
I would sit and sing the whole of the day;
I would fill the sea-halls with a voice of power;
But at night I would roam abroad and play
With the mermaids in and out of the rocks,
Dressing their hair with the white sea-flower.

I knew what he was doing. But trying to make me laugh wasn't going to work. Nothing could take my mind off Connor.

Calder had explained to me, months ago, how mermaids hunted. Somehow, the way he explained things, it sounded almost excusable. Now having seen the wasted remains of their hunt, it was impossible to think about. More terrifying than the inescapable memory of Connor's vacant, milky eyes was the knowledge that he wouldn't be their last.

Calder slipped into Hopkins's "Epithalamion" without me noticing he'd turned the page.

. . . there comes a listless stranger: beckoned by the noise
He drops towards the river: unseen
Sees the bevy of them, how the boys
With dare and with downdolphinry and bellbright bodies
*   huddling out,*
Are earthworld, airworld, waterworld thorough hurled, all
*   by turn and turn about.*
. . . Here he feasts: lovely all is! . . .

"Lily? Are you listening?" I looked up without an answer. "Where's your head at?" Calder asked. "You're so distant."

"It's Father's Day," I said. "And Dad's not—" But before I could finish my thought, tires squealed around the corner and screeched to a stop punctuated by car doors slamming. Across the street, Gabby and Mr. Pettit hurried from their van toward the station.

"I wonder what that's about," I said.

"One guess," Calder said. "Come on."

I staggered to my feet, and Calder dragged me across the road. He paused in front of the building, lifting his chin and cocking his head to listen. Then he pulled me around the left side of the building and back toward the third set of windows, which were cracked an inch. Calder crouched below the window and gestured for me to do the same. From inside, Gabby's voice carried above the others.

"Are you trying to ruin my life, Jack? Y'know, it didn't used to completely suck being your sister."

"Quiet, Gabby. Don't make me regret letting you come," Mr. Pettit said.

"I'm sorry to have to call you down here, Martin," said an unfamiliar male voice.

"What else could you do?" Mr. Pettit asked. "Explain yourself, Jack."

There was a scuffle and the sound of a chair turning over. "Get your hands off me!" Jack said. "Someone's got to finally listen. I'm not crazy."

"This has got to stop. This time you've gone too far," Mr. Pettit said.

"Your father's right," said the other man. "Wasting my

time is wasting tax dollars. I've got a limited staff. What if a real emergency comes in and you've got my people dealing with your bogus pranks? I can't have that."

"Chief Eaton, I'm telling you that kid's death was a real emergency," Jack said. "A mermaid killed him."

"That boy's death was a tragic accident," Chief Eaton said.

"You'll be keeping Jack overnight, then?" Mr. Pettit suggested.

There was a pause. It seemed Chief Eaton hadn't been considering that. But then he said, "S'pose we could do a twenty-four-hour hold, if that's what you want. We can look at whether there'll be any criminal charges in the morning. Disorderly conduct most likely. And I'm sure the district attorney's going to want restitution for the handcuffs and the window."

"That's fair, Bob," Mr. Pettit said.

"Fair?" Jack cried. "Fair? I'm trying to stop a killer, and you're asking him to lock me up?"

"Oh, shut up," Gabby said. "Serves you right. I'm so out of here." Gabby's flip-flops slapped on the floor and faded away. Calder pulled me toward the front of the building to cut her off on the sidewalk. The heavy doors scraped open, and we heard Gabby's shoes on the concrete steps.

"Hey," Calder called. "Hey, Gabrielle! Wait up."

Gabby spun around and threw her hands in the air. "Oh, great. I was hoping I wouldn't see anyone I knew."

"What's going on?" I asked.

Gabby turned her back on us and kept marching toward their van.

"Gabby!" I called.

She stopped in her tracks and threw back her head. "Fine," she said. "You're going to hear about it sooner or later."

"Hear about what?" I asked, running around in front of her. It was a terrible performance on my part–playing dumb like that–but Gabby didn't seem to notice.

"Oh, I don't know. Maybe about Jack breaking in to the station last night. Or how about Jack handcuffing himself to a chair and swallowing the key. He's become completely unhinged."

"No way," I breathed.

"Way," Gabby said. "He refused to leave until someone agreed to investigate that Connor kid as a mermaid victim. God, I feel ridiculous even saying that out loud."

I massaged my temples. "What did they say?"

"They laughed," Calder said.

"If I could be so lucky," Gabby said. "No one's thinking this is funny anymore. I tried to talk to him. Nobody's going to ever take him seriously again. He told the chief it was only a matter of time before the next 'accident.'" She made air quotes with her fingers.

I put my hand on her shoulder as my insides twisted in knots. Gabby was in full rant mode now.

"Jack got in a huge fight with my mom and dad last night, too. They said he's throwing his life away. My dad's not going to let him use the boat anymore. Jack went ballistic, of course. Threw a kitchen chair. Stormed out. Mom and I waited up, but he didn't come home. Then this morning, Chief Eaton calls."

The front door of the station house opened and Mr.

Pettit walked out, pushing Jack slightly ahead of him, his hand clamped down on Jack's shoulder like a vice.

Gabby muttered, "So much for the lockup. I can't catch a break."

Jack stopped dead in his tracks and glared at Calder. "You," he said, his hands balled into fists.

Calder stared him down, his expression emotionless, while my heart crashed against my rib cage.

"Guess who came to see me last night," Jack said to Calder, spit flying with each word.

Pavati, I thought. *She made good on her promise to see Jack, after all.* Would this make things better or worse? But then I remembered what Gabby'd said about Jack's late-night trip to the police station, and I answered my own question. Calder didn't say a word.

"She got close enough for me to know she was there, but then she ran away."

"Enough," Mr. Pettit said, and he pushed Jack into the backseat of his car. "Sorry, Lily. Calder. I'd appreciate it if you didn't mention this to anyone."

Gabby shook her head and climbed into the front seat, folding her arms over her chest.

After the car pulled away from the curb and raced up the street, Calder pinched the bridge of his nose and walked back to the park. He found a seat on the ground and leaned up against a tree.

I stood in front of him and looked down on the top of his head. "Do you believe him?" I asked. "About Pavati?"

"I have no reason not to." He rested his elbows on his knees and laced his hands together, twisting his fingers.

"Do you think she knows that Jack's been revealing her secret?"

"Doubtful. She wouldn't risk being captured. She's just doing her best to fulfill her promise to see him. Sick compulsion. We'll go look again tonight. If Pavati came to see Jack, she might still be close. And if she's close, your dad's fast enough to catch up to her."

"That's good," I said.

The look Calder gave me told me it wasn't the same conclusion he'd drawn. I scrutinized his face to discern the cause of his conflict, but he didn't explain.

21

EAVESDROPPER

The willow tree north of our dock must have been hit by lightning at some point in its history. While the whole tree was a beautiful umbrella of green, part of the trunk was split low, throwing a branch across the water with young shoots all along its length. I walked it as if it were a knobby balance beam, picking my way to a place where I could sit and dangle my feet in the water but still hide should someone want to drown me like poor Connor.

Didn't work, though. Sophie found me. She followed, her arms held out to her sides, balancing, wavering, grinning at me. "Pretty dress," she said. "Going somewhere?"

I looked down at the white, tiered minidress. I wasn't going anywhere. With Calder gone, life–it seemed–had come to a standstill.

"Whatever you're doing, can I watch?" Sophie asked.

"I'm just sitting here, Soph."

"Really?" She scrunched up her face and sat beside me, kicking a spray of water out toward the dock. "You don't look like you're doing nothing."

"Sorry to disappoint you."

"Huh." She picked bark off the willow branch and threw it at the water. "I thought maybe you were thinking about looking for Dad. He's been gone a–"

"Yeah, I've noticed." Every time Sophie brought up Dad, it also brought a liquefying feeling to my stomach. I tried to suppress it, but Sophie wasn't fooled.

She said, "Settle down, Lily. I just thought maybe you could try looking for him. For Mom. She's really worried."

"If I could do something about it, I would have already," I snapped back. I looked up at Sophie, and two red spots were burning in the center of her cheeks. "I'm sorry, Soph. But I don't have any idea where to search."

Sophie studied the water and nodded seriously, then, after a while, asked, "Do you wonder what Dad and Calder are doing?"

"What makes you think they're together?"

She sighed dramatically and wiped her eyes with the backs of her hands. "Never mind," she said. She got up.

"Sophie, what are you trying to say?"

"I'll go. I can tell you don't want me here."

Her curly blond ponytail bobbed as she jumped from

the branch down to the sand and walked up the yard. Before she reached the porch, she turned and yelled, "So are you going swimming or not?"

"Not!"

She ran into the house and slammed the door. I understood her frustration. By my count, it had been eight days since we'd seen Dad around the dinner table. I hadn't seen Calder in a few days either. Not since our run-in with the Pettits at the police station.

But what did Sophie expect me to do about it? Even if I let her in on my secret experiments, it wasn't like I could just go swimming after them. Holding my breath and searching three thousand cubic miles were two different things. Plus, there was Maris and Pavati to contend with. But maybe . . .

Maybe I didn't have to leave. I jumped off the branch without a thought for my dress. The water was just barely over my head. Deep breath, and I let myself sink under to sit cross-legged on the rocky bottom, pressing my hands against the underside of the willow branch to keep from floating.

I'd heard voices before. If Calder's theory was right, I should recognize Dad's thoughts, seeing as he was family, and I was familiar with his voice on land. Maybe I could . . . if I strained. . . . At the very least I could practice my breath control.

The underwater experience always started the same for me: The crush on my ears. The metallic ringing. The low, humming vibration. I had to push past all that to hear anything else. The pips of lake trout. The brushing grasses. The tumble of small stones under my feet. Only when I searched beyond the expected could I discover the unexpected.

But today there was nothing.

I pulled out from under the branch and pushed myself up to the surface. Water streamed down my hair and down the lengths of my arms. I stared down at the water. My face reflected back at me. When did I start looking so serious?

I ducked under the branch again. Crush, ring, hum, pip, brush, tumble, then suddenly the hard bite of the *T* sound. I pushed further, straining to hear more. *Teh, teh*, the words *time* and *can't*. Then the slosh of a *J*.

The first voice I heard was Calder's. I'd know it any-where. But it was muffled and far, far away. It came to me broken and thin: *"Jas . . . iss time oo oh home . . ."*

Then Dad's voice, as clear as if he were standing right next to me: *"I told you. I can't."*

"Remem'er . . . Ba–and for . . . exerci . . . both muscles . . . impor'an . . ."

"I feel tight. I'm drying up. I need to stay in the water."

Calder's voice wavered even more. *"Thas nah . . . emo . . . Geh . . . ba . . . your family."*

They both went out of earshot. I pressed forward, keep-ing only one finger on the branch. Where did they go, where did they go? After a few minutes:

"Speaking of family," Dad said.

If Calder responded, I heard nothing from him.

Dad continued, *"What are your intentions regarding Lily? I worry I'm not there to supervise."*

Oh dear God, I thought. *Oh, please, no. Dad, do not embar-rass me. I'm begging you.*

"What was that?" Dad asked. Still nothing from Calder.

A long, painful pause. For a moment I assumed they'd swum out of my range. Then:

"I think my daughter might love you," Dad said.

Sweet Jesus.

"She does," Calder said, completely confident.

"And what about you?" Dad asked.

Again, a humiliating silence filled the seconds. Had Calder responded? Was he considering his response? Did he say yes? No? *Geez, Dad, I could kill you right now. Get out of my business.*

"What is *that?"* Dad asked again. *"Don't you hear that?"*

"Jason, focus . . . go home."

"I told you. The more I'm gone, the worse Carolyn reacts. The worse she reacts, the harder it is to look at her. And that just makes me need the water more. The more I need the water, the more I'm gone. It's a vicious circle."

". . . ly . . . break . . ." I was losing track of Calder again.

Then Dad said, *"Do you think I should tell Carolyn the truth?"*

"NO, Dad!" He couldn't tell Mom! What was he thinking? Surely Calder wouldn't let him. That would be too much for her to bear.

"Damn it, what is *that? Is that Maris? Do you think I'm finally hearing them?"*

"No," Calder said. *"I heard . . . time, too. . . . eavesdropping . . ."* Then Calder's voice turned from confused to sad. *"Lily, is that you?"*

I stood up, bashing my head on the underside of the branch, and ran, wet and heavy, into the house to hide and wait for his retribution.

22

BOUND

Surrounded by dog-eared books and crumpled paper balls, I barricaded myself in my room to await my sentence for spying on Dad and Calder. Two days had passed. If I didn't miss him so much, I would have applauded Calder for his sense of justice; punishing me for eavesdropping with the silent treatment was pure poetic genius.

While I waited for him to return—and for him to tell me how he'd answered Dad's questions—I reread the same Emily Brontë poem I'd been reading since breakfast:

There is not room for Death
. . . .
Thou art Being and Breath,
And what Thou art may never be destroyed.

I couldn't have agreed more. In recent days, I'd never felt stronger. Maybe not indestructible, but I was definitely not as afraid of Maris as I should have been. Or Pavati, for that matter. Calder might be mad about my newfound listening skill, and that scared me a little—he'd probably be even madder when he learned about the rest of my breath control experiments—but there was no denying that I could serve a valuable purpose.

Dad and Calder might not be able to find Maris to warn her about Jack, but I could. Or at least, I was pretty sure I could if Calder would let me. If I could find Maris, if I could reason with her that there was no more room for death, maybe no one else would have to die.

Reason with Maris. Yeah, I hated to think what Calder would say about that.

"Lily!" Mom's voice called up the stairs.

Why was it I could never get five minutes to put a solid thought together? "What?"

"Could you come down here? Sophie has something she wants to do for us."

"Yeah, I'm kind of busy," I hollered back.

"It will only take a second."

I tossed my book to the end of the bed and protested by clomping down the stairs more loudly than necessary. Mom was sitting on the couch. Sophie was standing in front of her with a poster leaning up against a chair. Rainbow beams of light circled the room.

"What's all this?" I asked.

"Your sister is going for her Science Investigator badge, and she's giving her presentation to her troop tonight. She wants to practice on an audience."

"I was kind of in the middle of something," I said, glancing back toward the stairs and the solace of my room.

"Sit," Mom said.

I barked once and found a seat on the floor by Mom's feet.

Sophie smiled and cleared her throat. Her blond curls bobbed at her shoulders.

"Have you ever wondered how a rainbow works?" she asked, her voice bubbling over with a forced enthusiasm. I immediately picked up on the intonation she'd stolen from kids on TV. It made me want to say, "No, I never did!" but I kept the sarcasm to myself.

"*I* did," continued Sophie, answering her own question, "and that's why I did *my* science project on rainbows. Tonight I'm going to demonstrate for you the science behind rainbows, using *this*." She held up a pear-shaped crystal hanging from an invisible string. It spun in front of her face, casting red, blue, and green squares around the walls.

"A crystal is a prism, and because it has all these different cut sides, it bends light. Here's what happens:

"Light travels at different speeds when it goes through different things, like the air or the rain or this crystal." She glanced down at her notes.

"Think of it like this: You move differently on different things. You move one way when you're walking on an icy sidewalk. You walk a different way on a sandy beach. And you walk a different way when you're pushing something. If you pushed a baby stroller through sand, sometimes the wheels get caught and you go sideways." She demonstrated, lurching her body around, which made me laugh. Mom slapped me on top of the head.

Sophie wasn't rattled. "That's what happens with light. When light is going through the air, it's white. But when it goes through something else, like raindrops, or this crystal, it changes speed and bends and goes sideways. Different speeds and different angles make different colors."

She put the crystal down, consulted her notes, and then picked up the crystal again. "Sometimes, like in this prism, the light bends twice, and that's why you can see more than one color at once. That's what happens in rainbows, too. All those raindrops act like thousands of prisms that separate all the colors out of the white light, all at once."

Then she bowed, and Mom clapped like her baby had won an Academy Award. I clapped, too. It was actually pretty decent. Sophie blushed as Mom went to check the clock.

"Mrs. Larson will be here soon to pick you up," Mom said. "Make sure you have everything you need."

"So you think it was good?" Sophie asked.

"Actually," I said, "it was. I am very, very impressed."

"You gave me the idea," she said.

"I did? How?"

Sophie smiled and didn't say anything more. She threw her notes and the prism into her backpack, carefully rolled up her poster, and raced out the door.

Before I could give her any more thought, the phone

rang. It wasn't on the charger. The muffled sound came from under the couch cushions. I dug around, finding it just in time.

"Hello?" I huffed into the receiver.

"Lily? Oh, good! I need a huge favor. Huge!" It was Gabby.

I groaned mentally. I really didn't have time for a favor. "What?"

"I'm in Duluth with some friends, and Brady Peterman called."

"So?" I asked. I walked into the kitchen and I hoisted myself up onto the counter to sit.

"He's totally drunk."

"I'm not following you, Gabby, and I'm kind of busy." I twirled my hair around my finger and flipped the ends back and forth against my nose.

"He said a bunch of them were up at Marsden's Orchard. He said I need to get up there and pick up Jack, but I'm too far away, and if Jack's in half the shape Brady's in, he won't be able to get himself home. Obviously I can't call Dad."

I rolled my eyes and exhaled. "Where exactly is he?" There was leftover mac and cheese in the pot in the sink. I dug out a mouthful.

"Brady said Jack's still at Marsden's barn. Can you go get him? He's not answering his phone. I'm afraid he passed out or something."

"You *so* owe me," I said, sucking my fingers. "*Both* of you. Maybe Jack should have thought about this before he got lit."

"Great! You're a lifesaver, Lil," Gabby said, and she hung up before I could say goodbye.

The car keys hung on a peg in the kitchen. I tossed them in the air, catching them with an overhand grab, and walked out the door. Turning the key in the ignition, the car stutter-started, vibrating under the soles of my feet. The gas gauge hovered around empty, but there was enough to get me up to the orchards.

Marsden's was two orchards past the strawberry fields and hard to miss because of its old red barn that doubled as an everything-apple retail store. The faded and peeling paint made it look more pink than red, and the long, rectangular MARSDEN's sign hung left of center over the barn door.

The gravel parking lot was empty and a cardboard Closed sign sat propped against the window.

"Great," I said to no one. "Awesome." The place looked deserted. Maybe Jack managed to stagger home on his own after all.

I got out of my car and crossed the parking lot to the barn. I peered into the dark windows, but it seemed empty. "Jack!" I called, cupping my hands to the glass. "Jack, are you in there?"

"Here," said a voice from behind a dilapidated outbuilding, twenty yards from the barn. "Help me."

I strode toward his voice, preparing to scold him for being so stupid, but what I saw stopped every scathing word in my throat. "Holy . . . ! Jack! Are you okay?" I ran to him and dropped to my knees.

Jack Pettit lay flat on his back, stripped naked. His hands were tied over his head to a rusty ring on the side of the building, his legs tightly bound together with bright blue duct tape that came up past his waist, immobilizing him with a sadistic merman's tail. Someone had written *FREAK* on his chest in black Sharpie.

How many people did it take to hold him down? Gray dirt caked his face. Tears plowed wide tracks down his soiled cheeks. I couldn't help but take a breath at the realization that Jack was–in this grotesque state–closer to his original desire than he'd ever been before. If Pavati came back . . . if she said that she wanted him after all . . . would he want this life? Now that he was vulnerable and beached, would he choose this life if she wanted him in hers? Would I, if the choice was mine?

My hands came up to do something–anything–but I stopped at the prospect of pulling all that tape off. What would come with it? "Please tell me you're wearing shorts under there."

"Damn it," he said, fighting back tears. "Why did it have to be you? *Why you?*" Veins pulsed at his temples.

"You don't want my help? I can leave, y'know."

Jack looked up at me, panicked.

"Gabby called," I said. "Brady called her and told her where you were."

"Don't tell my dad about this," he whispered.

"Why would I do that?"

"Or Gabrielle."

I promised, although I didn't think he stood any chance of having Peterman keep his mouth shut. Chances were he'd sent pictures to everyone he knew. There were probably pictures popping up online already.

I surveyed the bindings and tried to figure out how to get him free. I couldn't find where the tape started.

"Cut it," he said. "Don't rip it." Sweat beaded above his upper lip.

"I don't have anything to cut it with," I said.

"Check your glove compartment. Check your trunk. You've got to have something."

I ran back to the car and frantically checked every storage place I could find. Single socks, hair binders, and gum wrappers . . . those I had plenty of. *Sharp, sharp, something sharp.* I came up with a paper clip and some nail clippers.

I raced back and started puncturing and cutting the tape. At one point I bit at it. Picking and tearing, I made slow progress. When I got it down to a thin-enough layer, I perforated the tape with the end of the paper clip and ripped up the middle, ankles to thighs, liberating his legs.

"Get my hands," Jack said. "I can do the rest."

I tore at the tape around his wrists and cold gray fingers. "Jack, you've got to let up on this obsession. Things are only going to get worse for you if you keep trying to convince everyone there are mermaids in the lake."

"There *are* mermaids in the lake. I know it. You know it. Why aren't you siding with me on this? Forget about Calder White." He made the last name sound like a curse. "His sisters are dangerous. He'll turn on you, too. Just like Pavati turned on me."

I closed my eyes and shook my head. I'd heard all this before.

When the last bit of tape gave way, Jack yanked his hands free and the iron ring creaked on its rusty hinge. He rubbed the circulation back into his hands, then started peeling the layers of tape off his belly gingerly, pulling off hair and skin.

He cringed and made strangled cries high in his throat, grimacing and sucking at his teeth. Watching the agony on his face, it reminded me of an actual merman transformation.

Jack paused to gather himself before he started to pull off the tape on his thighs.

"Maybe if you rip it off fast it won't hurt as much," I said.

His face glistened with sweat and he eyed me cruelly. "Don't watch," he said. "Go find my clothes. I think they threw them behind that old gas tank."

I got up and searched, grateful for something else to do. When I came back, a T-shirt and swim trunks in my hand, there was another angry ripping sound, fast and loud. He screamed; then his back hunched before he rolled over and puked in the grass.

When there was nothing more but dry heaves, Jack sat in the dust, covering his nakedness. Filthy and bleeding, he spit and wiped his mouth. I stayed back and tossed his clothes to him. He pulled on his shorts and then curled into a fetal position, his head on his knees.

"She said she loved me," he said, his voice low. "We had plans. I put everything on hold for her. She said she wanted a baby. We were going to be a family."

Jack's confidences made me feel young and naive. But he must have misunderstood her. Pavati wasn't the mothering type. And Jack was only nineteen.

"Then it got cold. And she left," he said.

"But she must have told you she'd come back with the spring migration."

"That's what got me through the winter. But all spring I watched for her. She never came back. Or, I should say, she never came back *for me.*

"I don't know what I was thinking—trying to have a future with her. She betrayed me. She's not *normal.*" His face clouded over, and I could almost taste the bitterness on the air. "If I can't have her . . ." But he never finished the thought.

We both sat in silence for several minutes. I rocked back and forth, trying to think of something reassuring to say, but I could come up with nothing.

Jack spoke first. "Whatever. I did what I could to warn everyone. I'm done trying. The next dead body is going to be on *their* heads. Not mine."

I shuddered at his complete lack of hyperbole. "That's a little extreme, don't you think?"

"It's a little too late to worry about what's extreme. This whole town can go to hell for all I care." He pushed himself to his feet and staggered into the woods.

"Don't you want a ride?" I called out to him.

"Just stay away from me," he said, leaving me alone on the bloodstained ground.

23

WITNESS

Big Mo's Pizzeria was short on tables. Fifteen people hovered around the hostess station waiting for diners to clear out. Twice in the last five minutes our waitress had stopped to ask if there was anything more she could get us, and although there was nothing, we didn't give any sign that we were ready to leave. The bill still lay turned over on the table and half the pizza remained on the round, aluminum disc. The cheese had solidified minutes ago, and pools of grease lay like millponds on the crusted pepperoni.

Jack sat across the table from Gabby and me and chewed

on his straw. Mr. Pettit was making Gabby keep tabs on her brother, so Gabby insisted I come along. It had been two days since I'd found Jack bound and bleeding outside Marsden's barn, and neither he nor I had spoken of it. In fact, we hadn't said much of anything at all. I stayed true to my promise, and Gabby was still in the dark. She attributed my silence to not wanting to be seen with Jack in public. She got that; she'd written the book on it.

I picked at my half-eaten slice and peeled off the cheese like the sole from a leather shoe.

"So," Gabby said. Neither I nor Jack expected her to say anything more, and we didn't do anything to help the conversation along.

In the booth behind me and Gabby, a young family was finally seated. They corralled the littlest kid into a wooden highchair and sighed in exasperation at the other two. "No," said the mom. "For the last time, we're not going swimming today."

"But it's hot," whined one of the kids.

Gabby reached over me and picked up the bill. She dug in her purse and said, "Seven bucks each, cough it up."

"Too dangerous," said the dad behind me, and Jack and I made eye contact for the first time that day.

I pushed my plate to the edge of the table as the waitress came over to check on us again. My phone vibrated. It was Jules.

JULES: Guess what?

I threw a five and eight quarters on the table and texted: What?

JULES: Phillip's uncle has a cabin on Madeline
   Island.
LILY: And?

The mom behind me responded, "Rip currents, honey. There's been another drowning. A big boy. And if it's too dangerous for big boys, it's too dangerous for you."

I watched Jack as the two conversations enfolded around me. His eyes hardened, glistening in the ambient light. For a second, I thought he was going to cry in public, and I desperately hoped he wouldn't because that would send Gabby over the edge, but then I realized I misread him. When the dad whispered to the mom, but loud enough for us to hear, "Rip currents, my ass," the corners of Jack's mouth twitched, and he guzzled back the rest of his Mountain Dew.

JULES: He's letting us use the cabin for a week.
   We're coming up to visit you!

I hastily texted back to Jules: Who is we?

When the waitress returned to collect our pile of money, I asked her if she'd heard anything about another drowning.

"Yeah," she said, lowering her voice. "Didn't you?"

Jack leaned across the table toward me. "Told you," he said, then to the waitress, "Tourist?"

"What's this?" Gabby asked.

"Did you know Brady Peterman?" the waitress asked solemnly. "A little kid found his body in the rocks under the fishing pier this morning."

I looked at Jack, and his face was ashen.

"The police are calling it an accident, but a lot of people are talking like they're not so sure," said the waitress.

JULES: All of us. Me Rob Phillip Zach Colleen
Scott. I got a new suit!!!

I tried to swallow, but my throat was too tight. It would be hard to muster up tears for Brady. A little malicious corner of my heart almost hoped "smug arrogance" had been a satisfying, emotional meal for Maris. I was pretty sure that was the best Brady Peterman had to offer.

But Jules's last message, and the thought of my friends being on the lake, eradicated any sadistic feeling that justice had been served. Instead, fear coiled in my belly like a little black eel.

"What are people saying?" Gabby asked.

The waitress looked surreptitiously at her manager and let a single word slip: "Murder."

Jack, Gabby, and I ran outside and down the street toward the lake. A flimsy yellow line of police tape fluttered in the breeze and did its best to barricade the fishing pier. Jack grabbed my elbow and pulled me and Gabby toward the park.

"I want to get a better look," he said.

"There won't be anything to see," Gabby said. "Besides, it creeps me out. I can't ever remember a summer like this. I'm thinking about moving to Kansas. There's no water there, right?"

"They won't let this one go by without some kind of

search," Jack said, breathing hard as he pulled us along. "People knew Brady. They're going to listen now." Then he put his mouth to my hair. His hot breath brushed my earlobe. "You tell Calder White the clock is ticking."

Jack ducked under the yellow tape. Gabby refused to cross, but I went after him. "Jack, we're not supposed to be this far."

Jack charged ahead, but I stopped in my tracks. My hand rose shakily to my mouth. A pale arm emerged from under the pier where the deck met the ground. The hand was palm up, its fingers curled eerily toward the sky.

"Hey, now, kids," Chief Eaton said, standing up and coming our way. I hadn't seen him there before. He'd been crouched down at the side of the pier with a camera. "Don't tell me you didn't notice the tape."

Jack's face went stony, and Chief Eaton squared his shoulders. "I'm not going to have any more trouble from you, am I, Jack? People in town are going to need some time and space to grieve. I don't want you flappin' your lips about any of your cockamamie stories. Respect. Do you understand me?"

"Loud and clear, sir," Jack said through his teeth.

"I've had a mini vacation planned for months," Chief Eaton said. "This new accident has set me back a day, but I don't want you ruining my fishing trip with any more unnecessary antics. No more. Got it?"

"I heard you the first time, sir."

Chief Eaton paused to assess Jack, who stared back unflinchingly, his jaw firmly set. It didn't take a genius to know what was really going on in his head. Even Chief Eaton could read *those* thoughts.

"You'd have to be cold-blooded to use a tragedy like this for your own sick gains," said the chief.

Jack's eyes burned with anger, and I gently turned him back toward the street. Gabby was standing there with her hands on her hips.

"And you should head on home, too, now, missy," Chief Eaton said.

"I will," I said, glancing back over my shoulder at him.

By the time we got to the car, Jack's mood had withered to a dark gloom. He muttered under his breath about something never being enough. I didn't want to ask. Instead I slid open my phone and saw I'd missed two texts.

JULES: Are you excited? It's going to be so great. I thought maybe you and your man could show us around. Phillip's uncle has a boat. We could check out some of those islands you were talking about.
JULES: Are you still there?

24

CONFESSION

A hand slapped down hard on the kitchen counter. "Tell me," Mom said. "Don't lie to me anymore, Jason."

"You're getting upset over nothing." Dad's voice was a cool contrast to Mom's frantic plea.

"Nothing? *Nothing?* What is wrong with you?"

Sophie and I crept down the stairs to listen. I held my arms open, and she crawled into my lap, burying her face in my neck.

"Where are you going?" Mom asked, her voice dropping an octave. "Every day you disappear. For hours on end."

"I told you, Carolyn. I'm working. Getting ready for classes." From where I sat, I could see Dad's face. It was barely recognizable. A person's soul is in their eyes, and his were all wrong.

"Bullshit," Mom said, and Dad winced, turning his back on her. I thought a curse from my mother's lips would make the earth crack open. Instead, the front door slammed with an enormous *bang*, sending vibrations up the wooden steps and into my backside.

I shifted Sophie onto the step and ran back to my room, throwing open my window to the crisp morning air. "Dad? Dad?" I called.

I couldn't see him, but he snapped back, "What?"

"You all right?" I asked, quiet and unsure.

"Perfect." He took three long strides down the porch steps and across the driveway.

"Where are you going?" I called.

"Out."

I took the screen off the window and crawled onto the porch roof just as Calder came around the side of the house. I hadn't seen him in days, and he ignored the fact I was even there.

He grabbed Dad's shoulder and stopped him in his tracks. "Give her another try, Jason. You need to give it time to work."

"I tried to do it like you told me, but it's no use. I only feel worse."

"Dad, please don't go," I said, creeping closer to the gutter. "I haven't seen you in two weeks."

He didn't turn around. He only shook off Calder's hand

and ran into the woods. I watched him go, forcing myself not to ask Calder the questions that hung in the air between us: Was Dad's betrayal complete? Had he left us for good? I knew the answers. To have Calder confirm them aloud would only make them more real.

Calder was smart enough and kind enough to be silent. He seemed to be listening for something, anyway–something too far away for me to hear. After a moment, he said, "That's that, then."

He hung his head and walked to his car. I watched as he climbed in the back and lay down on the seat. His feet hung out the door, and he threw one arm over his face. Only in that gesture did he answer me. Dad wasn't coming back. And I couldn't help thinking it was all my fault. If I'd never told him the truth about what he was, he'd be a normal dad, in the kitchen doing crossword puzzles.

Running back downstairs, I found Mom in the living room. When she heard me coming she drew the back of her hand across her eyes.

"Are you okay?" I asked.

"What does it look like?"

She was going to have to work harder to deter me. "He'll be back," I said, hoping it wasn't a lie. Even if I didn't believe it, I needed to get the words out for her. Even if she didn't believe me, she needed to hear them.

Mom moved slowly into the kitchen, wetted a rag, and started wiping down all the surfaces. "He's always gone. He comes home late, if he comes home at all. He hasn't slept here in nearly a week. I think it's pretty clear what's going on, Lily."

"No, Mom. It may be many things, but it is definitely not clear."

"Tell me I'm being silly."

"Dad's not having an affair, if that's what you're saying. I know that much for certain."

"He never used to lie to me. I know life hasn't been easy since I got sick. I wouldn't blame him if he wanted to leave."

"Dad loves you. He *needs* you to be happy. Try and fake it if you have to. I can't explain, Mom, but you have to trust me. If you're angry, if you're sad, it'll be harder for him to come back."

She laughed one hard laugh and threw the rag into the sink. "Seems a little circular, don't you think, babe? It's the coming home that will make me happy, not the other way around. I'm sorry. I shouldn't be having this conversation with you. Fine bit of parenting, isn't it? Never mind, never mind. I think I just need to take a bath. A bath and a nap."

A small whimper drifted down the stairwell and Mom rearranged her expression. "Can you take Sophie out for a bit? She's been cooped up with me so much. Go do something fun with her. That would help me a lot."

The noontime sun blazed down on us as we bobbed a safe thirty feet from our dock–me, Sophie, and Calder–in our small, aluminum fishing boat. A blue plastic cooler sat by my feet. Water sloshed gently against the hull. None of us spoke. Worry roiled in my head like storm clouds. I hoped that was the only reason Calder wouldn't look at me, and it wasn't that he was still mad about my eavesdropping, or worse, holding back an *I told you so. You should have never told your dad the truth.*

Why hadn't I believed him when he said it was a bad idea? Surely he had better instincts when it came to merman matters than I did. But no, I had to go plowing ahead, so certain it was the right thing. Dad would have never left if I'd only kept quiet.

Sophie reached into her pocket and pulled out the prism from her Girl Scout project. She dangled it over the side of the boat and let the sun work its magic. A spray of sparkling color reflected off the water and the side of the metal boat. Rainbow beams twirled around in a circle, hitting our faces, as the prism spun on its string.

"What are you doing, Sophie?" I asked.

"Fishing," she said, as if this should be obvious. She wouldn't look at me, either.

Calder shifted in his seat and kept his head buried in an old *National Geographic.*

"You'll have better luck if you put some bait on a hook," I said. "Maybe they'd like salami." I grabbed a sandwich from the cooler and broke off a corner for her.

"You fish your way," she said. "I'll fish mine."

Calder didn't seem as amused by her as I was, and seconds later the first lake trout darted toward the surface, knocking its side against our boat with a soft thud.

"See?" she said smugly. "They like the colors." My skin prickled when she added, "Isn't that right, Calder?"

Calder laid down his magazine but kept his eyes cast

down. He dragged his foot through the scattering of sand on the bottom of the boat.

Sophie continued, "I was playing with the prism one day when I was working on my Girl Scout project. A whole bunch of fish started circling around the dock. I put the prism away, and they went away. When I pulled it out again, they came back. Calder likes prisms, too." She looked up, seeing for the first time the way I stared at her.

"Don't be mad!" she said, looking away quickly. "I didn't mean anything by it."

Calder asked, "What do you know, Sophie?" His tone was serious but nonthreatening.

She shrugged. "I watch. People think I'm too little to notice stuff, but I know."

Sophie spoke only to Calder now. "You and my dad disappear. You're gone for a long time. When you come back, your hair is wet. When I hug Dad, he's cold. Once when you came back—you weren't here, Lily—you found my prism and dangled it over your head. I know what you are. I know Dad is the same."

"That's enough," Calder said, and Sophie shut up, her cheeks flushing scarlet.

I leaned forward, touching her arm. How long had she known? Why hadn't she come to me? She must have so many questions.

Sophie reached over the side of the boat and tickled a silver fish. "I watch you, too, Lily."

Okay. Now you can shut up.

"I know what you've been doing with the stopwatch."

Calder's expression went from sad to anxious.

"I tried to copy you," Sophie said, "but I couldn't do it. Besides, it's too cold for me. I guess I can only see the colors. She says it's because I'm a 'Half.'"

"She? Who's 'she'?" I asked. "What colors?"

Sophie swallowed hard. "I can see the prisms in people. That's why I wanted to do the science project. When you're happy, you look so pretty, Lily—like raspberry ice cream—but right now you don't look so good. Are you okay?"

I turned to Calder, but Sophie's question did nothing to shake the rigid set of his jaw.

Sophie was still talking. "But you don't look as bad as Gabrielle's big brother. It makes me sick to look at him."

"What have you been doing with the stopwatch?" Calder asked me.

This was not the way I wanted to tell him. Sophie realized a little too late that he didn't have a clue. She shot me an apologetic look before turning her attention back to the fish circling the boat.

"I've been experimenting to see how long I can go without air. My best time so far is four minutes, thirty-two seconds," I said sheepishly.

"No tail," he said, but it was a question, and the anxiety in his eyes needled me. Why didn't he want that for me?

Oh. I could read it there on his face. He was worried that if I was a mermaid, I would fall into their mental funk. Well, that was silly. Why would I need to look for energy in other lives when I was perfectly happy myself? Calder and I would still be enough for each other, wouldn't we? Even if his worry was justified, we could keep each other from hunting. Couldn't we? I was sure of it.

"No tail." Sophie sighed, reaching over the side of the boat and stroking a whitefish.

Calder exhaled and, bracing himself, asked, "Anything else I should know?"

I stared at my feet. "You and Dad aren't the only ones I can hear in the lake."

Later that night, after the sun set, Sophie crept into my room and slid under the covers with me. I dropped my book to the floor and wrapped my arm around her. Her skin was cool through her thin nightgown. She tucked her head under my chin, and I could feel the moisture on her cheeks against my chest.

I was about to fall asleep, when she spoke. "Do you think we should tell Mom the truth about Dad?"

"I don't think that's a good idea."

Sophie pulled out of my arms. "If she didn't cry so much, if she wasn't so sad, it wouldn't hurt Dad so much to look at her. Then he could come home."

"I get your logic, Soph, but how does knowing the truth make her cry less?"

"Wouldn't knowing the truth be better than thinking he's left us?"

"He has left us."

"No, he hasn't. He's probably swimming out in front of the house right now, probably waiting for your light to go out. I think he wants to come in. But he can't."

"No one's locked the door," I said.

She shook her head, and her eyes glistened in the dim light. "It gives me a tummyache to look at Mom. It's almost as bad as looking at Jack Pettit. I bet it's worse for Dad. I think it would be better if Mom knew the truth. I wasn't scared when I figured it out."

"And why is that, Sophie?"

She shrugged, her shoulders nudging the pillow. "I guess no one told me I was supposed to be."

"I've been pretty dumb about things," I said, tucking my blankets around her.

The moon shone through my window, lighting her face in a silvery blue. "Not dumb. But you don't trust people."

"What's that supposed to mean?"

"Remember when I fell out of the kayak?"

How could I forget? That was the night Calder's sisters almost succeeded in their plan to kill Dad. That was the night Calder confessed his part in their plot.

"Why did you come after me when Dad had already got there? Why did you jump off the cliff this spring?"

I closed my eyes tight, pushing out the memory. "Who told you about that?"

"Why did you do it, Lily?"

"I thought I was protecting the family."

"Mom's tougher than you think," she said.

I chewed on my lip until the skin tore. "You're sure he's really out there?"

Sophie pulled me out of bed and we tiptoed downstairs to the bedroom where Mom slept alone, her body curled around a pillow.

I shook her shoulder gently. "Mom? Mom, wake up."

"What?" She pushed herself up on her elbow. "Everything okay? Is Sophie okay? What's wrong?"

Sophie came around my right side and sat on the bed, taking Mom's hand. "Come with us, Mommy," she said. "It's about Dad."

Sophie and I helped Mom to her walker and out toward the porch. We eased her across the uneven front yard. She asked why we were outside, but Sophie stroked her arm and told her there was something we needed to show her. When we got to the end of the dock, I turned on the motion detectors. They'd been off since I left last spring. For now, the lake was a silent black pool. We sat in the darkness and waited for something to activate the lights.

Mom said, "I don't understand. What are we doing?"

"Like Sophie said, it's about Dad. What we're going to tell you, you know parts already. Other parts will be a surprise. We're hoping it's better for you to know the truth, than to imagine the worst. And Sophie thinks it was wrong of me to keep it a secret from you."

"The worst?" she asked. "What have you been keeping from me?"

I started the story. Sophie filled in parts I didn't know how she knew, like the part about Grandpa breaking his promise and stealing Dad away. Mom barely reacted. She stared straight ahead. Only occasionally did she raise her eyebrows or frown.

I hoped Sophie was right about Dad swimming in front of the house. We'd been out on the dock for twenty minutes and there was still no movement on the water. I got to the part about Dad rescuing me from the lake when there was a small splash against the dock. A mechanical buzzing followed, then a loud *clunk* as the motion detectors activated and the spotlights snapped on, illuminating the night. A dark shape breached and Dad emerged, head above the waterline, ripples sloshing against his shoulders.

Mom tensed and grabbed both Sophie and me by the knees. "Jason?" she called, terror in her voice.

Dad stared at us with a cool, blank stare. We might as well have been strangers for the amount of concern he showed us. There was no panic, no apology, no explanation. His face was devoid of all warmth, and I hoped I hadn't made the biggest mistake of my life.

There was an intake of breath–maybe mine, maybe Mom's–followed by a scream. "Jason! Jason! Oh my God, Jason!"

I counted to three, and Dad dove–a rippling bull's-eye marking his exit.

MY SCRIBBLINGS

An Unappreciative Man of Pure and Utter Suckage

Ozymandias may be dust but
he was a better man than you, who blew
away with wind and water.
So piss off.

Signed, your loving Daughter

MERMAID STATS

Best Swim Time: 4 minutes 32 seconds
Voices: √
Tail: Who are you kidding?

25

WORMS

The rest of the night I slept, or I didn't sleep, I don't know which. Between thinking about Jules and everyone arriving tomorrow and Mom's hysterics, there was nothing I could do to escape the incessant worry. I know I saw my clock turn to 2:15. And I also saw 4:27. But I must have fallen asleep at some point, because the next time I looked it was 10:41 a.m.

A caramel mocha latte sounded like the only thing that could reach me right now, and I doubted Mom would be needing the car. I rolled out of bed, threw on a Fleetwood Mac T-shirt, an embroidered skirt, and combat boots, and headed for town.

But when I got to the café, the door was locked. I shook the doorknob and checked my phone for the time. The neon OPEN sign was unlit, replaced by a St. Jude vigil candle on the window ledge. I peered through the glass, cupping my hands at my temples to keep out the sunlight. Inside it was dark but for a sliver of light from under the office door.

I shook the handle again and called through the glass, "Mrs. Boyd, are you in there? Mrs. Boyd?"

The office door opened and Mrs. Boyd stepped out. She stopped just beyond the counter and said, "Sorry, we're . . . Oh, it's you." She finished her walk to the door and unlocked it, opening it just enough to let me in. She tucked a wrinkled tissue in her bra.

"Good Lord, girl, you look awful. I'll have your coffee ready in two seconds."

I followed her to the counter. "Why are you closed? Everything okay?"

Mrs. Boyd bent over behind the espresso machine and got a gallon of milk from the refrigerator. "I'm always closed on this day."

I leaned against the counter and waited for her to finish steaming the milk. "Anything I can do to help?"

"That's sweet, honey, but no, thank you." From where I stood, I had a clear view of the office. Its door was still partially open. I'd never been inside; Mrs. Boyd always kept it locked. Through the gap I could see a bulletin board covered in faded photographs. Another vigil candle burned on the desk.

"Another St. Jude?" I asked, gesturing vaguely toward the office.

Mrs. Boyd looked, then went over to close the door. "St. Adjutor."

I'd never heard of him, but that didn't mean much. Mrs. Boyd handed me my coffee, put a day-old apple fritter in my hand, then practically pushed me out the door. Once she had me on the sidewalk, she locked the door again and pulled the shade.

"Okayee," I said to myself. "Don't let the door hit you on the way out, Lil." I headed toward a red-lacquered bench by the water.

It was almost the Fourth of July, but the lake air still kept the mornings cool. Halyards *ting-tang*ed off the sailboat masts in the marina, and cars rolled idly through town. There was an *Eeyaw, aw! Yaw!* and two seagulls landed a few yards from me, eyeing my breakfast with tilted heads.

Hungry? They took two synchronized steps toward me, so I pinched off some of the fritter and tossed it their way.

"Feeding the birds, Miss Hancock? That's very Franciscan of you."

I shielded my eyes from the midmorning sun and found the speaker, a man dressed in worn sneakers, khaki pants, and a jean jacket. Underneath, he wore a black shirt and white collar.

"Father Hoole! I didn't recognize you at first."

"Ha! A full cassock seemed a little formal for a walk in the park."

"Yeah, guess so."

He sat down beside me, and I shuffled to my right. "Am I disturbing you?" he asked.

I shrugged and threw the remaining pastry to the

birds. They fought over it, snapping at each other in turns. "Not really."

"I didn't see your family at Mass this morning. I haven't seen your dad in a few."

"Oh, is it Sunday?" Father Hoole leaned back to see if I was kidding. "Sorry, Father. I guess we all forgot. Rough night."

"Anything you'd like to talk about?"

"You mean like a confession?"

"Well, if you'd like to go up to the church we can, but I was thinking more like a conversation."

"Oh. Okay." I fingered my necklace absentmindedly, trying to think of a good explanation. "Let's just say I've let some things get a little out of hand."

Father Hoole shifted his weight and looked out across the lake. He was right. This might be easier if we didn't look at each other. "I see. Maybe you could define 'out of hand.'"

"What if I told you I was hearing voices?"

Father Hoole's shoulders relaxed. Apparently he preferred this question to the direction he thought our conversation was going. "Ah. Well. The prophets heard voices."

"They heard God," I said.

"Fair enough. Are you hearing God?"

I shook my head and kicked at the seagull who'd lost out on the meal. "I seriously doubt it."

"Are the voices coming from a place of love?"

"Exact opposite. They sound angry."

"Ah. Common misconception." Father Hoole leaned forward and rested his forearms on his knees, his fingers clasped together. His khakis were frayed at the bottoms. "Anger is

213

not the opposite of love. The opposite of love is indifference. Indifference, neglect . . . these things can do terrible damage to a person. Apathy can suck the life right out of someone."

Apathy? Maris and Pavati could be described in many ways, but apathetic was not one of them.

Father Hoole sat back again and folded his arms across his chest. "Find out what the voices care about. If it comes from love, I wouldn't worry too much about it."

In the distance, I saw Calder approaching us slowly. "I've got to go, Father." I pointed to Calder. "Some friends of mine are coming up for the week. We're meeting them at the ferry in a few minutes."

"Ah, well, you have fun. I think I'll sit here for a while longer. Oh, but hey, how'd you get Mrs. Boyd to make you a coffee? Isn't she closed today?"

"I guess I was just being pushy. I didn't know she wasn't open."

He eyed the seagull that was now tugging at the laces on my boot. "Huh. Maybe I can convince her to make me a cup. So we'll see all the Hancocks at Mass next Sunday?"

"Um, yep?"

"I'll take that as a yes."

I dropped my empty cup into a trash can and jogged over to Calder, who slipped his fingers through mine. "Who's that?" he asked.

"Father Hoole. He noticed we weren't at Mass. Dad still hasn't come home. Have you seen him?"

Calder squeezed my hand and looked out across the lake. "I heard your mom saw Jason in the water last night."

"You *did* see him!"

"Do you think that was smart to tell her?" he asked.

I thought of my mom crying into the morning hours. "Jury's still out on that one. By the way, it was Sophie's idea to tell her. She thinks Mom will feel better . . . eventually . . . now that she knows."

"I'll see what I can do to help that along," he said.

About fifteen minutes later, Zach's familiar blue van rolled up to the ferry dock.

"That them?" Calder asked.

"That's them," I said, trying to muster up some enthusiasm. It seemed like an invasion, this other part of my life arriving uninvited. Not like I owned the town, but it still felt weird. And it made me nervous to have them here—now— with crazed mermaids on the loose.

Calder rubbed my shoulder, trying to relax me. "Come on, babe," he said. "Get it together. You're muddying up."

"Right," I said. "Happy thoughts."

He kissed my hair, and it must have improved my color, because he groaned quietly under his breath.

The sliding side door opened, and Jules practically fell out of the van. Rob tumbled out behind her, laughing and pushing her. Jules ran toward me, yelling, "Lily! Lily! We made it!" but Rob held back to talk to Phillip at the driver's-side window.

For a second, Jules's excitement stripped away my fears and made me laugh. "Did you think you wouldn't?"

She rolled her eyes in an exaggerated way and pulled her dark hair into a ponytail. "Phillip was driving the last hour. It was a leap of faith," she said.

I hugged her. "You seem to be in one piece."

"Barely."

Rob came up behind her, his face tense—hopefully he was embarrassed by his behavior the last time I saw him. "Hey, Lil."

"Hey, Robby. You remember Calder?"

"Yeah. How you doing, man?"

Calder didn't answer. His attention was on Jules. "So you're staying on Madeline?" he asked. "What side?"

"I don't know," Jules said. "Phillip said it's past a marina and a golf course. There's room for you two if you want to come stay at the house."

I glanced at Calder, and then Jules was begging. "Please, Lily? We've got to catch up."

"That sounds like a great idea to me," Calder said.

"I'd have to ask my mom," I said, hedging.

"She already said it was okay," Calder said.

I looked at him, silently asking, *She did?* But Calder wasn't looking at me. He was staring directly into Jules's eyes, her pupils dilating. *Hmmm.* So it was Calder's idea to invite us to the house—not Jules's—and Rob wasn't exactly comfortable with the idea. He shifted in his shoes and scowled at the ground. What was Calder's angle?

"The van's kind of crowded," Rob said.

"That's okay," Calder said. "We'll find our own way there."

Phillip came over as the ferry crew started loading cars. "Hey, Hancock!" He gave me a big hug.

"They're going to stay at the house," Jules said.

Phillip's eyebrows rose. "Oh yeah? Hey, that's awesome! My uncle's got a ton of room, and it's easy to find. Take

Middle Road until it Ts. Hang a left and we're on the lakeside. I'll park the van at the end of the driveway."

"Between Chebomnicon Bay and Big Bay Point?" Calder asked.

"Um, I guess," said Phillip. "I only know the roads."

"We'll find it," Calder said. "No problem."

"Guys! We're loading!" yelled Zach, now in the driver's seat. Colleen waved at me through a back window.

"See you in a bit, Lily," Jules said. "We're cooking out. Don't be late."

"Absolutely not," I said, and Calder raised a hand to wave goodbye.

Zach tentatively pulled his mom's van onto the ferry and followed the crewman's direction to even out the weight. The ferry groaned as it rubbed against the black rubber bumpers lining the pier.

"That boy's a nervous wreck," Calder said.

"That makes two of us. But you should cut him some slack. It's his first time taking a car on board."

Calder shook his head. "What's the worst that could happen?"

"Oh, I don't know, Maris hijacks the ferry and pulls them all out of the van and down to the bottom of the lake."

He grabbed my elbow. "My God, Lily, that's brilliant."

"Brilliant?" I snorted. "It's my worst nightmare."

"No, it's genius. You know how to catch a fish?"

"With bait?"

"You got it, babe. We want to catch Maris, and that van is the biggest can of worms I've ever seen."

* * *

217

Later that afternoon, I was zipping a sundress, purple high tops, and a faux-fur shrug into a large waterproof bag. Calder watched me with amusement.

"What?" I asked.

"You're serious? That's what you're packing?"

"It could get cold at night."

Calder shook his head and added a pair of shorts and one of my band T-shirts to the bag, sealing it shut with duct tape.

The rich, tongue-coating smell of melted chocolate wafted upstairs. As soon as we'd got back from the ferry dock, Calder had, as promised, "helped" Mom deal with our revelation about Dad. In his usual way, he'd convinced her that Dad would come back soon and that baking would speed things along.

Five minutes later, she'd given in to a compulsive desire to feed people. Already there were six dozen peanut butter cookies cooling on the counter, and the oven was full of brownies, their molten crusts splitting, releasing an aroma that made me want to stay home.

"Why can't we just take your car over on the ferry?" I asked.

"Swimming is faster. And cheaper," he said.

"And wetter," I added, grousing at the bag. I still couldn't figure out how we were going to explain our soaking wet arrival. No doubt Calder could make it look good. Amazing, even. I was going to look like a drowned rat.

"True, but I want to test something out. You wanted to help. Let's see how talented you are."

"I told you. I'm not going to help you use my friends as bait."

"Think of it as you getting to help me stop Maris from killing anybody else."

"It sounds better the way you say it, but I still don't like it."

We came down the stairs and Sophie looked up from her book.

Calder said, "When the brownies cool, tell your mom that Lily and I have gone to look for your dad. Tell her we'll be back sometime tomorrow."

"Where are you really going?" she asked.

"We're going over to Madeline to have dinner with Lily's friends."

"What's the big deal? Why don't you just tell her that?" she asked.

"She'll want to send food," I said. "We're traveling light."

"You're swimming over?"

Calder winked at her, and Sophie lowered her voice so Mom wouldn't hear. "When will you take me with you?"

"When you're older," Calder said.

Sophie stuck out her tongue and went back to her book.

Once outside and out of Mom's view, I stripped down to my bathing suit and stashed my clothes in the bushes next to Calder's. He was already in the water waiting for me with our watertight packages in a messenger bag strapped across his chest. "Come on," he said. "Don't be nervous."

"I'm not nervous," I lied as my chin shook and my teeth crashed together with a mixture of anticipation and uncertainty.

"Are you cold?"

"No. Now be quiet and quit harassing me."

He waited patiently as I waded in until I was waist deep. I dropped under the waterline. When I stood up again, chin leading, my hair fell smoothly against my back and I was ready.

"Come on," Calder said, coaxing me forward. His voice was deep and soothing, and I felt the hypnotic pull of his thoughts invading my mind. I saw myself in his arms, and I wanted the feel of it as quickly as I could make it a reality. I stared into his eyes and walked a few more feet, until I fell forward into the water and took ten long strokes out to him. He took me in his arms.

"Did you feel that?" he asked.

"Of course. You've done that to me before, remember? But you don't have to. I'll always come to you."

"I wanted you to have a recent hypnotic experience to draw on. Now here's what we're going to do. What I did there, I projected my thoughts into you."

"Like you did with Jules."

He winked. "Right. In the air, the thoughts only go in one direction: out. In the water, it's like osmosis; the thoughts go freely back and forth, from one mind to the next. But not with me and Maris and Pavati. Not anymore. But you . . ."

"You think it's really *them* I'm hearing?"

"You said you've heard other voices before—not just mine and your dad's. Who else would it be? We're going to go out into the channel. I want to see if you can hear them, but I don't want them to hear you. Receive; don't project. Not yet. I want you to keep your thoughts completely blank."

"How do I do that?" I couldn't imagine how that would

be possible, particularly when I was out in the middle of the lake in the arms of Calder White.

"Picture your mom's canvases."

"Which ones?"

"The blank ones. Think big, white, and blank. Don't try to put any pictures on them. Keep the canvas as clean as you possibly can."

"I think I can do that," I said. "For a while."

"But at the same time, I want you to listen. You've got to listen without reacting. As soon as you react, it will be like slapping paint on the canvas. Don't be afraid. Don't get mad. Don't get curious."

"That sounds harder."

"Very. But it's important. Can you do that?"

"I'll try."

"'Do, or do not. There is no try.'"

"You're quoting Yoda?"

He smiled.

"Okay. I'll do it."

When we were an even distance from both the mainland and the Madeline Island shoreline, Calder looked at me with a serious look. "Exhale," he said. "Blow it all out."

"I'll need air," I said.

"You're only doing it to relax. Blow everything out of you. Think blank canvas. Then fill your lungs and I'll take you down. We're going to go for a short time. Fifteen seconds. Obviously you won't have any trouble with that. When I take you back up, you can tell me if you heard anything."

I nodded, inhaled, and then slowly let everything out.

Once I'd pushed all the thoughts from my head, I inhaled deeply, and Calder took me down.

Blank, I thought. *Blank canvas.* I let the canvas grow bigger, wider, pushing everything else from my vision. And then I was above the waterline again.

"Anything?" Calder asked.

"Nothing," I said. "I guess you were wrong."

"I'm not wrong," he said. "We'll go to another site."

We swam north along the shoreline toward Basswood, and I could feel the tension building in his arms the closer we got.

"Would they keep the same campsite?" I asked.

"Your dad and I have already searched the most obvious places. Still no sign, but we're habitual by nature, and you have an uncanny way of running into them." He stopped with a nervous glance at Basswood. "Are you ready?"

"Yes," I said, exhaling, letting the canvas expand in my mind until I was looking into clear, bright light. My head was a vacuum and the world was silent. Calder brought me under, and a tinny ringing filled my ears. And then one word: *Die.*

I must have flinched, because Calder had me into the air with such a burst of speed I choked on the water.

"Die," I said. "They're dying."

He shook his head. "*Someone's* dying," he said. "It's not them."

"I don't know. It sounds like they're in pain."

He looked confused by that. "That's enough," he said. "I think we've got our proof. Your range isn't very good, but if you can get close enough to hear them, they can hear you. Next time, no blank slate. We're going to send them a message."

"When's next time?"

"You said your friend has a boat?"

"That's what Jules said."

"Then we're taking them on a boat tour tomorrow. And they should bring their suits."

The next time we came up for air, we were on the southeast shore of Madeline, right before Big Bay Point. Calder studied the shoreline, looking back and forth between several houses buried in the trees.

"There." He pointed to the largest house with a bank of windows facing the lake. "That one."

"You're sure."

"Absolutely. I can hear, what's his name? Phillip? He's got a big mouth."

I took the bag from Calder, swam to shore, and ripped the plastic bag open with my teeth. Calder swam up and down the shore, waiting for me to get dressed. I left his clothes in a pile on a rock and started up the long, splintered staircase from the rocky beach to the house.

When I got to the twelfth step, I sat down sideways and waited, picking at the shrubbery that threatened to overgrow the railing. Below me, Calder was pulling himself up onto the sand. His transformation played out in my mind; I didn't have to look. But I couldn't help myself.

He was in a fetal position. His broad back and shoulders curled around the rest of his body, with just a hint of a silver, feathery fluke showing. The tension in his muscles made the crisscrossing scars stand out red and angry. His body trembled like a timpani drum. He squeezed his arms around his knees, then exploded outward, his body going rigid and straight with a groaning strain and a wild pop.

No sound escaped his lips, but the pain on his face made me close my eyes and turn away.

When I looked back, he was standing, his torso tapering to slim hips and long legs, the muscles in his scarred shoulders jumping. He opened the bag and stepped into his clothes, his legs shaking as he carefully placed his bare feet on the rocky beach. He shook the water out of his hair and turned to face me.

"I forgot shoes," he said, but I didn't answer, too stunned by the beauty of his body. My insides twisted into a tight spring that, when released, was sure to send me sailing into the air. I only hoped he'd be there to catch me when it did.

He climbed toward me, looking exhausted. "Stairs are tough right now," he said. "I need a sec to acclimate. Maybe we could sit for a while?" He sat on the step below me and rested his head in my lap. I pulled him up so our faces were even. It hurt—the stair digging into my back—but I didn't care.

"Lily?" a voice asked.

Calder looked up as Jules and Rob came down the stairs.

"What are you doing down there?" Jules asked.

"Oh . . ." I looked at Calder for a little help, but he seemed to be enjoying something—my reaction or theirs, I couldn't tell.

"Did you knock on the door?" Jules asked. "We didn't know you were here yet. Were you swimming? You're all wet."

Seriously, Calder? A little help here. This would be an excellent time for that thought-projection thingy.

"We couldn't help but notice the view," Calder said. "We thought we'd come down and check it out before going inside."

"Us too," Jules said, and she took Robby's hand.

My eyes followed the gesture and then I looked up at Jules, who looked at me sheepishly. Her and Rob? Well, that was . . . unexpected.

"Come on," said Rob to Calder. "I'll get you something to drink."

Calder followed slowly, kissing my cheek as he passed. Jules and I watched them go, and then she turned to me with a whip of her hair.

"You and Robby?" I asked. "Since when?"

"I tried to tell you before, but I chickened out. I thought you might be mad."

"Mad? Why would I be mad?"

"Well, we got together just a couple days after you left, and I thought you kind of liked him. I thought maybe you'd been playing hard to get, but then you have Calder, so I . . ."

"Jules, you're worrying over nothing. I'm happy for you. Both of you."

"It's nothing serious. It's just fun to have someone to hang out with for the summer."

"Sure. Whatever you say. You guys look great together."

"Yeah, he's great." She watched Rob climb out of sight.

"Let's get up to the house," I said. "I don't want to leave Calder alone with those guys for too long."

"Yeah, God help their self-esteem," Jules said.

"That's not what I meant."

"Seriously, Lily. He's so hot. What's your trick?"

"I won him over with Tennyson."

"No, seriously," she said.

I threw my arm around her shoulder and we walked into the house together. I wasn't the least bit surprised to see Calder already in the thick of things—like one of the boys—laughing with Phillip.

"Hey, Hancock, Cal here says he can give us a tour of the islands tomorrow."

I bet he did. "Sounds great," I said, wondering which of my friends would pose the greatest lure for a bloodthirsty mermaid with death on her mind.

26

BAIT

The next morning I stumbled into the kitchen, where Jules was already up making French toast and bacon. Phillip and Rob were at the table, shoveling food in as fast as Jules could cook it.

"Are you two doing anything to help her?" I asked.

Phillip answered with his mouth full. "I opened the orange juice."

"Where's Calder?" Jules asked.

"Probably down by the water," I said. "I think he slept on the dock."

Jules raised her eyebrows and looked at Rob and Phillip, who stared at me for a long three seconds before going back to their food.

"He likes to sleep outside," I said.

"Yeah, sure," Jules said encouragingly. "That sounds great. We should all try that tonight."

Tonight. My stomach lurched at the word. Would they all be coming home tonight? What was I doing, using my friends as bait? This was twisted and wrong. They should at least be given the opportunity to choose. But who would choose to be a lure? I hated this plan. I had half a mind to call in sick.

"Eat something," Jules said.

"I'm not hungry," I said.

Colleen and Scott came out next, Scott's hair sticking up in the back and Colleen's mascara smeared under her eyes.

"Attractive, guys," said Phillip.

Zach trailed out behind them, scrubbing his finger over his teeth. "Did anyone bring an extra toothbrush?"

"Hurry up and eat," Jules said. "It's already ten. Half the day will be wasted before we get out on the boat." She flipped another eight pieces of toast onto a platter and blotted the bacon with a paper towel.

"Calder and I can start loading the boat up. Do you have a cooler?" I asked.

"Already packed," Jules said. "It's on the back porch."

"And my uncle said there are life jackets in a plastic bin out there," said Phillip. "There should be enough for everyone."

"I'm on it," I said, and I hustled out the back door. Calder was already waiting for me. He picked up the cooler without any effort, and I threaded eight life jackets onto my arms. Calder and I wouldn't need them, but it was good to keep up appearances, not to mention comply with the law.

"I'm going to have to get some of that breakfast," Calder said. "It smells amazing."

"You'll have to hurry," I said, and then, "Are you sure about this? It doesn't seem fair, not telling them what we're doing."

"You're going to have to trust me, Lily. I believe in *you*. You need to believe in *me*. I won't let anything happen to them. You've got two jobs: First, to keep them happy. Keep them laughing if you can, it will make the emotions stronger. Second, to send the message to Maris. Two jobs, Lily, and neither of them is to worry."

"What's the message going to be?"

"I'll wait to tell you that."

"Why?"

"A little faith, please."

I wanted to push him on it. It would help if I had more time to get the message firmly planted in my mind, to repeat it to myself over and over until I could think of nothing else. But I didn't have time to argue, because there was an explosion of laughter, followed by Rob, Phillip, and Zach pushing each other in a race down the stairs. Jules and Colleen walked serenely behind them. Scott brought up the rear, tripping occasionally because an armful of striped beach towels blocked his vision. A bee circled his head and then flew off toward the trees.

Calder and I had already pulled the rain tarp off the boat and loaded the cooler and life jackets on board. Phillip had the key on a flotation ring. He pulled a thin instruction booklet from his back pocket and flipped through the pages nervously.

"If you want," Calder said, "I can manage the boat."

Phillip looked only too relieved. "Yeah, that sounds great, since you know where we're going and all."

"That's what I was thinking," said Calder diplomatically. "You can drive us home at the end of the day."

Us, I thought again. Who would "us" be at the end of the day? Calder said to trust him. There was nothing else I could do. Well, yeah, I guess I could ix-nay this whole outing, but what explanation would I give at this point? Everyone had found their seat and kicked back. The guys were slathering on the sunscreen. Colleen dropped sunglasses over her eyes and tilted her head back to catch the sun. Jules handed Calder a muffin.

"You missed breakfast," she said. "This was all that was left."

Calder smiled one of those knee-weakening smiles, and Rob scowled. He repositioned himself next to Jules and threw an arm around her shoulders. His territorial behavior reminded me of a show I'd watched on Animal Planet.

Calder started the motor and let it idle. He untied the boat from the cleats, walking it away from the dock and then jumping on as the stern cleared the end. Rob and Zach leaned to their sides to give him room to step down and find his place behind the wheel. I had a sense of pride in how comfortable he was on a boat. I wondered when he'd mastered it. Why take a boat when you can swim? It reminded me how little I really knew about him, his past, the people he'd known, the girls. . . .

Calder reached out for me and took my hand. He pulled me close and had me stand in front of him, my hands on the wheel, his hands over mine. I wanted to turn around and face him, but he had me virtually pinned in position. It didn't help that his breath was gently grazing across the back of my neck and down my bare shoulder. It had to be intentional; it was almost cruel. I could imagine the smug expression on his face.

Seagulls sprang off the rocks, and although I was sure they were making an awful racket, it was impossible to hear them over the engines. It felt weird to be up so high. My view of the islands had always been at the water level—or below. With so much distance between our bodies and the water, the islands felt distant and impersonal. I barely recognized them.

The boat was fast. In no time, we rounded the northern tip of Madeline, and Calder pointed to a small strip of land to the Northeast. "Michigan Island," Calder said, yelling over the motor. Zach was the only one who really cared about the name. He was bent over a chart of the islands, and he put his thumb on the finger-shaped image.

Scott opened the cooler and threw a Coke to Phillip. Rob held up a finger and Scott handed him one, too. Calder cranked the wheel, sending Rob off balance and his hand plunging into the cooler ice. I would have lost my balance, too, but Calder held me in place. Rob pulled out his hand and shook off the cold.

He shot Calder an accusatory look, but Calder laughed it

231

off. "You'll need to get used to the cold if you plan on swimming," he yelled over his shoulder. "It's probably only about sixty degrees."

"Sixty?" Phillip yelled.

Calder laughed again.

Zach shook his head. "Say goodbye to your balls, boys."

Phillip tried to smile but looked out over the water with newfound concern.

"I thought we were supposed to keep them happy," I said so that only Calder could hear.

"Oh, they will be. That's Stockton Island," Calder said, back to playing tour guide. "Lots of bears. Good hiking."

"Where's a good place to picnic?" Jules yelled.

"We just ate," Colleen said. "God, girl, it's always food with you."

"I like to know where we're headed," Jules said.

Calder pointed to the channel between Stockton on our right and Hermit Island on our left. "Head for that split," he said to me, and he left me alone at the wheel. I glanced over my shoulder as Jules and Colleen separated so Calder could sit between them.

Make them happy. That shouldn't be too hard. Calder took the chart from Zach and showed the girls our route. He dragged his finger across the chart, indicating our intended anchorage—the eastern shore off Oak Island. I'd never been to Oak before. Did he think his sisters were this far north? I guess with all the scouting he and Dad had done, he'd ruled out everything to the south.

Jules and Colleen hunched over the chart with Calder, their three heads close together. I sighed. I knew it was all part of his plan, but it was hard to watch him working his charm on them. Even if he wasn't getting anything out of it (there was no tingle of electricity in the air), I knew what Jules and Colleen were feeling. Their boyfriends were only inches away, but Calder could be a powerful force of amnesia when he wanted to be. I wondered what images he was pushing on them. The need to take a refreshingly cold swim, no doubt. The sun was hot. That idea shouldn't take too much persuasion. Maybe images of happiness: puppies, chocolate, kisses. Army surplus stores?

Oh. That last one was for me. "Very funny," I said, and I wagged my finger at him.

He raised his eyebrows at me and mouthed the words: *Watch. Where. You're. Going.*

I looked back at the water in front of us. We were headed straight for a sailboat. I cranked the wheel and missed its stern by mere feet. The captain yelled and waved his fist at me. I yelled my apology, but I'm sure he didn't hear. The sailboat rocked violently in our wake.

Calder reached over Jules and slapped Rob on the shoulder. "You want to drive?" he asked.

The perma-scowl left Rob's face. He got up eagerly and took over the wheel from me. Calder left the girls and stood slightly behind Rob's shoulder, pointing ahead. If Rob had been irritated by Calder before, those feelings were long gone. Whatever Calder was saying, Rob was laughing like it was the most hilarious thing he'd ever heard. For the first time, I was getting a sense of how truly destructive Calder could be. What could he make me think, be, do, if he really wanted to? Could he have made me go to the Bahamas with him, even though he knew how important it was for me to come back with my dad? Could he have made me forget my family even existed, if it meant keeping me for himself? Hadn't he once told me merpeople were essentially selfish?

I watched him closely. Did it matter? If he wanted me for himself, wasn't that the same thing I wanted of him? As far as I knew, my free will was intact. My decisions were still mine, and yet . . . here I was, using my best friends as bait. Had I sunk so low? Was the situation really so desperate? Maybe we should turn back.

Calder reached in front of Rob and pulled the throttle back to neutral. He climbed over to the bow and dropped anchor, coming back to turn off the key. For a few seconds, we bobbed on the waves in silence.

"This is the spot," Calder said. We were ten yards from the Oak Island shore.

Jules said, "Are you going to bring us in a little closer? How do I get the picnic basket onshore?"

"You can swim off the swim deck on the back of the boat," Calder said. "There's a natural warm spot in the lake here because of the way the currents pass through these three islands. It's a comfortable temperature."

This was clearly a lie. The shallower water would help. No doubt it would be warmer than open water, but simply avoiding hypothermia wasn't exactly what my city friends would call "comfort." Could Calder actually trick their minds into thinking it was warm? I wouldn't put it past him, because we weren't here for the warm water. From here I could see the southern tip of Stockton, not to mention Manitou, Otter,

Raspberry, and Bear islands. We were here because it maximized the number of potential mermaid campsites.

I bent my head over the chart and measured the distance to the outermost islands. The closest of them, York, Rocky, and Ironwood, were at least five miles away. Too far.

My studies were interrupted by an enormous splash. *Oh my God.* It was starting already! I threw the chart on the floor of the boat as everyone else lined the port side to watch. Concentric circles faded out from a central spot that held everyone's attention. What had they seen? A tail, a beautiful face? Phillip emerged from the spot with a *whoop!*

"Come on in, it's fantastic!" That was all the convincing they needed. Everyone stripped down to bathing suits and jumped off the port-side rail and the swim deck. Calder and I remained in the boat. One of us was considering throwing up. What kind of person had I become? I would never forgive myself if anything went wrong.

Calder grabbed my hand and squeezed it. "Trust," he said. "Are you ready to send your first message?"

"Not even remotely," I said. He waited until I finally looked up and sighed in acquiescence. "Fine. What is it?"

"Anticipation."

"How's that a message?"

"It's a projection. You need to project the feeling of happy anticipation."

"I don't get this." I glanced at my friends splashing in the water, shrieking and diving. "Won't they put off enough emotion on their own? Shouldn't I send something more specific, like 'We Come in Peace' or 'Take Me to Your Leader'?"

"God, no, don't think anything like that. The message

has to be precise, and the timing has to be perfect. No errant thoughts. Remember your eavesdropping on me and your dad? We don't want anything that will connect the message to you personally. We don't want to spook Maris."

Scott swam in closer to shore and did a handstand. Colleen knocked him over.

"If Maris and Pavati are in close range, no doubt your friends would do an excellent job all by themselves, but since I don't know where they are, we're using you as an amplifier."

"Fine. I'm a megaphone, but I don't know how to amplify anticipation."

"Think Christmas. Remember when you were a kid?"

"Vaguely."

He kissed the worry off my mouth. "Close your eyes, Lily."

I complied.

"You're five years old. It's Christmas Eve. There's a big tree, with a star and silver tinsel hanging from all the branches. There is a pile of presents. Someone's playing carols on the piano."

"How do you know so much about Christmas?" I asked.

"The movies. *It's a Wonderful Life*. Now be quiet and concentrate. There's a ton of presents. You've checked them all. You've shaken some. They rattle. They have tags with your name on them. All you have to do is go to sleep. When morning comes, you get to open them. Do you feel that anticipation? Do you remember?"

"Yes. I can feel it."

"Then jump in the water. Go under and swim out a

hundred feet. Think only of that. Happy anticipation. Got it? I'll be close."

I dove, streaming through the water for what felt like a hundred feet, but I wasn't great at judging distance. I didn't think I was too far because I could still feel the vibrations in the water from my friends' splashing and kicking. There were other sounds, too. Squeaks and metallic sounds. Low groans. But no mermaid voices.

Happy anticipation, I thought, trying to push away the fearful image of a mermaid attacking Jules. *Happy anticipation. Christmas presents. Red and green ribbons.* I searched forward out into the watery expanse, but heard nothing.

Boxes rattling, I thought. *Tags with my name. No! Not my name. Calder said not to project my name. Christmas Eve. Waiting. Happy anticipation.*

When I couldn't sustain it anymore, I swam back to the starboard side and Calder pulled me back into the boat.

"Good?" he asked, wrapping me in a pink-and-white-striped towel.

"I don't think I'm doing it right. Any sign of them?"

"Not yet," he said, pulling a pair of binoculars to his eyes.

I waved at Rob as he beckoned me to join them. I held up one finger to buy some time. Damn him for looking so happy. I cringed at the thought of him in Pavati's embrace. I should be burned at the stake for what I was doing to them. "Should I try again?" I asked Calder.

"Yes. The next message is peace."

"I thought you said no 'We come in peace' messages."

"That's not the kind of peace I mean."

"You mean like world peace?"

He lowered the binoculars and let them hang around his neck. "Remember what you're doing. You're trying to entice them with the most positive human emotions. Like that movie *Jaws*. I'm picking the emotional equivalent of blood in the water. Emotional peace is what we're going for. Serenity. That's what Maris wants."

"Geez, Calder. Can't we go with plain old happy?"

"Too generic. We need something more satisfying."

"Okay, so maybe something peaceful like lying in a hammock?"

"That's good, but you need to add heat to it."

"Lying in a hammock on a beach in the Bahamas?"

"Come in, Lily!" Jules yelled. "What are you two waiting for?" She waved at me and I waved back.

"The Bahamas are good, but I was thinking of you in that bubble bath." He smirked.

"Whose happiness are we thinking of?"

"Yours. Think about a bathtub. You've got the water as hot as you can stand it. There's a mountain of white froth. Step in. Slide under. Let the water heat you to the core. Let all the tension of the day slide away."

"That last part will be tougher."

He pulled me closer as if he was going to kiss me, but his lips stopped a fraction of an inch from mine. We were nose to nose, his eyes burning into mine, until I could feel nothing but a slow, yearning heat in my stomach. He pushed the image of my bubble bath so smoothly into my mind that I silently stepped off the swim deck and let the water slide over my skin like silk. I sank below the boat, feeling the warmth in my cells slowly building into a sleepy heat. *Peace. Lying in a hammock. Lying in a bathtub. Under the bubbles. With Calder's hands slipping up . . . Ach! Damn it. What was it again? Oh, right, weightlessness. Heaviness. Relax, relax, relax.* I was doing a pretty good job. A few minutes more, and I might actually fall asleep. I had just enough energy for one last projection: *Serenity.*

I don't know how long I was down there, but it must have been too long because there was a jolt from above. Calder's arm plunged into the water and yanked me into the boat.

"Very good," he said, laughing, "but your friends are going to freak out if you stay under too long. God, that's impressive. Weird. But impressive."

I gasped at the air. "They're all okay? Everyone's still with us?"

"Of course they are. I told you to trust me."

I nodded. "So are we done?"

"One more. This should do it. But it's the hardest one."

"Great."

"Laughter."

"I have to laugh underwater?"

"No. It's not the sound you're going for. It's the feel. That's why it's hard. The thought of laughter is associated with the sound of it. You need to dig deeper. It's the pain in the belly I want you to go for."

"Pain? That doesn't make sense."

"It's a good kind of pain. You need to conjure that laugh-till-you-cry feeling."

"I know what you mean, but there's nothing funny about this situation."

Calder looked up to the sky. "I'm not going to be any help with this one, Lily. I haven't done much roll-on-the-floor laughing in my life, so you'll— Oh, man, here they come." He grabbed me by the shoulders and pulled me down low in the boat. We peered over the starboard rail toward Bear Island. Two heads emerged from the water. Two pairs of eyes were focused on my friends.

"What are they waiting for?" I asked. Jules and Colleen squealed and splashed water at Scott and Rob.

"I don't know, but they won't be waiting for long. You did an amazing job, Lily. They've got to be salivating."

"Then we should get out to them now."

"We need them to get a little bit closer still."

"No! That's far enough!"

"We need to maximize our time away from the boat without being gone so long your friends get worried. We can't waste time traveling. We need it for talking."

I counted in my head: *One Mississippi. Two Mississippi.* The heads disappeared and then came up again, four seconds later. "How close are they?" I asked.

"About a hundred and fifty yards," Calder said. "Let's go, but don't dive. I don't want your friends to notice us leaving."

"Is it time for a more specific message?"

"Nope. We're back to the clean slate. Blank canvas, Lily. Got it? You need to hear them, without letting them know how close we're getting."

I inhaled as deeply as I could, filling my lungs to capacity, and we slid noiselessly into the water. Calder swam with me, like a human, for twenty yards before he pushed me away and wriggled out of his bathing suit and kept it clutched in his hand. I swam next to him as he arched and bowed his body, swimming like a dolphin, until he exploded into merman form, the silver tail bright and flashing and reflecting filtered sunlight across my face.

He wrapped his arm around me and we swam at a speed I could not manage on my own. He circled around, coming at Maris and Pavati from behind. They had stopped to consult. I could hear them, or rather, feel their thoughts, which came in flashes like a slide show.

Hunger
Fear
Hunger
Death

The last one was so intense it almost made me gasp with pain. *Blank canvas, blank canvas.* I squeezed Calder's hand, and he brought me up for air.

"What is it?"

"We need to stop them," I said. "Now!"

We dove and raced toward the two figures who were facing each other, their fingers laced together. Calder hadn't told me to send any other messages, but I couldn't manage the blank slate anymore. My first thought sprang through the water like a shout.

Stop!

Maris and Pavati pulled away from each other and whirled around to confront us, their faces sunken and gaunt, their mouths gaping, like ghoulish eels. The change in their appearance was horrifying to behold.

Calder held his hands palms up. He kept his eyes locked

on his sisters and tilted his head in their direction, as if he wanted me to speak to them. Problem was, he hadn't told me what to say.

"Um, we'd like to talk," I said.

"What is this?" Maris asked, her voice echoing in my head as if shouted through a tunnel. *"What kind of creature are you?"*

Calder pulled me behind him, but I slipped around his other side. *"We need to talk. It's important,"* I said.

Maris and Pavati looked back over their shoulders at the churning water and pale, bare legs of my friends.

"Later," Maris said.

"Talk about what?" Pavati asked.

"It's important," I said. *"It's about your safety. All of ours. Are you camping on Oak?"*

"Yes," said Pavati, and Maris shot her a dangerous look. Calder was ignorant to the conversation. He could only read their expressions, and Maris was making him nervous.

"Can we go there? Calder needs to talk to you."

"Oh, that's rich." Maris laughed. *"He made his choice. So now he wants us when it's convenient for him?"*

Calder tugged gently at my hand and looked up at the surface, but I was still good for air.

"Please, it's important. We're only trying to help."

"We don't need your help," Maris said, and Pavati took two strokes in the direction of my friends.

"The island," I said. *"Now. This is about the survival of your family. Both of ours."*

Maris stared me down, her bony brow shadowing her

eyes. Something told me what words to use, and they were the right ones. Maris looked at Pavati and jerked her head in the direction of the island. Pavati gave one more forlorn look at their would-be targets, then followed behind Maris as she swam toward shore.

27

DEAD END

Calder and I sat on the Oak Island beach, around the point from where my friends still swam. We waited for Maris and Pavati to transform, find their clothes, and come talk.

"What's taking them so long?" I asked. "Jules is going to notice we're missing."

"Here comes Maris," Calder said, pointing north up the beach. She was stumbling toward us like a crazed bull.

"What's this about?" Maris's voice was as shrill in the air as it had been in my ears underwater. On land, I could see that it wasn't only her face that had changed. Her body was thin and angular. She leaned to the left. The ring around her throat was thick and black—more like a collar than its prior ornamentation. "What's going on with this girl? Why can we hear her?"

"You know who her father is," Calder said. "She's inherited certain traits. But that's not what we're here about."

Maris got within ten feet of us, then jerked to a stop. She crept closer as if it were me—and not her—who was to be feared. Her eyes rested warily on the pendant lying warm against my chest. Instinctively, I placed my palm over it.

Maris raised her arm and pointed at me with one scathing finger. "H-how . . . wh-why is she wearing Mother's pendant? She has no right to it. Give it back. Give it back!"

Their mother's? Calder squared his shoulders but didn't answer. Had he known all along? I looked sideways at him, but he didn't look at me. Why hadn't he told me? I hoped he wouldn't make me give it back. I squeezed the beach glass in my fist, and it gave me courage.

"We have more important things to discuss," Calder said.

Maris did not force the issue but kept her eyes riveted on me, watching warily, as if she expected me to make a sudden move. "I suppose you're here to say you've changed your mind and you're coming back?" Maris asked Calder.

Calder was losing patience. "Don't toy with me. You know what this is about. You and Pavati are getting out of hand. You've been hunting recklessly. You need an intervention."

"It's not me!" Maris screamed, dispatching a flock of grackles from the pine trees. They scattered in a cacophony of squawks and chortles.

Calder threw his hands into the air, his eyes flashing in

a way I'd never seen. "So that's it? You deny it? You realize you're going to get caught, don't you? You're going to end up betraying the whole community of merpeople."

Maris snapped her head to glare at him. "*I* betray nothing," she said.

"At the rate you're going, how long do you think it'll be before rip currents and hypothermia aren't good enough explanations for people? There can only be so many *accidents*. You've let four get away. They've talked to the police. News reporters. Now there are two bodies in the morgue. That's six in the last two weeks."

"So you've proven you can count."

"That's it?" Calder stormed at her. "That's all you can say? Jack Pettit is telling everyone and anyone who will listen that there are mermaids in the lake, mermaids attacking kayakers, mermaids killing swimmers. It's only a matter of time before someone takes him seriously—one more kill for the pendulum to swing from mocking the lunatic to searching for monsters. If you keep this up, people will come looking."

She rolled her eyes toward the sky and held them there. "And if they come? What will they find?"

"You tell me? Are you planning to *let* them find you?"

"We won't be found," she said, her voice flat. "Soon there won't be anything left of us. We'll be nothing more than wasted shells. And we're well aware of Jack Pettit's antics. That's why we've been keeping a low profile. If you can't tell, I haven't made a kill in over a month."

"Pavati, then."

Maris shook her head.

"I don't understand," Calder said, his shoulders falling heavily.

"Get this through your thick skull," Maris said. "It's not us. Something else has turned the lake into a killing ground, and its appetite has forced us to suppress our own."

"It's really rip currents?" Calder asked, almost too quiet to hear.

"Don't be a fool," Maris said, and she returned her gaze toward me. Her eyes narrowed again, studying the pendant and then searching my face. For what, I didn't know, but I didn't like the way she was looking at me.

I tugged at Calder's elbow. We'd found Maris and Pavati. We'd delivered our message. We'd warned them about Jack and the risk of hunting recklessly. "Let's go," I whispered.

"One second, Lil," he said, waving me off. "You weren't trying to spite me—leaving the bodies to rot so conspicuously?"

"We're not above spite," Maris said.

"But it's not you," he said, confirming something he could not quite rectify with his assumptions.

"No."

None of this made sense. If it wasn't them . . . I heard myself blurt out, "Then what?"

Maris whipped her head to glare at me again, her eyes blazing. "Maybe it's your father. Ever consider that?"

"That's impossible," I said, my voice more air than sound.

Calder looked at me nervously. "I've been with him. I've stayed close."

"Clearly, you aren't with him all the time," snarled Maris.

"Jason doesn't need to kill. His family keeps him happy," Calder said. "He can avoid the curse."

"Don't be a fool," said Pavati, finally walking up the beach on too-thin legs, scarlet and glistening in the sun. Her skin was more sallow than I'd seen it before, and her collarbones stuck out in dangerous points.

Dressed in tattered rags that barely covered her, she walked immodestly on the sand right toward us, without apology. I had to turn away, and I heard her chuckle under her breath. Calder seemed nonplussed. He barely acknowledged her presence.

"It's possible. I've done it," Calder said. "Jason can make his own happiness with his family."

"So he's spending his evenings with the family, playing Monopoly around the fire?" Pavati asked, stepping over a sun-bleached driftwood log.

"No," I said, and Maris flinched at the sound of my voice. Pavati, on the other hand, showed no discomfort.

"Give me another theory," Calder said. "One that makes sense."

"There's only one other option worth considering," Maris said.

Calder waited impatiently while Maris feigned a sympathetic look. "Aw, see? Isn't this so much harder, little brother? If you hadn't left us, all this information would be at your disposal. You really didn't think things through, did you?"

"I think you made it clear all the time I was growing up. Good instincts were never my strong suit."

Maris almost cracked a smile, but then a cloud descended over her face. "Maighdean Mara," she said as a sharp wind lashed around the point and sent sand stinging against my legs.

"What?" Calder asked, and his tone of incredulity dragged

my focus from the possibility of my dad as hunter back to the conversation.

"Maighdean Mara," Maris said again.

My hands shook by my sides, attracting Maris's gaze. I couldn't understand how guarded she was—so leery that my smallest movements did not escape her. She looked terrifyingly weak; if it came to a fight, I was pretty sure I'd be able to take her. At least on land.

"Maighdean Mara is a myth," Calder said. "And it isn't funny."

"Therein lies the problem," Maris said.

"Which is?" Calder asked.

"That you think I'm kidding. That we've always thought her to be a myth. That may be our problem."

"What is she talking about?" I asked, interrupting their tête-à-tête.

Calder answered me without taking his eyes off Maris. "She's blaming the attacks on the origin of our species, an ancient water spirit named Maighdean Mara."

I looked back and forth between their faces; their glares only intensified with the passing seconds. "Oh, come on," I cried. "You're not serious."

"You prefer the first option?" sneered Maris. "That your father is hunting this lake? Taking the most succulent morsels . . . ?"

"If you want to learn the truth," Pavati said, making us all turn in her direction, "go to Cornucopia. Someone there can tell you. I've tried to warn the boys myself, but . . ."

"But what?" asked Calder.

"Let's just say I'm not welcome in that town anymore."

She twisted her long dark hair around one finger, the memory of earlier flirtations lingering on her face.

"Who's this 'someone' we're supposed to talk to?" I asked, clenching my toes in the sand.

Pavati's eyes narrowed as she looked me up and down. The wind blew the tatters of her yellowed dress like feathers on a storm-mangled bird. "I don't remember his name. He's the woodcarver's youngest son."

"That's all you have to go on?" Calder asked.

"Blue eyes," said Pavati.

Maris said, "Calder, you do know what else you have to look for, don't you?" There was something soft now around her eyes, something I hadn't seen before. For a second, I thought she was worried about him.

"Seriously?" he asked. "Not all the legends can be true."

"If one is true, the other is, too, and you have to make sure she recognizes you as one of her own. There's no telling how she'd react if she sniffs out your human birthright. Don't look at me like that. I'm too weak to do it myself. You must find the dagger. You can't get to Maighdean Mara without it. Three green stones, Calder." Then she sighed deeply, adding, "I do hope you discover the truth. I don't think we'll last much longer."

Calder and I walked silently around the point and south toward the spot where Phillip's boat was anchored. Neither of us wanted to admit the impossibility of Maris's suggestions, but we didn't have much time to discuss it. As we approached the boat, Jules stood on the bow, yelling and pointing at me.

"Are you okay?" I called, cupping my hands on the sides of my mouth.

"You! Where were you?"

"We swam to shore and took a walk," I yelled back.

"A little private time," Calder added, but Jules's hysteria had her immune to whatever projections he was trying to make. Or maybe we were still too far away. Calder grabbed my hand and we jogged the rest of the way down the shore.

"Enough with this wandering off without saying where you're going!" screamed Jules. "We got cold and realized you weren't here. We thought you both drowned! None of us know how to start the boat." Then she paused. "What the–? Oh, for crying out loud, now where did Scotty go?"

Zach stood up and dropped the towel he'd wrapped around his shoulders. "Wasn't he over there?" he asked, pointing a short distance toward shore. "He was a minute ago."

"Damn it, all of you quit fooling around," Colleen said. "It isn't funny. I want to go." Phillip and Rob jumped back in the water. Rob yelled for Scott. Phillip turned in the water and yelled toward shore. I felt all the blood drop out of my head as if I were a human thermometer plunging toward zero.

"You're serious?" cried Colleen, now panicked. She held Scott's glasses tightly in her fist. "Scotty!"

There was a boat anchored nearby, but I couldn't see that anyone was on board.

Colleen yelled, "Somebody do something!"

Phillip and Rob got back into the boat. Calder ran into the water and made a shallow dive, swimming under the boat and popping up on the other side. He shook his head at me.

"Scott!" I cried from shore. My worst nightmare. Coming true. How had they done it? We'd been with them the whole time. Except for Pavati . . . she'd come later. . . . Could she have acted so quickly? Water spirit, my ass. This was Pavati's doing.

A hundred feet down shore, an oblong shape on the sand caught our collective attention.

"Scotty!"

My friends all jumped in the water and raced for it. Calder got there first. He lifted Scott's limp body off the sand, cradling him in his arms.

"Is he alive? Is he okay?" Colleen asked.

"I can feel him breathing," Calder said.

"Scotty, c'mon, man. It's me, Rob. Wake up. Should we slap him?"

Calder's eyes met mine as Scott coughed up water and rolled toward Colleen's voice. "Big," he said. "Big fish."

28

CONVINCED

My friends didn't stay the week. Instead, they packed quickly and headed home the next morning. Jules looked at me expectantly, as if she wanted me to come home with them, too. I didn't make eye contact with her as Calder and I waved from the ferry office, watching the van turn left at the stop sign and head out of town, back to their lives where the worst they had to worry about were dead cell phone batteries.

When they were out of sight, Calder said, "I know what you're thinking, so stop it."

"You said I could trust you. You said my friends wouldn't get hurt."

"I said Maris and Pavati wouldn't get to them. And I don't think your friend is *that* hurt."

I shot him a scathing look. "Pavati attacked him."

"It wasn't them. We were with them the whole time."

"Not Pavati. She came late."

"It wasn't them. It hasn't been them. Not once this whole time. I made the wrong assumptions. Maris told us the truth. They haven't hunted in a while. They're so past gone they can't even bring themselves to *eat*. You saw what a mess they are."

"A less experienced hunter then," I said, my voice falling low.

Calder grabbed me by the shoulders and spun me around to face him. "It wasn't your dad, Lily. He isn't hunting, and even if he was, he wouldn't take one of your friends."

"How can you be sure? Maris was right. You can't monitor him twenty-four/seven. And how is he supposed to live off the happiness of his family"—I choked on the sarcastic sound of my words—"when he's never home?"

"There *is* another explanation."

"Don't make me laugh." I couldn't believe Calder was buying into this. "Don't go grasping at fantasy. You can't go blaming five attacks and two murders on a mythical being."

"It wasn't so long ago you would have said *I* was mythical," he said.

I turned and walked away, marching up the hill. Calder didn't let me go that easily. He was right at my side before I'd taken four steps. I fought back tears and refused to look at him.

"You," I said. "You're buying into Maris's lie because you can't face the truth. We've lost Dad forever."

"I'm not ready to believe it, Lily. It took me forty years to find a father, and I won't give up on him now."

I stopped and turned around to face him. "You think that's what I'm doing? Giving up?"

"Well, aren't you?" He cocked his head to the side.

"I'm trying to be realistic."

"Since when?" he asked, without a hint of sarcasm.

"Since now."

He smiled and drew one finger through my hair. "I like the girl who welcomes fantasy better. Where is she?"

"To believe in a water spirit goes against everything I believe in."

"What did you tell me once? That *'God created the great sea monsters. . . . And God saw that it was good'*?"

I wasn't in the mood to be agreeable. "God made this Maighdean Mara to hunt people?"

"All creatures need to be tended and cared for. If Maighdean Mara has been neglected, wouldn't it make sense that she would set off to fend for herself?"

I sat down hard on a park bench, facing the lake. "You better start at the beginning for me. Is this thing one of those manitou stories Jack was telling us around the campfire in April?"

"You should know by now that Jack never gets more than half of anything right. The native people have their own legends, and maybe over the centuries there has been some overlap, but Maighdean Mara is from the North Sea.

"Supposedly, she migrated here during the Great Flood."

I crossed my arms and turned away. So far, his explanation wasn't helping.

"She mated with the native men and had three daughters: Odahingum, Namid, and Sheshebens. Maris and Pavati's ancestors, I guess."

"They're the half Jack got right," I said. "The mermaids who walk around like regular people."

"Right."

"So what did Maris mean when she said people were neglecting it . . . *her*?"

"The story goes that when Maighdean Mara died, she didn't leave. Her spirit increased in size and she became a guardian of the lake. Her descendants, and the descendants of the human men who loved her, paid her homage for centuries. They'd make offerings of tobacco or wild rice or copper. . . ." His voice trailed off, and I watched as his thoughts went far away.

"I remember Mother had a trove of Indian Head pennies. Old ones, from back when pennies were actually made of copper. She used to make an offering every year. But ever since she died, none of us ever did.

"That's what Maris meant when she said we'd neglected her. I always thought it was just a story. I mean, it was easy enough to think so. I've been swimming this lake for decades, and I've never seen any evidence of her."

I sank lower on the bench and groaned. "That's my point, Calder. You know why you haven't seen her? She's. Not. Real."

"C'mon, Lily. We came from somewhere. Let's keep the possibility open that she's the root of the problem. It beats the alternative. Have some faith in your dad. I do."

With those words, I felt as if I saw Calder for the first time. How he cared for Sophie and doted on Mom. How he trusted Dad, even now, when I couldn't.

With Calder, I didn't have to worry about things falling apart anymore. In some strange, unexpected way, he had become the glue that held us all together. He had faith in my dad, and I loved him for it. I really loved him.

So there was only one option for me now. Like it or not, I was banking on an impossibility.

29

CORNUCOPIA

Within the hour, Calder and I had driven the long and winding road up to Cornucopia. There was a crafts fair going on in the tiny hamlet, and people had parked their cars and RVs on every grassy inch alongside Highway 13, stretching a mile south out of town.

We parked and walked the rest of the way in, following the smell of wood chips, sugar, and hot oil, passing elderly couples headed back to their cars with the spoils of their day.

Calder held my hand as we weaved through row after

row of booths, finally making it to the center of it all. "See anything?" he asked.

"I don't even know what I'm looking for," I said. "A wood-carver's son? Was Pavati being literal or should I start looking for a freakin' Pinocchio?"

Calder frowned. "I'm hoping it's one of those things where we'll know it when we see it."

"Maybe we should ask someone."

"You go that way," Calder said. "I'll take this row. I'll meet you by the fry-bread stand."

When Calder left, I was consumed by the crowds: old women in embroidered sweatshirts, old men in suspenders, young mothers pushing strollers over uneven ground. I saw plenty of watercolor paintings, clocks mounted in driftwood, and ceramic garden gnomes, but I didn't see any marionettes, or any kind of wood-carver's son, for that matter. There was nothing here that might give us answers. That is, unless the secrets of the universe were hidden in a tchotchke.

Wandering aimlessly, I found myself standing near booth 124 and a line of RVs where the vendors camped for the weekend. I caught a glimpse of Calder just as a little girl in a purple dress ran by, clanging and ringing with a hundred metal tassels sewn to her skirt.

"So cool," I said under my breath.

"It's a traditional Ojibwe jingle dress," said a guy behind me. I turned to find Serious Boy lighting up a cigarette and leaning against a silver-bullet Airstream trailer. "They're doing a dance demonstration over at the park."

I gotta get me one of those, I thought.

"Forget it," said Serious Boy, reading my expression. "You'd never be able to sneak up on anyone again."

"I don't sneak."

"Puh-lease." He blew a cloud of smoke in my face, and I waved it away. "You were made for sneaking. And why would you want a jingle dress when you look so good in band T-shirts?" He pointed at me with his pursed lips. "Where'd you score the Grateful Dead? That looks legit."

He dropped his cigarette into the dirt and ground it out with the toe of his boot. I looked away and, in doing so, caught a glimpse of a wooden wind chime. A beautifully carved mermaid wearing an intricately braided crown of copper wire dangled from its center.

"That's pretty," I said.

"It's one of my dad's carvings. They're very popular; he sells a ton of them."

Serious Boy was the wood-carver's son? He was one of Pavati's boys?

"So," I said, not really knowing how to start this conversation, but hoping I was right and he'd have the information I needed. "You're from Cornucopia."

He narrowed his eyes as if to say, *All right, I'll play along.* "Grew up here."

This was a good enough start. I wouldn't have to look anywhere else for a while. "My friend and I are here doing a project for summer school." I gestured at Calder, who was about twenty yards away now, picking through a table of wooden birdhouses.

Serious Boy looked where I pointed, then choked on air. The choking morphed into laughter. "You are, are you?"

"Yeah, do you have a problem with that?"

He dropped his chin and shook his head, still laughing softly to himself. "If that's what you want to call it, that's fine with me."

"What else would I call it?"

"I know how you operate. The question is, does *he* know what he's dealing with?" He tipped his head in Calder's direction and when I didn't answer, he grunted and walked away.

I grabbed his hand, and he snatched it back as if I'd burned him.

"Careful," he said. "You trying to kill me?"

I mentally smacked my hand to my forehead. All the stares, all the weird behavior and innuendo. How could I have been so dense? Fine. If Serious Boy thought I was electric, if he thought *I* was a mermaid, I could play that trump card.

He got in my face, slight grimace, slight smile. "Listen. I could smell you coming a mile away. I know what you are. I know what happened to that boy on the island. And I know what you're doing here."

Well, that's one of us. "You do? And what's that?"

"Are you Pavati's sister?" he asked.

"Depends."

"Is she coming back?"

"I don't know. Pavati doesn't usually share her plans with me. You know how she can be."

He nodded just as a terrifying man with his hair spiked out like porcupine quills came walking quickly toward us through the maze of booths.

Serious Boy looked at his watch and said, "That's my dad. It's time for my shift. Meet me at Big Mo's. Noon. Tomorrow."

Then he ran up to his dad, who tapped aggressively at his watch and smacked him on the back of the head.

The Coca-Cola clock over the jukebox at Big Mo's read 12:21. My cup read pathetically empty. I'd slurped at the melted ice enough times that people were starting to turn and stare. I smiled apologetically and folded my napkin into a sailboat.

Calder didn't think his presence would help me get any information out of Serious Boy, and yet he was nervous about leaving me alone with him. "Pavati makes friends easily," Calder had said. "But if Jack is any measure, she makes enemies just as well. Be careful." Neither of us was clear on how things stood between her and the Cornucopia boys, but Pavati hadn't given us any confidence that they were good. Now and then I'd look up to see Calder walk past the restaurant windows, casually leaning into the glass to check on me. I'd give him a small wave and check the clock.

I shook my glass and the remaining bits of ice settled. I drew my fingers together and dug in the glass for the cherry when the door opened, and Serious Boy slid into the booth.

"Listen," he said, as if our conversation hadn't had a twenty-four-hour interruption.

Two other boys came in, one of whom I recognized from the camping trip on Manitou. They looked around the room, then marched toward us and slid in next to him. I felt conspicuous and awkward, alone on one side of the booth, facing the brewing threesome. This gang up inspired more stares from the families in the restaurant, and I glanced up at the windows, but there was no sign of Calder.

"It's taken me all year to get my head on straight," Serious Boy said. "I'm not letting any more of your kind mess me up." I got the impression he was saying what the other two boys wanted to hear, rather than what he really meant, because he was leaning so far across the table at me I had to pull back for a little personal space.

"And *we're* not going to let you," said one of the other two.

"My brothers," Serious Boy said.

"Maybe we could try again with names. I'm Lily."

"Daniel Catron," Serious Boy said. "My friends call me Danny."

The brother I didn't recognize coughed and said, "Guess that means you'll be calling him Daniel."

Daniel punched his shoulder, saying, "My oldest brother, Christian, and Bernard, he's the middle. They wouldn't let me come alone. They're only twice as annoying as they seem."

"Listen," I said, doing my best not to sound desperate. "I'm not here to mess with you, or cause anybody any problems. I just need some information."

"Then ask your question and get back to the lake," said Bernard.

I made my eyes wide and offended. "But I just ordered you a pizza."

"You eat pizza?" asked Christian, who was sitting in the middle, his broad shoulders crowding out the other two.

"Of course. Who doesn't? But it's all yours," I said. "We'll call it a trade. Pizza for information."

This seemed to work for them, and when the pie landed in the middle of the table, six hands lurched forward and gooey strings of mozzarella dripped across the checkered tablecloth.

"Back at your trailer," I said. "Was that wind chime, was it a representation of something called . . . called . . ."

Three heads bobbed and chewed. "Maighdean Mara."

"So do you . . . have you, like, seen any evidence of . . . her *activity* lately?" I could feel my face burn as I asked the question.

Christian and Bernard choked as they swallowed.

"What are you playing at?" Bernard asked, folding his arms over his chest.

"Just answer the question, please," I said with a sigh.

"We haven't seen her," Daniel said. "Nobody has. Our dad's grandfather used to back in the day."

Bernard chimed in, "Or at least according to our dad."

"There used to be a line of devotees in our family," Christian said, "but our dad's the last of that line. Now he says it's just campfire stories."

"So you don't have any infomation for me?" Why had Pavati sent us looking for these boys? They were useless.

Daniel wiped his mouth on his sleeve. "Wouldn't you know more about her than us?"

I clenched my teeth and tried to figure out how to end this conversation gracefully.

"Hypothetically," Bernard said, "if she really exists, they say she lives in Copper Falls and no human gets in without an offering."

Christian pulled off another piece of pizza and folded it in half before shoving it in his mouth.

"You'd have to be an idiot to go looking for her," Daniel said. "Even for your kind. She might have been a guardian at one point, but she's turned into a monster. Her eyes bulge, and she has six-feet-long arms, with gnarled claws. She can swipe you out of a boat like *that*!" He snapped his fingers.

"What are you talking about?" Christian said, taking another piece before finishing the one he held.

"I don't know about that," Bernard said, "but they did find human skulls around the falls about ten years ago. Even if she's only a myth, it's still dangerous to go there."

"So where is this Copper Falls?" I asked with a sigh. It looked like it was the only solid lead they were going to give me.

"On the Minnesota side. Just north of Duluth," Daniel said. "But it's not enough to go *to* the falls. The story is you have to get *behind* them."

"That's where she hides her magic," Bernard said. "Behind the curtain of water." He wiggled his greasy fingers in a mystical way.

I closed my eyes and took a calming breath. I didn't think I could suspend my disbelief much longer. I'd gone along with this Maighdean Mara thing—tried to make myself believe that a mythological water spirit was to blame for Connor's and Brady's deaths—but this was getting ridiculous.

I exhaled slowly. "And how do you get behind the falls?" I asked, opening my eyes again.

"Don't ask us," Bernard said.

Just then the air in the restaurant turned dry and static on my skin. Bernard reached for the metal napkin holder, and a blue spark zapped in the air. The hair on my arms rose to attention, and all three boys' spines stiffened against the booth. They stared at me, silently asking what they'd done to get me so uptight. Of course, it wasn't me filling the air with electricity. Calder was standing inside the doorway.

Yeah. Time to go. I laid a twenty on the table.

"You're sure you don't want any?" Daniel asked. "Stay a little longer."

I slid my legs out of the booth. "It's my treat."

"So is she coming back?" he asked.

"Who?"

"Your sister," he said with annoyance. "Pavati."

Christian backhanded Daniel's head.

"Um. Don't think so," I said, looking back and forth between the three brothers and Calder's urgent expression. "She doesn't think she's welcome in Cornucopia anymore."

Christian and Bernard exchanged a look while Daniel asked, "It's that other dude's fault, isn't it?"

I glanced again at Calder, who rolled his lips inward and jerked his head toward the door.

"You mean Jack Pettit?" I asked.

"Last summer Pavati was looking for . . . *a mate.* Don't look at me like that, I know what we are to you."

"Do tell," I said.

"Us guys, we're either mermaid Prozac or the Baby Daddy. That's what she told me. I know how this works. I thought it was going to be me, but then she met that Pettit kid, and I never saw her again. I don't know what happened between them, but something bad. She'd probably come back if it wasn't for him."

I held one finger up at Calder and leaned across the table toward the brothers. They inhaled sharply and leaned toward me, their eyes half closed, drinking it in. I knew they were only smelling Calder on me, but I used it to my advantage.

"What do you know about that, *Danny*?" I asked, imitating Pavati's seductive voice as best I could.

Daniel swallowed and wiped his mouth with the back of his hand. "I know that Pettit kid's not doing himself any favors. Pavati's not going to go anywhere near someone putting off that much negative energy. We all saw him on the news, and then on the island. I made a point of pumping him for information. He's got the wrong approach."

"You know us pretty well, don't you." I meant it to flatter him, and it seemed to work. His cheeks flushed until his skin look like a roasted chestnut.

"I told you. There was a reason I was so messed up."

"Lily," Calder said. "Let's go."

Daniel turned around at the sound of Calder's voice. He grimaced, saying, "That's no summer-school partner."

Bernard and Christian turned, too. One of them said, "Ah, man. There are dudes, too? We'll have to lock up the women."

I ran to the door to meet Calder. "What's the rush? Where are we going?"

"Copper Falls."

"You mean *now*? Wait. You heard all that?"

"Of course. And if there's any truth to Maris's theory, we've got to hurry. Chief Eaton's fishing vacation ended badly. His body just washed up on the beach."

30

MYTH

It took a second for my eyes to adjust from the dark restaurant to the midday sun. I squinted at the back of Calder's head as he led me to the car parked half a block away.

"Wait," I said. "What are you saying? Chief Eaton's dead?"

"I don't think I can say it more plainly, Lily. We've got to get moving."

"You mean we're going looking for this . . . this thing now? As in *now*, now? Don't we need to prepare?" I stopped walking and pulled back on Calder's hand. His expression was more serious than I'd ever seen it, and that was saying something.

"Calder, we need . . . well, I don't really know what we need. A plan, I guess."

"We don't have time for planning."

"But I'm not ready. What do we do on the off chance she's real?"

He pulled me the rest of the way to the car and pushed me into the passenger seat. Paper crunched under me, and I pulled out the road map.

"It's a ninety-minute drive to the falls," he said, putting the car in gear. "That'll have to be enough time for you to get ready."

I pulled my knees up to my chin and inspected the map. "Copper Falls. Didn't you say you were supposed to offer her pennies? Is it possible this is just some made-up legend to get people to throw coins into the lake? Like a giant wishing well? I bet the City Council would love to harvest that every fall. Maybe it's just a scam—"

"Lily."

"What?" I asked.

"You're not making sense."

"Like any of this makes sense!"

"Settle down," Calder said.

"Settle down? Awesome. I'll get to work on that. I'm trying really hard to believe you, but there's not exactly a winning option here. Either Maris is wrong and my dad's turned into a serial killer—"

Calder shot me a scathing look.

"—or she's right and, at least, according to Daniel—"

"Who?"

"The wood-carver's son. According to him, this thing could get us killed!"

"Not *us*," he said. "This is the only way to know for sure what's going on. It's the only way of stopping it, but I'm doing this alone." Calder clenched his teeth, and bands of muscles flexed across his jaw.

"Alone? Then why are you bringing me with you?"

"I need someone to report back if things . . . don't go well."

"Hold up. For one second, just stop, will you? What's this really about?"

He kept his eyes on the road and tightened his grip on the wheel. "It's about stopping the killings. What else would it be about?"

"It's not that you're . . ."

"What?"

"Never mind," I said. If Calder was still feeling bad about not having rescued me before, if he was now trying to prove something to himself, or to me, or to my family, well . . . I wasn't going to stand in the way of him giving it his absolute, most testosterone-fueled best effort. If this Maighdean Mara was real, if Daniel was right and we were heading off to face a killer, I sure didn't want Calder to hold anything back.

He drove west, speeding as much as he dared in between the towns, then dropping the speedometer down to a crawl through each one. He stared at the road in front of us. He didn't have much more to say to me, which gave me plenty of time to think.

One thing that had been bothering me was something Maris had said. Actually . . . lots of things Maris had said, but one thing in particular, so I broke the silence and asked him.

"So are you going to tell me what Maris meant by 'three green stones'?"

Calder pressed his lips together and downshifted as we entered the next town.

"It's just another story, something our mother used to tell us when she put us to bed. I told you that Maighdean Mara had three daughters. Well, she became paranoid that others of her kind would move west to take over her domain. You know, interfere with her hunting rights. So she decided to give each of her daughters a gift that—should they ever get separated from her—they could show her when they returned, and she would recognize them as her own.

"She gave Odahingum an iron chariot to travel the lake and survey the boundaries of their kingdom. She gave Namid a necklace that she wore above her heart to collect and store the histories of our people, and to her youngest, Sheshebens, she gave a small, copper-handled dagger with the words *Safe Passage Home* written on it."

"Okaaay," I said. "What about the stones?"

Calder looked at me sideways and rolled his eyes at my impatience. "Then, one November, the lake was threatened by a sea monster."

"Are you freakin' kidding me?"

"It had already wiped out every living thing east of the Pictured Rocks, down to the smallest fish. To keep it from crossing into their territory, the three sisters stirred up a terrible storm.

"They shook and split the trees. They made waves leap thirty feet into the sky. The great monster was thwarted, but Sheshebens was also lost. Her sisters found her dagger settled in the sand beneath the battle waves.

"They held out hope that she'd return someday, so the two remaining sisters buried her dagger under three green stones on the bank below the falls."

"And Maris thinks that dagger is still there?" I asked.

"She thinks if I can find it, it's all the proof we need that the legend is real. And if Maighdean Mara is real, I'll need the dagger if she's going to recognize me as one of her own. It's my ticket to getting close to her without getting killed in the process."

Less than two hours later, we pulled off Highway 61 and into a wayside rest stop. The area was dense with white and Norway pine. The smell of tree sap drifted through my open window. I got out and slammed the door behind me. Bees buzzed in the lilac and honeysuckle planted alongside the parking lot, but the air was full of a much bigger sound. In fact, it reverberated as if a freight train were rushing by, or a low-flying airplane. In my mind's eye, I could picture the black river churning on the rocks, recklessly rushing for the precipice before becoming Copper Falls. If Maighdean Mara didn't kill us, it would only be because we were already cut to ribbons.

I looked up at Calder, questioning.

"We're not going to swim over the falls, Lily. Unless, of course, you have a death wish." He looked down at me. "Don't answer that."

"I guess I assumed that was the only way down."

"If Maighdean Mara exists, all the stories say she lives *behind* the falls. Not at the top and not in the falling. Besides, check out all the cars. Tourists aren't really big on witnessing double suicides."

"Just the sadistic ones," I said.

"I'm going in from underneath," he said, "and we're hiking down."

Calder took my hand and pulled me toward a brown state park sign that marked a break in the trees and a path that wove down a steep cliff toward the water. Cuts had been made in the side of the hill that were supposed to be steps, but there had been so much erosion over the spring, they were little more than places to catch some traction. I used saplings and pine branches to hold myself from skidding all the way to the bottom.

The sunlit entrance to the path vanished behind me, and the shadow of the woods grew deeper. I stopped midway down and picked up a half-empty pack of cigarettes some careless hiker had dropped. The topsoil slipped below my feet and I stopped again, my ears picking up a high-pitched *click*. A stick snapping underfoot? I searched the woods but could see no one. Still, the back of my neck prickled. I could swear someone was watching. I started to ask, "Calder, do you–?" but he'd already reached the bottom.

I sidestepped the rest of the way, catching my feet on lichen-covered stones. By the time I reached the rocky shore, my hands were covered in pine sap and embedded with grit and silt. But I couldn't be bothered to scrub them in the lake.

The scene blew my mind. Above us, the black river hovered at the crest before plunging fearfully to the jagged rocks below. The copper-colored water rolled and thrashed. Enraged, it roared and twisted through the gorge, transforming into a silvery spray that vaporized on the air. At our feet, the water seethed as if it were boiling.

"Makes the hike down look like a wise choice, doesn't

273

it?" Calder yelled as he crouched at the water's edge, turning over large, round stones and digging underneath. I watched impatiently as Calder proceeded to excavate the dark rich earth, coating his bare arms.

I would have helped, but I didn't know what I was looking for. After a while, I sat down on a rock. Minutes turned into an hour of rock turning and muck burrowing. Calder moved several yards away from me, raking through a layer of small stones with his fingers. Then he stopped.

He looked back at me, then at the ground. I watched as he dug his hand into the soft sand and turned over a large stone heavily coated in black silt, but I thought I saw a green glint in the filtered sunlight. He thrust both arms down into the muck, elbow deep. "Holy . . . I can't believe it."

"What is it?"

"No way." His fingers scraped at the ground, digging a hole in the saturated earth that kept collapsing in on itself, but he kept digging, finally exposing a long handle, decorated with agates and a thick copper wire wound into complicated spirals and coils.

He tugged, huffing with exertion, the ground sucking back, until he fell backward and, like the boy King Arthur, held up his prize: at the end of the copper handle was a twelve-inch dagger engraved with ancient runes.

"Are you kidding me?" I yelled, barely able to hear my own voice.

"I can't believe it," he said again, turning the dagger over and over in his hands. "Geez, it's got a vibration to it. Like it's humming." Then he made a swiping motion, as if he were plunging the dagger into someone's heart.

"Oh, no, no, no. You said it was our ticket in. Please tell me you're not going to try and kill her." I couldn't imagine how, even armed, we stood a chance. "Is that possible? How do you kill a *spirit*?"

"You're right. It's only supposed to be used to identify myself, but if it doesn't work, or if Maighdean Mara's too far gone to care . . . Well, if I can't *reason* with her, I'll do what I have to do to stop her." Then, seeing my expression, he said, "Don't worry, Lily. I know what I'm doing."

Trouble was, I'd been able to read Calder's face since the first time I met him. He might have been giving me his best reassuring smile, but I could see the lie beneath. Three days ago he hadn't believed in this so-called Maighdean Mara. Obviously, this encounter wasn't something he'd ever practiced.

His smile faltered, and he crouched down to rinse the grit from the handle. The copper glistened in the sun.

"So how do we get behind the falls?" I asked.

"I told you. There is no 'we' in this. You're staying on-shore. If I'm not back in an hour, I need you to tell Maris what happened. It'll be up to her if Maighdean Mara can be stopped."

Calder stripped off his T-shirt, kissed me, and holstered the dagger through one of his belt loops. He ran into the lake and made a shallow dive. I gasped as the last ripples disappeared, terrified that I'd seen him for the last time.

Without a second thought, I peeled off my sweatshirt and ran in after him. Jagged rocks cut my feet. Stones turned under my weight, and I wavered like a tightrope walker before diving in. Calder must have sensed me in the water. As soon as I was swimming, he closed the space between us.

"No, Lily," he said, his eyes like cold fire.

"You need my help," I said.

He shook his head, sending water droplets flying off his chin. "I won't let you go into the falls. It's too dangerous." I started to protest, but he stopped me, saying, "If I let you help with the first part, will you promise to do what I say after that?"

"That depends."

"Lily, please . . . ," he said, his exasperation clear.

"What do you need me to do?"

He sighed. "Your hearing has been awfully good lately."

I pushed my hair off my face. "What am I supposed to listen for?"

"I want you to shut your eyes and listen," he yelled in my ear. "If you keep them open, your sense of sight will dominate, and you won't be able to hear what I need you to hear."

"If you think I'm going to be able to hear her over this—"

"Not Maighdean Mara. I need you to listen for the gap. Mother always talked about a gap of sound. A gasp of air, I think. I need to hit that gap to get behind the falls"

My eyes drifted up the nearly two-hundred-foot fall. All I could hear was a constant, roaring growl. It drowned out the higher pitched spray and muted the gulls circling overhead. If Calder thought I could hear anything more, he was overestimating my senses.

"I don't understand," I said.

"Lily, close your eyes, please."

He pulled me against his chest and supported me so I wouldn't have to tread water. I wrapped my arms around his neck and kissed him. He hadn't transformed. I could feel his legs against mine. The blade hung heavily against his hip. If he was going in without me, if this was, perhaps, our last kiss, I wanted to make it worth it. He must have felt the urgency, too, because he kissed me back, more fiercely than ever before.

When he let me go, I took a deep breath and tried not to be afraid.

"Be still, Lily. Can you hear it? I can't."

"I don't hear anything," I said, which was a lie. I could hear the raging growl of the falls. I could hear my heart beat in my ears. I could hear his breath, raspy in his throat. I could feel someone staring at me. I searched the shoreline, then turned around to see the lake behind us. Nothing. No one.

"Listen," Calder begged. "Try hard." He turned me around so he was behind me, his warm hands encircling my waist, and I was facing the falls. I wanted to hear what he thought was there, and at the same time, so desperately did not. It was all so jumbled in my mind. If I could hear a space of silence amid the roar, it would bring me one step closer to believing. But if Maighdean Mara was real, that meant facing a monster. On the other hand, if there was no gap in the watery curtain, if there was no Maighdean Mara, the monster I needed to face was more terrifying to imagine. The ancient mermaid might kill my body, but knowing my father was a murderer would kill my soul. My heart crumpled in on itself, and I nearly sobbed at the thought.

But then I heard it.

Like a hiccup.

As if Copper Falls was catching its breath, before crying

aloud itself. The sound—or rather the absence of sound—was gone before my mind registered it, but I knew it as certainly as if it had lasted a full second.

My body must have reacted, because Calder asked, "Did you hear it?" His voice was both amazed and terrified.

I didn't answer him, listening for it again. I counted in my head so I could pace it. *One Mississippi. Two Mississippi. . . .* I got to twelve, and this time tried to determine its exact location. But it was too quick.

I counted to twelve again. The third time, I picked up the source, low and to the left, behind an enormous black boulder.

I raised one shaking hand and pointed.

"You're sure?" he asked, and I nodded.

"Make sure," he said. "I've got one shot at this."

I could see what he meant. Anything that got caught in the turbulence would be battered and beaten against the razor-sharp rocks, and the gap was so quick—a fraction of a second—there was no room for error. "How do you get in?" I asked.

"I need to make a beeline for the gap. If I hit it at the right moment, I should get sucked in behind the falls."

"And if you don't hit it?"

"Seriously, Lily, you should go."

"I'm not going to leave you."

"You think it's by that boulder?" He didn't look convinced. "I'll have to be quick."

"Positive," I said.

His breath came out slowly against the back of my neck. "Good girl." He took off his watch and handed it to me. "Take this and go back to shore. Give me an hour. If I'm not back by then, well . . ."

I strapped on the watch and Calder left me, diving down deep. I watched for some sign of him—a splash, a flash of arm, but I heard the gasp of air and never saw him again.

Panicked, I counted in my head and timed my dive, swimming as fast as I could for the boulder, praying I could hit the spot right as my internal timer hit the twelve-second mark.

It couldn't have been more than twenty feet deep here—nothing compared to the depths we'd dived to before—but the velocity of the falls churned the lake into a watery nightmare. It pounded at my temples and bellowed in my ears. The currents pulled me toward the boulder's center, tossing and pinning me down.

The force of the falls pressed me to the rocky lake bottom. My fingertips met the boulder. *Twelve,* I thought. I waited for that infinitesimal vacuum of sound and air. When I heard the gasp, the falls parted and sucked me through.

31

LAIR AND LIAR

I was inside the cave behind the falls. I whispered Calder's name, but only the walls whispered back. Dank and rough, as if carved by a giant pickax, the rock walls seeped to the point of dripping in the small puddles around my feet. The aroma of rotted fish coated my mouth and a coppery tang settled behind my teeth. Pinprick beams of light crisscrossed through the cavern where moles had burrowed through the surrounding ground, finding weak spots in the rock. Their toothpick bones crunched under my bare feet.

I waited for my eyes to adjust to the darkness, but

there was nothing to see. Whispering Calder's name again, I felt him reach for my hand and pull me to his side. He shook his head in apparent exasperation, but he didn't scold me. He couldn't have believed I would let him go in alone.

Neither of us dared to speak too loudly or too much. This was hallowed ground. Had any human being come so far before? As far as I could tell, there were no large bones on the floor.

"We should have brought her an offering," whispered Calder. "How stupid can I get? I guess I never really thought . . ."

"Wait, I have this," I said, digging in my pocket. "It's not much, but it *is* tobacco." I handed him the pack of cigarettes I'd found on the hillside, and he sniffed at it before slipping the four remaining cigarettes into his hand. He tore off the filters and peeled the wet paper.

"Follow me," he said, and we crept deeper into the cave, my hands on his back. He stopped, reacting to something I couldn't see. He ground the wet tobacco between his palms and sifted it in a line across the stone floor.

"What do we do now?" I asked.

"We wait."

"How long?"

"Not long. If she's here, she already knows we've come."

We slid down the wall to wait. Calder rolled the dagger's handle around in his hands. The only sounds were the constant dripping and the muted roar of the falls above us, like traffic on a distant highway.

Calder grabbed my wrist and took back his watch. He hit

a button and illuminated our faces. "Forgot this had a light," he said. "Sorry, that would have been helpful before."

Only then did I see the worry on his face. I almost wished he'd turn off the light. Calder bent his head and whispered something in an unfamiliar language, repeatedly. Although I couldn't understand him, I was certain he was practicing for the confrontation.

After what felt like a very short time, he stopped whispering and checked his watch. "It's already been an hour," he said. He held his wrist up and aimed the light around the cavern. The carpet of bones reflected back the light. Below them were thousands of small, green-patinaed discs. Calder reached forward and raked his hand through some of them. He crawled away, scattering the bones as he moved.

"What are you doing?"

"There's nothing here," he said.

"What are you looking for?"

"Your soggy cigarettes are the only offering here. There's nothing else. No new copper, no tobacco, no wild rice . . ."

"I don't know about the copper, but wouldn't tobacco and rice have rotted over time? You don't really expect that to still be here?"

"That's my point. It's been a long time since anyone has made any offering. Anything dropped over the falls would have been sucked inside like we were. There's nothing here."

"So what does that mean?"

"Maris was right. We're not the only ones who forgot about Maighdean Mara. Her human followers have forgotten her, too. She's been neglected for a very long time. No wonder she's gone off to fend for herself."

"If she's not here, how do we find her?" I asked.

"We're going to need more help."

Later that night, after Calder had left to look for Dad, I sat on the porch roof, utterly defeated. In all of Calder's years in the lake, he'd never seen sign of Maighdean Mara. In all the searching Calder and Dad had done for Maris and Pavati, they'd never seen any evidence of her. In all my experimentation, I'd never once heard the voice of a monster in the channel. What chance did we really have of finding her? And if we did find her, what chance did we have of stopping her?

Doubt weighed heavily on my thoughts. We stood a much better chance of stopping the killings if Dad was behind them. But I couldn't go there. Try as I might, it was impossible to imagine him that way—snatching Scotty so quickly no one else noticed. Bringing him down so deep, the surface was undisturbed.

I forced my thoughts back to Maighdean Mara. The dagger was real after all. And so was the cave. But other than the wind-chime carving, I had no clear image of what Maighdean Mara even looked like. Every time I tried to picture her as a killer, it wasn't a monster I saw. Instead, I imagined a staggeringly beautiful face, with dark spiraling hair and violet eyes that evoked the sky after the rain. Pavati.

Outside my open window, there was no wind, no birds, no June bugs bouncing against the screen. It was easy to hear the water lapping at the shore, and with it an unfamiliar humming. When the humming turned to soft laughter, I moved to the window. The outdoor lights were off, but the moon beat a path of light across the water to our dock. I thought I could pick out some dark shapes near the shore. Dad?

I snuck outside, being careful not to let the front door slam, and picked my way across the yard. As I got closer, I heard bits of conversation, an "I can't" and "It's too hard."

It wasn't Dad. It was Sophie. She sat cross-legged in the dark at the end of the dock, centered in the beam of moonlight, talking to herself. I'd never known her to sleepwalk.

"Sophie?" I whispered through the night air. She didn't respond.

I crept closer. More indistinct murmurs. I thought someone said "sunglasses" (or "fun classes" or maybe "my guess is"). And then another voice, raspy in the night. "You have to set it up. Two days should give me enough time to prepare. Tuesday at dusk. Can you do it?"

Sophie said, "How am I supposed to–"

"Tell him to go to the flat rocks–south of town–he'll know the place. You *must* get him there."

"And if I do, you think you'll be able to convince him?" Sophie asked.

"Sophie," I called again.

This time Sophie startled and whipped around, half crouched, half ready to bolt. There was a small splash from the water, but when I got close enough to see, there was nothing there.

"Who were you talking to?" I asked.

"No one."

"Don't lie to me. Was it Dad?"

"It wasn't Dad," she said.

"Someone else then?"

There was a small *pip* of a sound, and Sophie turned toward the lake. I was not entirely surprised to see Pavati's face emerge from the inky blackness–I had been imagining her so clearly just moments before. She folded her arms across her withered chest and tapped her fingers against her arms, making it clear that my presence was unwanted. Her face, yellow as the moon above her, squinted at me from the darkness, her eyes sunken in the sockets, her cheekbones protruding.

"I've always liked your sister better," she said. "You've been problematic since the beginning." She rose a few inches higher in the water, and her dark hair lay flat against her razor-sharp jaw and over her pointed shoulders.

I pulled at the back of Sophie's pj's, trying to get her to retreat, but she must have been transfixed, because she refused to move.

"What do you want?" I asked, not wanting the answer because there was nothing I was willing to give her. "Are you here to kill us?" My body buzzed with a dark, prickly heat.

Pavati grimaced as she sensed my mood, and she looked away without a word. Sophie made an apologetic sound.

"Then what?" I asked, thankful that the sight of my terror repulsed her. Right now, it was my only weapon.

"Girl talk," said Pavati through gritted teeth. She serpentined through the water in front of our dock, back and forth, in a fluid motion.

I took another step toward the house, pulling Sophie with me. Sophie tried to pry my fingers away.

Pavati closed her eyes and turned away from me in disgust. Sophie groaned, too, as Pavati said, "Would you please relax, Lily Hancock? You look disgusting. Deep breaths."

She squinted at me again, then slammed her eyes shut like the doors to a vault. "God, I must have really scared you. I told you. I'm just here to talk. Your sister is hardly afraid."

Sophie whispered, "Please, Lily. Just relax. It's okay. Pavati is my friend."

Pavati looked over her shoulder at me and turned around with a thin smile as my anxiety turned to a less repellant aura of confusion. "Why are you here?" I asked. "What do you want with Sophie?"

Pavati stopped swimming and laid her arms flat on the top of the water. "Based on what I've known about your sister, and based on what I saw of your talents last week, you two might be exactly what Maris needs."

"I don't follow. Why are you here?"

She sighed as if I were being unbelievably obtuse. "Mermaids need family, Lily Hancock. We've lost fifty percent of ours. Looks like you're our key to gaining our brother back."

"That's not what we were—" Sophie said, but Pavati cut her off with a look.

"I don't have any influence over Calder that way. He's pretty stub—"

"I mean our *other* brother," Pavati said quickly.

I set my jaw and ground my teeth. If she thought I was going to turn over my father, she must have short-term memory loss.

"Easy, girl," said Pavati. "Let me put it this way. Your

skills as Halfs have me wondering about him. You say he isn't hunting. I'll take you at your word."

I swallowed hard, wishing I could just as easily accept that as the truth.

Pavati continued, "But is he . . . normal?"

"Define 'normal.'"

"Once Maris explained the truth to me about your father, I naturally assumed, since he never came back to the lake . . . all those years . . . that he wouldn't be able to make the change."

I stared at her without speaking.

"But Calder suggested that wasn't the case. My next assumption was that delaying his natural development would have had some debilitating effects. Perhaps he is a little impaired?"

"He's fine."

"Is he sane?"

"Sane enough."

"His brain hasn't been addled by malice?" When I didn't respond she started ticking things off on her fingers. "He isn't unnaturally sadistic, melancholy, morbid, masochistic, neurotic—"

I held up my hand and stopped her list in its tracks. "*Unnatural* is an interesting word. He's just going through some . . . growing pains right now."

She sighed knowingly. "Maris said she always assumed he'd be a freak."

"I don't believe you," I said.

"What part?"

"I don't believe any of what you're saying. You're not

here because Maris wants to bring Dad—or Calder, for that matter—back into the family."

"Why would you say that?" asked Pavati, her voice a velvety seduction.

"If that were true, you wouldn't have been so hard for them to find. Calder wouldn't have had to use me, my friends . . ."

"You've got that backward," said Pavati. "I think you mean if Calder hadn't left the family, we would have been easy for him to find. And vice versa. And I promise—"

"Promises! What about your promise to Jack? What about the promise you made this spring?" I asked, and Sophie drew in a quick breath behind me. "Did you really go see him two weeks ago? Jack said you did, but Calder had a hard time believing it."

Pavati tipped her head to the side like a seagull examining an apple fritter. "Jack saw me? He knows I came?"

"He said you came, but then you ran away."

She sighed and looked at Sophie. "I'm trying to make good on my promise. I *need* to make good on that promise. But the timing is out of my hands," she said. She moved her arms gently across the surface of the water, bringing her hands together, palms up.

"Whose hands is it in?"

She stared intently at Sophie in a way that made me squirm. Instinctively, I positioned my body between my sister and the emaciated mermaid. "Easy," Pavati said. "I've always had a soft spot for your sister. She knows I would never hurt her."

"Why was it so easy for you to leave Jack?" I asked. It was a question that had bothered me for months—ever since Jack first told me his history with Pavati. It was the question that had allowed me to doubt Calder's feelings for me.

"I don't understand what you're asking," she said, her gaze moving from Sophie to me. The water rippled softly across her shoulders.

Her confusion made me more uneasy than the expected answer. "You loved him."

"If you'd like to call it that," she said, shrugging. Her eyes burned like the aurora borealis.

I wondered how she'd feel if she knew it was Jack who killed Tallulah. Would she want to kill him just as they'd wanted to kill Dad? Was there enough love between Pavati and Jack that she'd feel at least a little bit bad when she dragged him under?

Pavati dropped lower, the water now grazing her chin. "I understand you went looking for Maighdean Mara today."

"How did you know that?" I hadn't made any attempt to hide my thoughts yesterday. Calder had never asked that I "blank canvas" my mind. Had it been Maris and Pavati watching us? Had they watched ambivalently as we risked our lives?

"Did you find her?" she asked.

"We did not," I said, my face and voice like stone.

"Hmmm. Maybe Coyote has a better idea."

"Coyote?"

"Go see Jack's dad. He knows him," she said, her Cheshire-cat smirk disappearing in the darkness.

MY SCRIBBLINGS

I do not need to breathe
to write these lines because air
is a luxury for the weak
and if I haven't mentioned it,
that's not me.

MERMAID STATS

Best Swim Time:	5 Min. 52 secs
Voices:	Able to Project and Receive
Tail:	None

32

COYOTE

The Pettits' house was a two-story farmhouse close to the lake. Calder wouldn't go to the door, but he got out of the car and listened from the woods. I'd been here only once before–the night Calder attacked Jack–and it looked different in the daylight. I found the door, but I was too short to look through the three small square panes at the top. On the other side of the glass, the lights were off, although I could hear that the TV was on. I looked for a doorbell but, finding none, knocked several times. The sound was low and heavy against the solid oak door. No one came, and I knocked again.

I was about to leave when the panes vibrated with approaching steps.

The door opened slowly, and Mr. Pettit peered out. "If you're here to cause trouble . . ."

"Mr. Pettit? It's me, Lily Hancock."

"Oh. Oh, I'm sorry. Come on in, Lily. I'm afraid Gabrielle's not here and Jack, well . . . who knows where he is these days."

"I don't want to bother you, but I was wondering if you knew a . . . a *coyote*." The question sounded more ridiculous out of my mouth than it did in my head.

"Are you talking about Everett Coyote?"

"Oh!" This whole time I'd been picturing an animal. This wasn't going to be as embarrassing as I thought.

"He's my dentist. Let me go look in the kitchen. I think he has an ad in the phone book. I'll be right back."

I'd never been inside the Pettits' house before. Dark brown shag carpeting led from the front door down a long hallway. The TV blared from a room on the left.

"Your dad told me about your Minneapolis friend," called Mr. Pettit from the kitchen. "I hope he's okay."

"Yeah, he's okay. You saw my dad?"

"Ran into him at the IGA. He was in a really good mood."

"Oh." I was already clinging to Calder's Maighdean Mara theory by a thinning thread. A happy merman meant one of two things, and since Dad hadn't been spending any time with Mom, that didn't bode well for my exercise in denial.

While Mr. Pettit fumbled in drawers in the kitchen, I wandered farther down the hallway, pulled by the childhood pictures of Gabby and Jack hanging on the wall, an eight-by-ten glossy marking each year of school. Gabby's room was just past the last frame, judging by the band posters and pile of clothes on the bed.

A second door was opened a crack. I peeked in. A blanket hung heavily over the window, making it seem more cave than bedroom. The light from the hallway raced in—breaking across the walls, exposing a floor-to-ceiling collage of Jack's artwork. I slid my hand along the wall inside the doorway, searching for a light switch. I flipped on the light and drew in a sharp breath.

It was like being underwater. A blue light flooded the room. Seconds later, a lava lamp sent a pulsing pattern of bubbles across the ceiling. Pictures of mermaids, some beautiful, others terrifying, plastered the walls. He'd drawn some images on full sheets of paper, others cut out precisely along their exquisite shapes. Charcoal drawings, oil paintings, sculpted pieces that reached toward the center of the room.

I walked in, holding my breath. On a bookshelf beside the bed, a battered sketchbook lay open. I flipped through its pages. Every single drawing was of Pavati, her blue-sequined tail unmistakable. Her lavender eyes stared out from the paper as if she could leap at me as soon as I turned my back. Page after page. Until I got to the back cover and found something I would have never expected.

There, Jack had stashed at least two dozen letters, all sent from a P.O. box in New Orleans. The postmarks indicated weekly letters through last fall, but then they tapered off. There were six weeks between the last two. Pavati had sent her final letter just two weeks before my family arrived. I pulled it from its envelope.

Jack,
   Don't send any more letters like the last one. Get a grip or you'll ruin everything.

                                                              P

   Oh, poor Jack.

   "I see you've found my son's room," Mr. Pettit said.

   I jumped and slammed the sketchbook shut. "It's beautiful."

   "It's a nightmare," he said. "Ever since his friends all left for college he's gotten stranger and stranger. I keep telling him he's got talent. He should pursue this art thing if that's what he wants to do. *So what* if he's a year behind now? People go to college later in life all the time these days. But there's no talking to him."

   Mr. Pettit handed me a torn piece of paper. "Here's Dr. Coyote's address and phone number. Are your teeth bothering you?"

   "Something like that."

   I found Calder pacing in the woods beyond the car, pitching pinecones against the trunk of a tree. When he saw me coming, he lobbed one over my head and reached for the piece of paper I handed to him. He read it quickly, nodded, and said, "Let's roll."

The sign read DR. EVERETT COYOTE—THE GENTLE DENTIST. It seemed like an oxymoron to me. Calder pushed open the door and a string of bells announced us to the receptionist. Calder walked quickly into the office and put both hands on her counter, leaning toward her with a wide smile.

"Do you have an appointment?" she asked.

"No," Calder said. "We were hoping to speak to the dentist."

"Oh, well, you'd have to have an appointment to do that."

"It's important," Calder said, and I felt the temperature tick up a degree or two.

The receptionist's eyes widened and her cheeks flushed scarlet. "Well, I suppose I could go see. . . ."

A man in a white lab coat came into the lobby through another door. His gray hair stood off his head like a puffy dandelion gone to seed. He pushed the last third of a sandwich into his mouth and picked up a magazine from the coffee table.

"Dr. Coyote?" I asked.

"Hmmm? I'm sorry." His words came out garbled. "I was just finishing my lunch. I didn't know I had another appointment so soon. Let me clean up and we can get started."

"I'm not here about my teeth," I said.

"Well, honey, I'm sorry, that's all we do here," he said, and there was a twinkle in his eye. "I can't help you with much else."

"Actually . . . we thought maybe we could talk to you about Maighdean Mara?" Calder asked. He leaned in and focused his eyes on the doctor's.

Dr. Coyote's caterpillar-like eyebrows shot up; then he chuckled and diverted his eyes. He wiped his hands on his wide-wale corduroys and glanced at his receptionist. "Why don't you kids come on back. We can meet in private." Calder and I exchanged looks as the dentist led us to a small office decorated in pastel dentist chic. Two chairs sat opposite the desk, and Calder and I fell into them.

Always blunt, Calder cut to the chase. "We're told you know something about her, the legend, I mean."

"Some might call me a bit of an expert," said Dr. Coyote. "I come from a long line of devotees."

His gaze settled on my pendant. "Who sent you?"

"My aunt suggested you might know where to find her."

Dr. Coyote looked me hard in the eyes, then got up and went to a bookcase behind his desk. Most of the books had the same ADA label on the spine, but up high, in the top right corner, were some smaller, older books, with cracked and broken bindings.

"You'll like this," he said, pulling one down and opening it up to a page marked with a red satin ribbon. "It's a children's book. Easily overlooked, but still useful for the basics, and even more if you read a little deeper." He opened the book and turned it around so we could see the pictures: charcoal drawings of a beautifully fearsome creature taming a storm.

"See here, that's Maighdean Mara," said Dr. Coyote, pointing as if we could have missed her. "Her mother was Talamh, 'The Earth,' and her father was Gailleann, 'The Tempest.'

"She also had a brother named Dóiteán, which means 'blaze.' They were fire and water, and they hated each other. One day they got in a terrible fight and Maighdean Mara ran far away. She came west and found the cave behind Copper Falls."

Calder took my hand, fumbling with my fingers.

"Back in the day, my grandfather always told me that Maighdean Mara was the ancestor of . . . the others."

"The others?" I asked.

"The others. Those creatures who are part woman, part animal." He discreetly stole another glance at my pendant and caught my eye for just a second before looking away. "Excuse me, but shouldn't you know all this already?"

"I heard these legends go back to the Great Flood," I said, ignoring his question. "As in Noah's ark."

"What I've told you is ancient legend. But she has been seen as recently as the late eighteen hundreds. After World War I, there was even a paper written, analyzing the scientific evidence and suggesting Maighdean Mara was still living, deep within the lake." Dr. Coyote smiled and pulled another book off the shelf. "It's all in here. You read it."

"Some boys from Cornucopia suggested she was a monster," I said.

"Oh, no, no, no, no, no. She's a great benefactor."

"But that could change, right?" I asked. "If people stopped paying attention to her, she could, like, retaliate?"

My question seemed to make Dr. Coyote uncomfortable. He frowned at his desk and closed the book without answering.

"Dr. Coyote," Calder said, "if someone were to look for her, where would you recommend he go?"

Dr. Coyote flipped open the second book to a page with a nautical chart of the lake. "Here," he said, marking a spot between Isle Royale and Thunder Bay with his finger. He wrote down the coordinates on a piece of scrap paper, slid them to Calder and said, "That would be *my* first stop."

Dr. Coyote narrowed his eyes. "If you do go looking . . ." He got up and opened a drawer, pulling out a linen bag that bulged at its seams. He untied the string and dumped a pile of Indian Head pennies on the table, many tinged green with patina. They rang out as they knocked together. "My grandfather gave me this bag when I graduated from dental school. They were *his* father's before that. He said to give some of them to Maighdean Mara every year to thank her for my good fortune."

"And did you?" I asked.

"I was young. I was embarrassed by an old man's foolishness." He scooped the pennies back into the bag and handed it to me. "When you get there, give her these for me. They're long overdue."

"We couldn't take those. You should offer them yourself," I said.

"I'm sixty-three years old, and I've lived here my whole life." He pressed the bag of copper coins into my palm and folded my fingers around it. "If I haven't got myself up there by now, I never will. I leave this in your capable hands."

He lightly brushed one finger against my pendant, then looked me directly in the eye so I'd know it wasn't an accident. He said, "I'm sure she has no interest in me now that I'm an old man, but if you think of it, say hi to Nadia for me."

33

NEGLECT

When we got back into the car, I pulled the map out of the glove compartment and started to plot our route. Calder kept his eyes straight ahead and left the car in park. "It'll take us six hours to drive to Thunder Bay, and that's just one way," he said.

I looked at the legend and walked my fingers down the interstate. "Twelve hours? Plus who knows how long it will take us to find her. My mom's never going to let me be gone that long."

"Have you tried calling for your dad again?"

I folded up the map deliberately, taking my time to line up the creases before I answered. "No. Have you?"

"I've tried, but he's not responding. I thought maybe you might have had better luck."

"We don't need his help," I said.

"He's not the bad guy," said Calder, leaning toward me. "He's just a little lost right now." He pressed his head to mine. "Three searchers are better than two, particularly when one can't swim very fast."

I gave him a little head butt and he sat back, rubbing his forehead. "Okay, fine. I get it. You don't want his help."

"How far a swim is it to Isle Royale?" I asked.

"Just because driving would take too long doesn't mean we're swimming. It's over a hundred nautical miles. That's too far for you."

"I can handle it," I said.

"No."

I pushed harder. "Our little boat can't make it that far. It's too small to cross that much open water. Swimming is our only option."

Calder shrugged and adjusted the rearview mirror. "No problem. I'll get us a bigger boat. There's plenty to choose from in the marina."

"Let's not add to our troubles, okay? Maybe the Pettits would lend us their Sun Sport."

"Which one of us is better equipped to ask for it?" asked Calder, chuckling low under his breath.

"Let me try the traditional way," I said. "I'll ask politely. They might say yes."

He wrapped his arm around my neck and pulled me close. "Gotta love your optimism. Just let me know when you get the no, and I'll pick us up something nice."

＊　＊　＊

In the end, I was right. Jack might have fallen into hysterics when I told him why we needed the boat, but he handed me the keys anyway, saying "You're delusional. We both know who's behind it all. Quit being so gullible."

I ignored Jack and prepared for our trip, packing food and putting on the best fate-tempting outfit I could find: a Jimi Hendrix Isle of Wight Festival T-shirt, dated August 1970. If this was going to be our last hurrah, so be it.

Calder didn't seem as fatalistic. I wondered if he planned on leaving me alone in the boat while he searched. If he did, he was a slow learner.

Calder checked the gas tank and filled an extra can. He spread maps on the captain's stand. "I've never gone that far north above the surface," he explained. "I need to get my bearings."

"How long will it take to get there?"

"About three hours if we really power it."

"That's still so long." I lifted the seats and pulled out the white vinyl cushions, uncovering Jack's cinder-block anchor, and his dad's scuba suit. Calder started the engine, and I leapt off the boat to untie the dock lines. As Calder backed from the slip, I walked the boat back, holding the line just as I'd seen Gabby do, and jumped onto the side rail as it pulled away.

"Very good," Calder said. "I'm impressed."

Once we cleared the no wake zone, Calder pushed the throttle forward and headed north, toward Basswood. The closer we got, the more the muscles in Calder's jaw flexed and jumped.

"What's wrong?" I finally asked over the drone of the engine. "You know Maris isn't there. They're probably still camping on Oak."

"Just bad memories," he said.

"Tell me."

He looked over at me with a frown, sighed, and cut the engine. The momentum of our wake caught up with us and the boat bobbed several times before the water settled.

"This is where they trapped me. This is where I was when I heard you agree to jump."

"Oh." I should have known by the look on his face not to ask. I got up and reached for the key to restart the engine. We didn't have to talk about this. It was better that he kept his mind clear. We had other things to worry about than the past. But he caught my hand.

"This is where I was when I saw you, through Tallulah's mind, at the top of the cliff, and realized I could never make it back in time."

"You did make it back."

"Not in time to save you." He bowed his head and scowled at the floor of the boat.

"That's not the way I remember it."

"You were barely conscious, Lily. How would you remember anything?" He seemed mad now, and I sat down on the seat.

"Okay. I'll bite. What's this really about?" I asked. "You should be focused on other things right now."

"I wanted to be a hero, but I couldn't do it."

"I didn't want to be saved," I reminded him. "*I* was trying to do the saving. If you had interfered, they'd still be after my dad."

Neither of us spoke for a while, and the waves sloshed rhythmically against the hull.

"I'll never understand you, Lily. No ordinary girl would have done what you did."

"I've never claimed to be ordinary."

"Right," he said, drawing out the word. "You're a Half."

"What do you think that means, exactly? That's what Pavati called us, too."

"Pavati?"

I forgot I hadn't mentioned her little visit. I kept going. "Aren't we *all* half? Except for you, of course, but Maris, Pavati, Dad—they all had human fathers and mermaid mothers. They're Halfs, too. If Pavati was to have a baby—"

"Don't make me laugh, but, yeah, I see what you're saying. The thing is, you're the reverse. You have a merman father and human mother."

"And that makes a difference?"

"Apparently, it makes a very fortunate difference. It's what's keeping you from busting out with a tail."

"I don't see that as a good thing. If I could swim faster . . ."

Calder started up the boat again, drowning me out, and followed the Bayfield Peninsula around to Raspberry Island, cutting north between it and York. The farther north we traveled, the more my muscles tightened with trepidation. Calder must have been nervous, too, because he barely spoke over the next few hours, except to shout out meaningless comments about the islands, or the depth of the water, or finally the Rock of Ages lighthouse off Isle Royale.

Just north of the lighthouse, Calder slowed the boat and quieted the motor. He picked up our earlier conversation.

"I've been thinking, Lily, that it is a very *good* thing, you

303

being a Half. If you were a full-on mermaid, think what that would mean. That would mean the whole package. The whole enchilada. You'd be miserable. I'd be right back where I started. We'd both be hunting the lake for kayakers."

"I can't speak for you, but I doubt *I'd* be miserable. As long as we were together, we'd still be happy."

"I'd like to think so, but the truth is we have no way of knowing. This is going to sound harsh, but based on everything I've been taught, you and Sophie shouldn't exist. Remember I told you mermen aren't supposed to reproduce? That's why Maris was so skittish around you on Oak Island. You were wondering about that, weren't you? She doesn't know what to make of merman offspring. She thinks you're a freak of nature or something."

"That's a bit ironic, don't you think?"

"To you, maybe."

I laced my fingers through his. "Do you think I'm a freak of nature?"

"Absolutely. Just my type."

Your type, I thought. *Is that the best you can do?* "Remember when you busted me for eavesdropping?"

"Vividly."

"I heard my dad ask you . . . about how you felt about me?" *I should be thoroughly flogged. Why am I doing this? Just shut up, Lily. Shut up before it's too late.* "I never heard your answer."

Calder turned the key and cut the engine. The silence was startling.

"You know how I feel about you," he said. I couldn't help but notice the strange tightness in his eyes. "I've made no secret about it."

"You need me," I said.

"Yes."

"People *need* lots of things."

The corners of his mouth flinched upward, but if it was supposed to be a smile it was barely perceptible. "What do you want me to say, Lily?"

Say that you love me. Before I do. Say it out loud. "It doesn't matter what I want you to say. It matters what you want to say."

"This isn't exactly the right moment," he said.

"We're about to go looking for a potentially killer water spirit. There might not be any other moments."

I didn't see where he pulled it from, but Calder rolled the dagger handle around in his palm. "Your dad wanted to know my intentions. But what I want doesn't matter in the end."

"The end of what?"

"Summer." Calder motored our boat slowly across the water now. It barely felt like we were moving. "When fall comes—assuming we're both still alive—I'll need to look for warmer waters. It'll be time for you to start college."

"I don't need college if I'm going to be a poet. All I need is inspiration."

"Don't you think you're being a little naive?"

"Wherever you go when summer's over, I'm going with you," I said, my voice raising an octave.

"You are?" Then his face fell. "I can't have you do that."

"Why? Would I cramp your style in the Bahamas?"

He scowled at me. "This isn't a joke."

"No," I said. "It's not. I love you, Calder. And I want to hear you say you love me, too."

"It's just a word, Lily."

"So you're telling me you can't say it."

He shifted his shoulders and fidgeted nervously with the nautical charts, folding them messily and storing them away. "I've said it. Once, when you were asleep. Just to see how it sounded.

"Thing is, Lily, I never thought love was possible. Not for me. Not for my kind. Then you came along and changed that. I *have* allowed myself to love you—" He broke off and looked at me, his eyes full of pain. Then he sighed in exasperation. At me? At himself?

"Please understand," he said. "It feels too dangerous. When I look back on my life, I've lost everyone I've ever loved. I can't lose you, too.

"Not saying the word out loud . . . not admitting it to the universe, maybe it's stupid, but this is my way of keeping you safe."

"I appreciate the sentiment, but—"

"I can't think about this now, Lily. We're here. This is the spot Dr. Coyote marked. It's time to go in."

His words caught me unprepared, and I looked around nervously. Dr. Coyote's approximation of Maighdean Mara's whereabouts seemed more likely to be accurate than the Cornucopia boys', but did that also mean she wasn't the monster they thought she was?

Dr. Coyote had called her a benefactor. I didn't like the idea of attacking something that had taken such care of human beings. But then again, if she had turned on us, if she was now a killer . . . Once more, I hoped the dagger was sufficiently sharp.

Calder busied himself with the anchor, then found some tiebacks to strap the dagger to his arm. He looked at me with purpose and put both hands on my shoulders. "Ready, then?" he asked.

Those two words imbued me with confidence. He was not going to argue with me about staying behind. We would do this together. I put one foot up on the rail and, keeping my eyes on his face, stepped up and over the side of the boat.

I sliced through the water, feeling everything rush upward—my blood to my ears, my hair trailing. I don't know how deep I plummeted. The water here was different than anywhere else I'd been. Neither cold nor warm, it felt—if it was possible—alive. I could recognize each molecule individually as it bumped and trembled along the length of my limbs. The humming made the water feel dry, as if a thin layer of air outlined my body.

The only disruption to the steady vibration was when Calder shot through the water and exploded in silver shards of light. I shielded my eyes, feeling shrapnel of pure energy penetrate my skin. When I dared to look, Calder was inches from my face.

His hand slipped behind my neck and he kissed me hard, crushing his lips to mine. Only then did I truly feel what he'd been trying to tell me before. To lose him now would be impossible to bear.

Calder pulled back from the kiss and unsheathed the dagger. He held it firmly in his hand and pulled me along beside him toward the source of the heat.

As we dove deeper, the water swirled into unnatural patterns of lilac and green, and then intensified by the fathom to violet and jade. As the color deepened, my skin burned. The vibrations burrowed deep into my flesh, making their way into my bloodstream and racing for my heart. What was this place? There were no underwater landmarks; the surface seemed miles away. The sun was nothing more than a pinprick from another galaxy, and still I had no need for air.

Calder led me on, nearing the lake floor, to a large boulder, which hummed like a beehive. As we closed in, Calder abruptly dropped my hand and put on the brakes, skittering backward a few strokes before hesitating and leaning forward again. He reached, hands trembling, toward the boulder.

It was black and lichen green with coppery flecks, oval in shape, like the deformed egg of some prehistoric bird. When his fingers met the boulder's surface, he jerked his hand back and studied his fingers. He touched the boulder again, caressing it along its humped back. Then his shoulders slumped.

Calder let his hands gently follow the smooth surface, investigating all sides. He pressed both hands against it and pushed. It was as big as my twin bed, so I was surprised by how easily it rolled. Calder treated it gently, respectfully, letting it rest on its side. It was so light, so delicate, I wondered why it didn't float.

Calder spread his arms wide, slid them under the boulder, and carried it to the surface. I followed him, quickly retracing the trail we'd taken down. When I emerged from the water, I sucked greedily at the air, taking my first breaths since leaving the boat. I didn't even want to think about how long it had been.

Calder dropped the dagger onto the floor of the boat and

rolled the boulder gently onto the swim deck. But it was no boulder. The boat barely acknowledged the extra weight.

Calder watched my face closely as I drew my finger over its porous surface. After only a few seconds of examination, I began to see the line of an arm, the curve of a knee, the turn of a face, although the features were long since lost. It was more human than animal, but more stone than human. Looking at it now, in this fetal position, curled like a sleeping giant, I knew it was ridiculous to think she could have ever been responsible for the attacks. Even in her dark stony corpse, I knew she was a peaceful thing.

"It's her?" I whispered, afraid my voice would wake it.

"Yes."

"Is she asleep?"

"No," Calder said, and there was a deep mourning in his voice that was beyond even what I was feeling. "Maighdean Mara isn't the killer. She didn't leave the cave to fend for herself. She left the cave to die."

"What killed her?" I asked.

"We all did," Calder said, and tears welled in his eyes. "Neglect."

"We need to put her back," I said. "She belongs in the lake."

I rolled her off the swim deck and into Calder's arms. He returned her to her resting place while I climbed into the boat and retrieved Dr. Coyote's pennies. I dropped them one by one into the water and watched as they chased Maighdean Mara all the way to the bottom.

34

DEFEAT

It was a quiet three hours back to Bayfield. There would be another attack, another body. What did it matter if it was someone I didn't know? Whoever it was, it would be someone else's best friend or neighbor, sister or brother. It was only a matter of time. All I knew for sure was that we were back to where we started, and I had run out of good options. There was no one left to blame.

My fingers rubbed nervously at the beach glass around my neck. It heated at my touch and gave me comfort. I'd wanted to ask Calder about it since our confrontation with Maris and Pavati on Oak Island, and even more so since he told me the story of Maighdean Mara's three daughters, but I'd been afraid he might make me give the pendant back to Maris, and it was my last connection to Dad.

Still, now, in the silence, seemed as good a time as any for the inevitable. "What do you know about my pendant?"

Calder glanced down at it and furrowed his brow. He looked at the water in front of us and said, "I never saw it in real life until you and I were on our way back up here, but I've seen it plenty of times in Maris's memories. It was our mother's. She was a direct descendant of Maighdean Mara's daughter, Namid. I don't know how you came to have it."

"I told you. It was a graduation present. Dad said Grandpa gave it to him, to give to me."

"Yes, but how is it that Tom Hancock had it?"

I didn't know the answer to that. "I think your mother is in the glass," I said.

"She's not in the glass. I know where she is."

"I don't mean literally, I mean . . . I think she's with me, somehow. If I'm afraid, she calms me. She's what drew me to the water . . . the day Maris attacked. I knew it was wrong, but I couldn't help myself. She made me go in."

"You think my mother set up an ambush?"

"That's not what I'm saying. I'm saying—if I had to guess—I think she's glad we're home. When she called me into the lake, I think she was calling me *all the way* home."

Calder pulled me in front of him, wrapping his warm

arms around me as he steered the boat. The early-evening air was clean and cool on my face.

"That's how I feel when I'm with you," he said. "All the way home. And I don't want to give you back, either."

I leaned against him, letting him support me. My lids grew heavy. Each time I opened my eyes, the sun seemed to have lunged farther across the sky. By the time we pulled into the marina, the light was fading to purple.

"Do you think Maris knew Maighdean Mara was dead?" I asked, breaking the silence as Calder finished tying the dock lines at the Pettits' slip. "Do you think she was mad about me having the pendant and she was tormenting us with a big wild-goose chase?"

"I don't think so," he said grimly.

I looked at my fingers. My nails were lined in a dark, chalky substance. Traces of Maighdean Mara—a mystical creature reduced to gritty residue. "Neglect is a terrible thing," I said, holding my hand out in front of me.

"Yes," he said.

"It's scary. None of us is meant to be alone. It was a mistake for you to leave your sisters."

"No. I've made plenty of mistakes, but that's not one of them."

"You said yourself you couldn't make it on your own. That you just wandered aimlessly, and when you did search for something, you searched for family."

"I have a new family now."

"Mine? Look at us. Right now, the epitome of neglect. I've seen my dad once in the last three weeks, and that one time he was saying goodbye."

"He's around. You know he's around. He'll come home as soon as he can manage."

"You're missing my point."

"What's the point, Lily?" He reached for my hand and helped me step from the boat to the dock. We held hands as we walked slowly, defeatedly, back to the car.

"Your sisters are neglecting their natures, and they're near death. Now Maighdean Mara"–I pulled my hand free and held it up before he could interrupt me–"I have no idea how great she once was, but now there is nothing left of her. Neglect, Calder. It's a destructive thing."

"Where'd you hear all that?"

"Father Hoole told me . . . that day you saw us talking . . . the day Jules and everyone showed up. But listen to what I'm saying. This senseless killing, it comes from somewhere. It comes from hurt. It comes from some great neglect."

"We've all been neglected at some point. You can't justify this, Lily."

"Not justify. Explain. Crazy is crazy, but hurt comes from somewhere. What does that level of hurt *look like* to you?"

"Hurt so great you'd kill? That kind of negative energy would be impossible to look at. At least, not directly, and not without getting sick. I'd need to prepare . . . wear sunglasses or something. It would take some serious prep time."

And that was all it took. In that moment, I knew. I knew who the killer was. And I knew where I needed to go. The only question was, did Sophie know what she was walking into?

"What day is it?" I asked.

Calder scrunched up his forehead. "Tuesday. I think. Why?"

"We need to find Pavati!"

He almost laughed. "Lily, I can't find her just like that." He snapped his fingers for emphasis.

"It won't be hard this time. Jack told me back in the spring that he and Pavati used to meet on some flat rocks. Just south of town? I'd bet anything that's where she is."

"I know those rocks. They're about a quarter mile past the fishing pier."

"Thanks!"

"Thanks? Lily, what's going on?" he called as I ran ahead of him, as fast as I could, across the lot to the car. I jumped in the driver's seat and fished around under the mat for the key. The car started up on the second try, and I peeled out, leaving long black lines on the road and Calder looking frantic in my rearview mirror. People turned to watch as I sped down the county road. I pulled my cell phone out of the center console and saw three missed calls from Mom. I hit Send.

"Mom? Is Sophie home?"

"She said she was going for a walk. I was baking. Now I'm in the back painting, but I don't think I've heard her come in. Are you driving? You know I don't like you on your phone when you're driving."

I turned off my phone and tossed it in the backseat. How could I have been so stupid? I could now see how Pavati had worked it all out with Sophie two nights ago. Sophie was bringing Jack to Pavati so she could make good on her promise. But did Pavati know how truly dangerous Jack had become? Somehow I couldn't believe Pavati would intentionally put Sophie in danger. I only hoped I wasn't too late.

In less than two minutes I found Jack's van pulled off the county road. I slammed on the brakes and turned sharply into the drive. The car behind me laid on the horn.

The dirt road ended abruptly after the spot where Jack had parked. I skidded to a stop, kicking up a cloud of dust that engulfed the car. I couldn't believe Sophie would have got in a van with Jack Pettit, but every fiber of my being knew I was fooling myself.

The road narrowed to a footpath that twisted its way through the woods toward the lake. I raced down its length. With each footstep pounding the hard-packed ground, my muscles ached, my lungs burned. The wind pulled tears from my eyes. *Please, no. Oh, please, no. She wouldn't be so stupid.*

I followed the path east, until I saw them.

For half a second, I forgot my fear. The beauty of the scene overtook my senses. I could see why Pavati and Jack had made this *their place.* A sentry of pine trees, their branches heavy and drooping with long, hair-like needles, shielded the spot from boats and errant hikers. Spider-webs hung like wedding veils from the smaller trees, their silver threads shimmering with mist from the lake. The ground—a flat plate of brownstone—soaked up the heat of the sun and ran smoothly into the lake, barely six inches above the water level. Thick spongy patches of moss grew under the trees and made soft places to lay one's head.

The sky opened before me, the gray water deep and choppy beyond.

Where the brownstone met the water, two bodies stood at the edge. One tall, one small. The smaller figure leaned away from the other, her face turned away from the despair that only she could see.

"Jack, no," I said, but neither of them flinched. Maybe I hadn't actually spoken. Maybe the wind drove my voice back into the trees. By Jack's feet was another chain and cinder block—just like the anchor he kept in his boat.

"What are you doing?" I said, this time louder. I searched the water for any heads breaking the surface, but there was no one out there.

Sophie twisted around to look at me, but Jack did not.

"The mermaids are dangerous," Jack said, his voice eerily calm. "I need people to believe me."

"The mermaids aren't killing anyone," I said, closing the gap between us.

"They have before," he said. "They will again."

"Tell me what you want. Just let Sophie go."

Jack tightened his grip on her wrist, but Sophie said, "Stay away, Lily. Pavati needs to talk to Jack. I'm helping. I don't need you."

"I want the lake searched," Jack said. "I want her found. I want her to suffer for what she's done to me." He reached down for the chain and turned to face me. His face was sunken, his skin red and splotchy. "She promised she'd come back."

I took ten steps closer and Sophie said, "She did. And she's here again. Under the water." She pointed with her free arm down at the lake. I couldn't see the spot because their bodies blocked my view. Was Sophie trying to distract him, or was Pavati really there, using the lake as a filter so she could better look at Jack?

"If Pavati promised you," I said, holding my hands out, moving closer, "you know she'll make good on that."

"Then where is she?" His voice cracked, the pain cutting through as a dark head broke the waves. It was only a silhouette. I couldn't tell who it was, but whoever it was, he or she was listening. I was sure of that.

"She couldn't come before. You wouldn't let her come," said Sophie.

Jack jerked in surprise and let go of Sophie's wrist. "I've begged her to come!" he said as I silently pleaded with Sophie to run, but she stayed by his side.

"You've been too angry. She can't get close to you when you're like that," Sophie said, squinting at the ground. "Even now you're making it hard. Please look. She's there. She's trying her best."

He raised the chain toward Sophie's neck while I ran toward them.

"Run, Sophie!" I slammed into Jack and shoved Sophie out of the way, but Jack lunged for me. One second later, I was in a choke hold, staring out at the lake.

"Let me go! This isn't going to help." Jack yanked me closer to the edge. I struggled and he tightened his grip. "Even if you convince someone the mermaids exist, even if they search the whole lake, what is catching Pavati going to do? You know she'll end up dead in the end."

"Good!" he said, spit flying past my face. "If I can't be

with her, no one can. Besides, we don't belong with their kind. You don't know how they mess with our minds. Not yet anyway. I'm doing you a favor. I'm putting you out of your misery." He dragged me a few feet to the right and grabbed the length of chain from the ground.

"No, Jack. Don't! Pavati. She's there." I was gasping. Tears distorted my vision.

"She wants to be with you," Sophie said, pulling at Jack's fingers around my arm. "She came. She just can't get close to you when you're like this. Calm down."

"Shut up! Shut up! You've learned to lie too well." He yanked my body, tossing me off balance. "I suppose he taught you how to do that." The chain looped around my neck and shoulder. Sophie closed her eyes and pulled at his elbows, but he kicked her aside.

Jack shoved the cinder block into my arms and pushed me closer to the edge of the rock. I planted my feet and refused to move. I tried to sit down, but he was too strong.

"I never meant to kill anyone," Jack said. "Connor was an accident. I kept him down too long. But then . . . at least that got people's attention. For a while. Brady and Chief Eaton—they were easier. People can't keep thinking it's an accident *forever*! But no. You wouldn't even side with me when I grabbed one of your own friends."

"Your mind is clouded, Jack. Open your eyes. Open your eyes! Pavati's there. Do you see her?"

"Shut up!" he yelled. "There's no one down there." I bent my knees, trying to anchor myself to the ground, but he grabbed me under the arms, lifting me off my feet.

For the first time I focused on the water, so clear I could see the bottom despite its great depth. Pavati stared up at me from the sand, through the rippling water, her eyes red with grief, her mouth open in silent disbelief at Jack's confession.

"Pavati, do something," Sophie yelled. "Now! It's your only chance!"

But Pavati was frozen, an icy pillar beside the underwater cliff face. If Sophie's invocation registered in Jack's mind, he didn't show it. If he saw the object of his desire in the water below, the damage was already done. My feet slipped, and I slid closer to the edge. There was no hope now. Had there ever been?

I squeezed my eyes tight and two large tears rolled down my cheeks. When I opened my eyes, it was just in time to see a blue angel burst from the waves, sailing through the air, arms outstretched. The most amazing sight, equal in both beauty and terror: Pavati arcing against the sky. She threw her arms around Jack as she rose over us, then turned, returning to the water with him, Jack's face glowing with fervent obsession.

Somehow, in that balletic maneuver, I was knocked off balance. One second I was mesmerized by beauty; the next, the world tilted on its axis. It was just one

staggering

step, but

now

I

was

falling.

Adrenaline raced to my brain, setting it abuzz–the chain still wrapped around my neck, the cinder block heavy in my arms. Stupidly, I clung to it like a life preserver. Above me, Sophie was watching. She was always watching.

I counted the seconds until Calder would save me: *One Mississippi. Two Mississippi. Three Mississippi* . . .

Jack, finally appreciating he was in the arms of his beloved, burst open with an enraptured light even I could see. I heard Pavati's mental gasp and then, overcome by starvation, she spiraled him to the bottom of the lake, crushing him to her until he was no more.

Eight Mississippi.
Nine Mississippi.
Ten . . .

I cried out, and a torrent of icy water rushed my lungs, drowning out any oxygen I might have been able to preserve. The seconds stretched out between my heartbeats, which slowed, then stuttered.

Twenty Mississippi . . .

Sophie screamed, her voice piercing the water.

Twenty-three . . .
Twenty-four . . .
Twenty-five . . .

The voices of *all* my family, some merely imagined but

others real and very close, called my name: Mom from the porch steps. Calder and Dad and Maris in the water. Pavati's sated sigh. Sophie from the rocks.

A high keening burrowed like a dentist's drill through my brain and out the top of my head. I called for someone—anyone—though no words escaped my lips. Instead, from my open mouth burst a light so brilliant the whole world burned white-hot. A ripple of spasms tore through my body and lifted me into the air, dropping me onto the rocks, gritty and wet and hard against my grasping fingers.

And then everything went black.

35

ACCIDENT

I drifted in and out of consciousness. Men were talking in mix-and-matched sentence fragments and non sequiturs. Some of the combinations made me laugh out loud, but laughing made me sound hysterical, and hysterics only increased the din of their concern.

"Explain this," said the angriest voice.

"I didn't do it," said the saddest. "I didn't do anything. I would never do this to her."

"You weren't trying to be a hero?"

"She didn't need one. She was still alive."

"Then what the hell is this supposed to mean?"

"I don't know. I've never understood her."

I arched my back and opened my eyes to a cloudless sky, patchy and blue through the tree branches. Skin pulled tight across my rib cage. I levitated. No, wait, someone was lifting me from a car. Gravel crunched under their feet as they carried me down a road.

"Careful, Lily. Be still. We've got you. You're home."

"Dad?" I croaked. "Where did you come from?"

"I've always been here. Now don't talk."

"Where's Sophie?" My throat constricted, and the words came out like a rasp.

"I'm not speaking to you," she said.

"Put me down. You don't have to carry me." I struggled in a net of arms, but Dad and Calder tightened their grip.

"Get in the house, Sophie. Tell your mom we're coming," Dad said.

My muscles seized, arching and twisting me in their arms. Pinwheels of light spun in my field of vision, and I squeezed my eyes so tight I feared they'd turn inside out. Blood filtered over my tongue as my teeth pierced my bottom lip.

"Let me go!" I cried, trying to break free of Dad's grip, but I couldn't feel my legs. For the first time, I was truly afraid. *Did the chain break my neck? Am I paralyzed? Is this why they are carrying me? Me and Mom both in wheelchairs?* It was too much to comprehend. "No!" I cried.

"Easy, baby," Dad said. "Everything's okay."

But I could hear the lie. Tentatively, I reached down, afraid of what I'd feel. Afraid of feeling nothing. My fists refused to unclench, but slowly I willed my hands to open, letting my fingers stretch to their full length. The first thing I found were the remains of my shorts, hanging in fringed tatters from the waistband. I combed the strips of cotton through my fingers and took a deep breath. If only I could feel my fingers against my legs, I knew I'd be okay. No one would ever hear me complain if it was just a broken leg. I laid my hands flat against my thighs, relieved to feel my palms hot against my skin, but gasping at the sensation, because beneath my fingertips was the familiar texture of smooth scales over compact muscle. In a panic, I replayed my slip off the rock, the sinking, the air burning up in my lungs. I remembered the flash of light.

"You changed me?" My voice was a coarse grating—like the bottom of a boat against the sand.

"He says he didn't," said Dad, whom I'd now located at my shoulders.

"I didn't!" Calder said, from my feet, or fin. . . . I didn't want to look, but peeked through my lashes. All I could see was a twitching blur of pink that caught the sun and flashed light in my eyes.

Calder and Dad carried me up the porch steps, and Mom called through the screen door. "Jason! Jason! Oh, thank God you're home! What are you–? What's wrong with her? Lily!"

Sophie held the porch door open, and Dad and Calder carried me in. The pain was unbearable now—like waves of broken glass pulsing through my bone marrow. I writhed and twisted as my skin pulled and joints strained in their sockets. Somewhere in my head, Mom was screaming.

"Blankets!" Dad yelled, and Sophie pulled quilts off beds and the afghan off the couch. My tail knocked over a floor lamp as I thrashed and seized uncontrollably.

Mom whimpered nearby while Calder cocooned my body with the blankets and placed couch cushions around my head to stop me from slamming it into the wood floor. Already, a goose egg rose up at the back of my skull.

"Shhh. Shhh," he said. "Just breathe. Deep breaths."

I screamed in agony against the ripping. Could they hear me tearing in two? It was so loud in my ears. Tears burned like acid behind my eyelids. "I don't understand!" I cried.

"You shouldn't have butted in," Sophie said.

"Not now, Sophie," Dad said. "Why is it taking so long for her to change back?"

"I don't know," Calder said. "I've never seen anything like it."

"Should I call the doctor?" Mom asked. "Maybe Father Hoole?"

"*No!*" sounded four voices in unison.

"No, of course, not," Mom said. "What was I thinking? I don't know what to do. Give me something to do."

"Take me to the lake!" I howled. "Get me back. I can't stand it!"

"How long has it been?" Calder asked.

"I don't know," Dad said. "Ten minutes? Fifteen?"

When I opened my eyes, Calder was my mirror. When I flinched, he did as well. Every movement I made, every grimace played out for me on his face. To both feel and see the pain doubled its intensity, and I gripped his arm with such force, he sucked air through his teeth.

"Please," I begged, digging my fingernails into his flesh. "Get me back to the lake."

Dad apologized. He didn't want to backtrack the process. Perhaps I'd made some progress that they just couldn't see; perhaps just another minute longer and I'd be back to normal, whatever that was.

I shrieked again as a tremor ran the length of my spine. If I didn't know better, my vertebrae were trading places. Calder scooped me up and slung me over his shoulder like a bag of laundry. Dad protested, but Calder wasn't listening. He ran for the lake.

I lifted my head off Calder's back just enough to see Mom and Dad through the kitchen window, Dad's arm around her back, supporting her as she stood, watching, her hand covering her mouth. She turned into him and buried her face. Through the window, I could hear her say, "Don't leave," and Dad's shaky voice say, "I never left." My face fell limply between Calder's shoulder blades. At least Dad was home. He and Mom would be all right. If I was dying, at least I could die happily, knowing they had each other.

I clenched my teeth to hold in another scream as my body stiffened. Calder adjusted me in his arms and slid me, ever so gently, out of the blanket and into the lake. I slipped in smoothly and all my muscles relaxed, my shoulders dropped. The pain dissolved like sugar into the waves, the water finding no resistance against my body.

Calder knelt at the edge of the dock with his face inches from mine. "If I leave you, you're not going to go anywhere, are you?"

"What do you mean, 'if I leave you'?" I asked.

"Just for a second. I'll bring the blanket back to the house, check in on your parents. I worked too hard with your dad to make this reunion happen. We hadn't counted on your little . . . accident. I'll be right back. Don't go anywhere."

His hand brushed across my back, raking his fingers through what was left of my tattered shorts. "I've never seen a mermaid in a Hendrix T-shirt before. Or with a tattoo. I wondered if that would stay."

"You've been wondering if this would happen?"

"Worrying is probably closer to the truth. Now stay here."

I watched him run back to the house, his arms pumping and his muscles flexing, his skin smooth and glistening in the sun. The front door slammed, and I was alone.

It was peaceful. Right now, the trials of the landlocked world were as foreign to me as life on the moon. I ran my fingers over my tail. It was dark raspberry with iridescent pink, possibly the most beautiful thing I'd ever seen, next to Calder's.

I swam away from the dock. Just a little. While I waited for Calder, I turned in circles, flipping over and around, trying out new muscles, wondering, wondering. I swam out deeper and dove down to skim along the bottom. I held my breath— too afraid to see how imperfect the transformation had been. How embarrassing would it be to try to breathe underwater only to come up choking and sputtering?

Out of the corner of my eye, I sensed a movement. The floodlights were off, and a cloud blocked out the moon. The water was a black, matte canvas. Still, there was something there. In the distance. A dark shape. At first I thought it was a submerged log, but it was moving fast. And then I knew. My thoughts must have been too loud for Maris not to notice me.

"Well, well, well, Lily Hancock. Aren't you just full of surprises."

My instincts were to retreat, but she did not hold the same threat she once had. Maris was visibly weak, while my muscles twitched with pent-up energy. *"Calder will be back soon,"* I said.

"Doesn't that sound lovely," she said, drawing close. I tried not to show my surprise at her appearance. I could count every one of her ribs. Her eyes bulged in sunken sockets. Her pale, milky hair floated sparsely around her face.

"What do you want?" I asked. *"Where's Pavati?"*

"She's already left," Maris said. *"She couldn't stay a minute longer now that . . ."*

"So she did *love Jack after all."*

Maris rolled her eyes. *"She chose him, yes. But she had no choice but to end him once she heard his confession. His mind was too addled. I'd warned her about that when we left last fall, but she never listens. There would be no reasoning with him, and we can't afford for him to continue to interfere with our hunting schedule. Humans have a way of ruining the best laid plans."*

I didn't know exactly whom she was referring to, there were so many options at this point. My name was probably at the top of her list. Although, was I still human? How did that work?

"Where did Pavati go?" I asked.

"She's hoping to pick up with that blue-eyed boy."

"Daniel Catron?"

"Is that his name? He's her Plan B."

"I'm sure he'll take it," I said, although I couldn't help

thinking, *Poor boy.* I was pretty sure I knew what Pavati's intentions were in regard to Daniel, but it was still impossible to imagine him fathering Pavati's child, let alone parenting it for its first year. Daniel was just a kid. But, then again, it wasn't like he was going in blind.

Maris laughed condescendingly. *"Of course he'll 'take it.' Pavati's completely intoxicated on what she absorbed from that Pettit boy. She'll stagger into Cornucopia, and that blue-eyed boy will scoop her up so fast. . . . After the deed is done, she'll head to New Orleans. I'm meeting her there in a few weeks."*

"So you're leaving, too?"

"Maybe no one believed what Jack Pettit was saying, but the results of his actions have put people on edge around here." She pulled her arms through the dark water, drawing herself closer to me. *"There's no good hunting these days. Tomorrow's the Fourth of July. There will be a lot of party boats on the St. Croix River. I've got a favorite spot just north of the Stillwater lift bridge. Lots to choose from. That should sustain me until I get to the Gulf."*

"Uh-huh." I shuddered, trying to picture it. Clouds shifted and let the moonlight shine through, dappling the space between us. For a second, it made Maris almost pretty. Like she used to be.

I wondered when the emotional cravings would start for me, or if they would at all. I couldn't imagine being miserable as long as Calder was with me. So far I felt nothing but awe and amazement.

"Calder says he didn't change me. Was it you?"

Maris smirked and said, *"No. You changed by yourself. Strange, that. I would have thought if it was going to happen, it wouldn't have taken so long. But Calder was ridiculously slow when he started out. . . . Still, I don't think I've ever seen a mermaid whose transformation skills were so delayed. Must be your diluted genetics. Hmmm. No ring,"* she said, touching my throat. *"I didn't want to go before I knew my family was all right."*

"All right?" I sounded like an idiot, but I hoped her assessment meant I wasn't so delayed to be stuck like this.

Reading my thoughts, she smiled apologetically. *"All I ever wanted was for my family to be together. That's what's most important. Our family looks different today than it did a few months ago, but I can be flexible. No one can replace Tallulah, but Mother would want us to be together. You, your sister, your . . . dad."* The concept was obviously still difficult for her to grasp. *"Calder, too. Oh, speak of the devil, here he comes."*

Calder's dark hair streamed behind him as he swam a torpedo's course toward my side. My anxiety subsided at the sight of him—transformed—his silver-sequined tail bending the water.

"Calder, it's all right," I said, repeating Maris's assessment. *"She's just leaving."*

"I'm sure you're not sorry to see me go," Maris said, but he did not react to her goading. *"Oh, that's right. Lily, you'll have to translate for us."*

"Ask her why you can't change back," Calder said as he pulled me to his side.

Maris appraised us with mocking eyes. *"You two were made for each other. Slow and sentimental."*

"What did she say?" Calder asked.

"She says I'll get faster with practice." My blood cooled at the thought of having to practice that torture. Couldn't I just stay in the lake forever?

"If you want," Maris said, reading even the thoughts I didn't intend for her to hear. *"You're welcome to join me."*

"Join you?"

"No," Calder said in response to my question, and with a flash of his silver tail, he took a defensive position between me and Maris. *"I won't allow it."*

Maris shrugged and looked past Calder to me. *"I can see you're curious about the possibilities, Lily Hancock. I'll be back in the spring. We can see how things are then."*

"What is she saying?" Calder asked.

I wished it were daylight so I could better read her expression. I said, *"Maris misses her family."*

"I don't know what she's playing at," Calder said, *"but tell her she doesn't fool me."*

"Calder misses you, too," I said.

Both Calder and Maris twitched, and she leapt into the night air, bending into a back dive. We surfaced just in time for her black tail to slap the water and send a stinging spray into our faces. We watched the telltale signs of her path—the dark shadow, the disturbed current—until she was gone.

There was a moment of silence before I asked, "So what happens next?"

Calder didn't answer, and I knew he was wondering the same thing. Would I ever regain my legs? Could I avoid the need to hunt? But when I turned to face him, he was taking in every detail of my new body. He smiled a closed-lip smile and said, "Just when I thought you couldn't get any more beautiful . . ."

He pulled me against his body and took me under the

331

waves, our tails entwining, feathery flukes undulating under us. His kisses were deeper, sweeter than ever before. His thoughts resonated in my mind. At first they were a mere vibration, a D string, a sonnet, and then they were a ballad, and the chorus was *"I love you."*

MY SCRIBBLINGS

A Mermaid's Love Song

She is fast, but he is faster
A million bubbles flying past her
as they stream through archipelago
moonlight sets the water's edge aglow
Down they dive their arms entwined
like a fruitful, ample vine
To their castle, pale and green,
chasing their forbidden dreams.

                  -Lily Hancock, "Mermaid"

ACKNOWLEDGMENTS

Writing a novel can make you feel a little crazy sometimes. While I was writing *Deep Betrayal,* Lily kept waking me up at night and telling me how things were supposed to go down. I'd say, "Really? Are you sure? Wouldn't you rather . . ." This is where I get to thank all those people who told me to shut up and keep out of Lily's way.

So here's to you: Nina Badzin, Heather Anastasiu, Kristen Simmons, Deede Smith, Beth Djalali, the Minneapolis Writers Workshop, and Dave Meier for telling me that the opposite of love is not hate, but indifference.

Thanks to Jacqueline Flynn, Joëlle Delbourgo, Françoise Bui, Paul Samuelson, Sonia Nash, Random Buzzers, Kathleen Eddy, Holly Weinkauf, Amy Oelkers, Pamela Klinger-Horn, and Rachel Bongart and to YA book reviewers, bookstores, librarians, book clubs, and readers everywhere who love Calder and Lily as much as I do and who forgive them their mistakes.

Thanks to the Apocalypsies for all your support, guidance, Thursday-night chats, and crude jokes.

Special shout-outs to the kids in my life who have provided inspiration along the way, especially: Sammy, Matt, Sophie, Zach, Marie, Kelly, Andreas, and Sam.

Finally, my gratitude to Greg, without whose love I wouldn't know what to write.

※ ❧ ❧

COMING IN
SPRING 2014!

Don't miss the conclusion of Lily

and Calder's gripping story in

Promise
Bound

❧ ❧ ❧

ANNE GREENWOOD BROWN

(annegreenwoodbrown.com) lives in Minnesota with her husband and three children. She has worked as a lawyer, a teacher, a bartender, a ski instructor, and a chicken farmer. More than anything, she loves to tell stories. *Deep Betrayal* is the sequel to *Lies Beneath*.